THE
STATIONERY
SHOP

THE
STATIONERY
SHOP

MARJAN KAMALI

G

GALLERY BOOKS

New York   London   Toronto   Sydney   New Delhi

G

Gallery Books
An Imprint of Simon & Schuster, Inc.
1230 Avenue of the Americas
New York, NY 10020

This Gallery Books Canadian export edition June 2019

GALLERY BOOKS and colophon are registered trademarks of Simon & Schuster, Inc.

For information about special discounts for bulk purchases, please contact Simon & Schuster Special Sales at 1-866-506-1949 or business@simonandschuster.com.

The Simon & Schuster Speakers Bureau can bring authors to your live event. For more information or to book an event, contact the Simon & Schuster Speakers Bureau at 1-866-248-3049 or visit our website at www.simonspeakers.com.

Interior design by Davina Mock-Maniscalco

Manufactured in the United States of America

10 9 8 7 6 5 4 3 2 1

Library of Congress Cataloging-in-Publication Data
Names: Kamali, Marjan, author.
Title: The stationery shop / Marjan Kamali.
Description: First Gallery Books hardcover edition. | New York : Gallery Books, 2019.
Identifiers: LCCN 2018052061 (print) | LCCN 2018053604 (ebook) | ISBN 9781982107505 (ebook) | ISBN 9781982107482 (hardcover) | ISBN 9781982107499 (trade paperback)
Subjects: | BISAC: FICTION / Cultural Heritage. | FICTION / Family Life. | FICTION / Contemporary Women.
Classification: LCC PS3611.A4645 (ebook) | LCC PS3611.A4645 S73 2019 (print) | DDC 813/.6—dc23
LC record available at https://lccn.loc.gov/2018052061

ISBN 978-1-9821-2986-6
ISBN 978-1-9821-0750-5 (ebook)

For Kamran
You are my love

They slipped briskly into an intimacy from which they never recovered.
F. Scott Fitzgerald, *This Side of Paradise*

———————

There is nothing new in the world except the history you do not know.
Harry Truman

Part One

Chapter One

"I made an appointment to see him."

She said it as if she were seeing the dentist or a therapist or the pushy refrigerator salesman who had promised her and Walter a lifetime guarantee of cold milk and crisp vegetables and unspoiled cheese if only they would buy this brand-new model.

Walter dried the dishes, his gaze on the kitchen towel and its print of a yellow chick holding an umbrella. He didn't argue. Walter Archer's penchant for logic, his ability to let reason trump all, was a testament to Roya's own good judgment. For hadn't she married a man who was reasonable and, my goodness, unbelievably understanding? Hadn't she, in the end, not married that boy, the one she had met so many decades ago in a small stationery shop in Tehran, but lassoed her life instead to this Massachusetts-born pillar of stability? This Walter. Who ate a hard-boiled egg for breakfast almost every single day, who said as he dried the dishes, "If you want to see him, then you should. You've been a bit of a wreck, I'm afraid."

By now Roya Archer was almost American, not just by marriage but by virtue of having been in these United States for over five decades. She could remember a childhood spent in the hot and dusty streets of Tehran, playing tag with her little sister, Zari, but her life now was carefully enclosed in New England.

With Walter.

One visit to one shop a mere week ago—to buy paper clips!— had cracked everything open. Once again she was mired in 1953. Cinema Metropole in the middle of Iran's largest city that contentious summer. The red circular sofa in the lobby, over which a chandelier's crystals glistened like corpulent tears, smoke from cigarettes floated in wisps. Up the stairs and into the movie theater he had led her, and there on the screen, stars with foreign names caressed each other. After the film, he had walked with her in the summer twilight. The sky was lavender and layered with shades of purple so varied, they seemed impossible. He had asked her to marry him near the jasmine-soaked bushes. His voice cracked when he said her name. They had exchanged countless love letters, planned their union. But in the end, nothing. Life had pulled out from under her everything that they had planned.

No worries.

Roya's mother had always said that our fate is written on our foreheads when we're born. It can't be seen, can't be read, but it's there in invisible ink all right, and life follows that fate. No matter what.

She had squished that boy out of her mind for decades. She had a life to build, a country to get to know. Walter. A child to raise. That Tehran boy could very well be squeezed to the absolute bottom of the bucket, like a rag useless and worn out and pressed so far down into the depths that after a while he was almost forgotten.

But now she could finally ask him why he had left her there in the middle of the square.

⌒⌒

Walter maneuvered the car into the slippery spot narrowed by snowbanks. When they jerked to a stop, Roya couldn't open the car door. Somehow, during their long drive together, they'd become locked in.

He came around and opened the car door because he was Walter, because he had been raised by a mother (Alice: kind, sweet, smelled of potato salad) who had taught him how to treat a lady. Because he was seventy-seven and couldn't comprehend why young men today didn't handle their wives like fragile glass. He helped Roya out of the car and made sure her knitted scarf protected her nose and mouth against the wind. Together they walked carefully across the parking lot and up the steps of the gray building of the Duxton Senior Center.

A burst of overheated air greeted them in the lobby. A young woman, about thirty, her blond hair in a bun, sat behind a desk. A plastic badge with the name CLAIRE was pinned to her chest. Flyers tacked onto a bulletin board behind her desk exclaimed "Movie Night!" and "Bavarian Lunch!" all with exclamation marks, even as the edges of the flyers furled, even as crumpled people in wheelchairs inched their way across the linoleum floor and others pushing walkers steadied themselves so as not to fall.

"Hi there! Joining us for Friday lunch today?" Claire's voice was loud.

Walter opened his mouth to say something.

"Hello, he won't," Roya quickly said. "My husband is going to try the famous faux lobster roll at the Dandelion Deli. I looked it up on the Yelp. So rare to find lobster roll served in the middle of winter, don't you think? Even if it's fake." She was rambling. She was trying so hard not to be nervous. "It was given five stars."

"That deli?" The receptionist looked surprised.

"Their lobster roll," Roya mumbled.

Walter sighed. He held up five fingers to indicate to Claire that his wife believed in the five stars.

"Oh, okay! Lobster!" Claire nodded. She pronounced it *lobstah*. "Have to trust those Yelp reviews!"

"Go on, then," Roya said gently to her husband. She raised herself on her toes to kiss Walter's freshly shaven cheek. The crepey skin, his Irish Spring soap scent. She wanted to reassure him.

"Righty-oh." Walter nodded. "You got it. Off I go, then." But he didn't move.

She squeezed his hand, the familiar soft grip of her life.

"Don't let her get into too much trouble now," Walter finally said to the receptionist. His voice was strained.

A blast of cold air filled the lobby when Walter walked out the double doors and descended into the icy parking lot.

Roya stood uneasily in front of the desk. She was suddenly overwhelmed by the smell of ammonia and some kind of stew. Beef? Definitely beef with onions. The heat, cranked up to compensate for the New England cold, made the stew smell overpowering. She couldn't believe she had actually come here. The radiators hissed, wheelchairs squeaked, it all suddenly felt like a terrible mistake.

"And how may I help *you*?" Claire asked. A gold cross hung around her neck. She looked at Roya with a strange expression, as though she knew her.

"I made an appointment to see someone," Roya said. "One of your assisted-living patients."

"Ah, you mean a resident. Great. And who may that be?"

"Mr. Bahman Aslan." The words came out of Roya's mouth slowly, like rings of smoke, visible and real. It had been years since she'd said his full name out loud.

The cross on Claire's neck glinted under the fluorescent lights. Walter would be out of the parking lot by now.

Claire got up and came around the desk to face Roya. She gently took both of Roya's hands in hers. "It is so nice to finally meet you, Mrs. Archer. I am Claire Becker, the assistant administrator at the Duxton Center. Thank you for coming. I have heard so very much about you. It means a lot to me that you are here."

So she wasn't the receptionist—she was an administrator. How did Claire Becker know Roya's name? It must have been in the appointment book. She had made an appointment, after all. But why did this young woman act like she knew her? And how had she heard so much about her?

"Please come," Claire said softly. "I'll take you right to him." This time she didn't add the obligatory exclamation mark that seemed necessary for covering up misery around here.

Roya followed Claire down a corridor and into a large hall furnished with a long table and plastic folding chairs arranged on either side. But no one sat at the table playing bingo or gossiping.

Claire pointed to the far end of the room. "He's been waiting for you."

By the window sat a man in a wheelchair next to an empty plastic chair. His back was to them; Roya couldn't see his face. Claire started to approach him, but then she stopped. She cocked her head and took in Roya from head to toe as if measuring her potential for safety, for harm, for drama. Claire fidgeted with her necklace. "Is there anything I can get you? Water? Tea? Coffee?"

"Oh, I'm fine, thank you for asking."

"Are you sure?"

"You are kind to ask. But no."

Now it was Claire's turn to linger. By God, no one wanted to leave Roya alone with this . . . resident. For crying out loud. As if she, a small woman in her seventies, held any kind of power over him or anyone else anymore. As if she, Roya Archer, could torch the place down with her presence, create a blast just by being there.

"I am good," she said. She'd learned to say that from Americans: *I'm good, I'm fine, it's all okay, okey-dokey.* Easy-peasy Americanisms. She knew how to do it. Her heart pounded, but she looked steadily at Claire.

Claire lowered her head and finally turned and walked out. The *click-click* of her heels as she left the room matched Roya's extra-loud heartbeat.

She could still follow Claire and leave this smelly place, catch up to Walter before he finished his lunch, go home, climb into bed, and pretend never to have made this strange miscalculation. It wasn't too late. She imagined Walter hunched over his ginger beer and lobster roll alone at that deli—poor thing. But no. She'd come here to finally find out.

One foot in front of the other, that was how you did it. She forced herself toward the wheelchair by the window. Her heels didn't click; she had on her trusty gray thick-soled shoes. Walter had insisted that she wear snow boots, but she had refused. She was willing to accept a lot of things, but seeing her old lover for the first time in sixty years while wearing fat Eskimo boots was one of the few things she could not accept.

The man was oblivious to her presence, as if she didn't exist.

"I've been waiting," a voice suddenly said in Farsi, and Roya's body buzzed. That voice had both energized and comforted her when they were inseparable.

It was 1953. It was summer. She was seventeen. New England melted away, and the cold outside and the false heat inside evaporated, and Roya's legs were tanned and toned, and they were standing, she and he, by the barricades, leaning onto the splintered wood, screaming at the top of their lungs. The crowd billowed, the sun burned her scalp, two long braids ended at her breasts, her Peter Pan collar was soaked in sweat. All around them, people pumped their fists and cried as one. Anticipation, the knowing of something new and better about to arrive, the certainty that she would be his in a free, democratic Iran—it was all theirs. They had owned a future and a fate, engaged in a country on the verge of a bold beginning. She had loved him with the force of a blast. It had been impossible to imagine a future in which she didn't hear his voice every day.

On the linoleum, Roya saw her feet, suddenly unrecognizable to her—in gray little-old-lady shoes with thick soles and tiny bows on top.

The man wheeled his chair around and his face broke into a smile. He looked tired; his lips were dry and deep lines scored his forehead. But his eyes were joyful and filled with hope.

"I've been waiting," he repeated.

Was it possible to slip so easily back? His voice was the same. It was him, all of it, the eyes, the voice, her Bahman.

But then she remembered why she had come. "I see." Her voice came out much stronger than she'd expected. "But all I've wanted to ask you is why on earth didn't you wait last time?"

She sank into the chair next to him, as tired as she'd ever been in all her years on earth. She was seventy-seven and exhausted. But as she remembered that cruel, disillusioning summer from which she'd never fully recovered, she felt as if she were still seventeen.

Chapter Two

The Boy Who Would Change the World

"I would like it," Baba said at breakfast, as they ate fresh naan with feta cheese and homemade sour cherry jam, "for you girls to be the next Madame Curies of this world. I would like that. Or even writers"—he smiled at Roya—"like that American woman: Helen? Keller?"

"I'm not deaf, Baba," Roya said.

"She's not blind, Baba," Zari said.

"What does that have to do with anything?" Maman motioned for both her daughters to eat faster.

"You have to be deaf and blind to be Helen Keller." Zari beamed, proud of her knowledge of American heroines.

"And mute. Don't forget mute," Roya mumbled.

"I didn't mean that part." Baba put down his tea glass. "I meant the genius part. I meant the writing eleven books part. That's the part I meant!"

Fate had given Maman and Baba only two children, and girls at that. Baba was remarkably, exceptionally enlightened for his time: he wanted his girls to be educated and to succeed. Education was his religion and democracy his dream.

As high school students, Roya and Zari were on track to get the best education a girl could get in 1953 Iran. The country was rapidly changing, opening up. They had a democratically elected prime minister: Mohammad Mossadegh. They also had a king, the Shah, who continued the advocacy for the rights of women that his father, Reza Shah, had begun. "The Shah's certainly a servant to the damn British when it comes to giving away our oil!" Baba always said. "But yes, he did help with women. I'll give you that."

Scorn and judgment from more traditional family members accompanied Baba and Maman's enlightened views. How could they, aunts in the kitchen whisper-shouted at Maman, allow their teenage girls to walk everywhere without chaperones? Maman became expert at laughing it off. She had dropped the hijab as soon as Reza Shah enforced a no-veil policy for women back in the 1930s. She welcomed reforms for the emancipation of women even as her more religious relatives cringed at *farangi* foreign-embracing ways.

Maman and Baba sent their two daughters to the best girls' high school in Tehran. Every morning, as Maman brewed the tea, Roya and Zari got ready for the day. Roya simply washed her face and braided her thick dark hair into two long plaits, but Zari dabbed a little color on her lips and proudly puffed into place the waves she created by pinning sections of her hair with newspaper scraps every night.

As her younger sister preened and primped, Roya looked at her own reflection in the mirror. Over the last year, Roya had changed a lot. Her face had lost some of its baby fat and her cheekbones were more prominent. Her skin, which had sometimes broken out with pimples, had cleared up. Her long black hair was naturally wavy, and she could have let it cascade over her shoulders as Zari so often recommended. But Roya still braided her hair. It kept her feeling more like herself, especially since the rest of her had changed so much physcially. She was still petite, but much more curvy and big-breasted—or, as Zari said, *developed*—these days.

Zari nudged Roya aside and took up all the space in front of the mirror. She patted her hair and pouted. "This hairstyle makes me look like Sophia Loren. No?"

What could Roya do but say yes? She buttoned her own long-sleeved cotton blouse, slipped on her uniform of *ormak* fabric, and pulled up the dreaded knee socks. Roya had to admit that even she wanted to wear ankle socks, "American" socks, as the girls called them, but the headmistress punished girls who wore short socks. Roya hadn't worked up the courage to walk into school, head held high, with tiny socks on her feet.

"He's our hope!" Baba stuffed his mouth with bread and feta cheese at breakfast. "Prime Minister Mossadegh nationalized our oil so we could be rid of the chokehold of AIOC." AIOC, the Anglo-Iranian Oil Company, was Baba's nemesis. "For the first time in decades, Iranians can feel in control of their own natural resources instead of being taken advantage of by imperialist countries. The prime minister is the only one who can stand up to the foreign powers. We'll be a full democracy in no time with Mossadegh leading us. Now, if you girls study history and chemistry and mathematics, you can join the best professional class this great nation has ever known. Can you believe it? Do you see what's available to you? The opportunities we have now for young ladies? What can I do as a government clerk? Push papers around? Sit and drink tea?" He took another long chug of his tea. "But you, my daughters! You will go further than your mother and I ever dreamed! Isn't that right, Manijeh?"

"One morning!" Maman said. "Can't we have one morning of no lectures? Just breakfast?"

Baba looked slightly wounded but did not stop entirely. "My Marie Curie!" He nodded at Zari. "My Helen Keller!" He winked at Roya.

The girls, eighteen months apart, knew all too well about their father's puffed-up hopes. Seventeen-year-old Roya tried to live up to Baba's wishes, but all she really wanted to do was read translated novels of writers named Hemingway and Dostoyevsky. Or poems of their own Persian greats such as Rumi or Hafez or Saadi. Roya also loved to cook, standing next to Maman, following the recipes for the best *khoresh* stews.

And her younger sister was far from becoming a future Madame Curie. Zari was obsessed with a boy named Yousof. She wanted to marry rich, to dance the tango and learn the waltz. She wanted to pay five *tomans* for a ticket at one of the popular kids' parties, jump into a samba, and impress everyone with her moves. Most nights as they went to bed, Zari laid out all her dreams in detail for Roya.

"Off you go then!" Maman kissed the girls' cheeks and took their tea glasses.

Zari saluted Baba in a mock expression of her devotion to his ideals. Instead of laughing, Baba saluted slowly and seriously back.

Zari glanced at Roya with a quick grimace only perceptible between sisters.

At the door, Roya and Zari put on their shoes. Even though Roya was a senior and Zari a junior in high school, they were still required to wear the black baby-doll leather shoes that were part of the school uniform. Roya pulled the strap and buckled tightly.

The girls walked from the inner *andarun* section of the house to the outer section, along a corridor, and down the steps leading into the garden. As they passed the turquoise-tiled koi pond, Roya envied the fish in it. All they did was swim in cool blue water. They weren't supposed to become successful members of the best professional class the nation had ever known.

Roya closed the gate and they went into the alleyway and then the main street. Here they stuck together, hugging their books to their chests.

There were no demonstrators this early in the morning, but the ground was littered with pamphlets from a previous rally. Photographs of Prime Minister Mossadegh—his sharp hooked nose, his erudite, world-weary eyes—littered the ground. Roya couldn't bear to see his face scattered like that where people could walk on it. She picked up a few of the papers, gingerly holding them face-side up.

"Oh, please, do you really think you can save him?" Zari asked. "There'll be a communist demonstration tonight. There'll be another one after that where the Shah's supporters will show up. You can't save the prime minister. He's outnumbered by two factions who want to see him gone."

"He has thousands, millions of supporters! The people, *we*, are behind him!" Roya said.

"The people have very little power and you know it. In this country there's too much deal-making and corruption behind the scenes."

Roya held her books and Mossadegh's pictures tighter to her chest as they continued to walk. Of course, Zari had a point. Just last week a special assembly had been called at school. The headmistress had stood onstage with her hands on her hips and demanded that the students identify who was circulating communist papers amongst them. No one had spoken up. Roya knew it was

Jaleh Tabatabayi who passed those pamphlets under desks and at recess, hidden in parchment. She wondered how Jaleh had access to such political papers. How she even dared to get them in the first place. Then, at dismissal, the police had shown up, bearing a megaphone, guns, and a water hose. Abbas, the school door guard, helped the thick-necked policemen attach the water hose to a faucet in the yard. Just as Jaleh walked out of school, the policemen turned on the hose and aimed the force of the water at her. At first, Jaleh's expression was one of wonder, a kind of awe. Then her expression changed to resolute will. She sailed into the air to avoid the hissing snake of water. She landed with a thud smack in the middle of its force. A few seconds later, Jaleh was entirely soaked, her uniform clinging to her curves, her hair dripping and soppy.

One of the policemen had said, "That'll teach you to disrespect your country by spreading communist lies. Don't think we won't eventually find every single one of you behind traitorous collusion with Russia. You girls need to focus on becoming decent young women instead of political donkeys."

The headmistress had clapped.

The pro-king girls, devoted to the Shah, clapped and cheered too as they stood as a group in the yard. Several of the pro-Shah girls were from wealthy families whose fathers worked in the oil industry. A few deeply religious girls clapped with them. For the first time in a long time, families of the clergy and fans of the Shah stood as one.

The pro-communist girls ran to Jaleh and huddled around her as soon as the police and headmistress had left the yard. They tried to dry her with their cardigans, their handkerchiefs, the hems of their uniforms. Jaleh stood tall, though dripping, and said not to worry. She even laughed. Roya knew Jaleh would only spread more Marxist pamphlets now, not less. That's how the *Tudeh* communist girls were. Fearless and resolute and always saying that Iran should follow in the steps of the Soviet Union.

Roya and Zari and the pro–prime minister girls had clustered in their own circle, shocked and shaken. If a fellow student asked whom she supported, Roya would say, "Prime Minister Mossadegh and the National Front"; to say anything different would have broken Baba's heart. Prime Minister Mossadegh could get their country to full democracy. He'd studied law in Switzerland, become foreign minister, and gone all the way to the United Nations in America to testify that the British Anglo-Iranian Oil Company should give Iran ownership of its own oil. Roya liked Mossadegh's independence and self-reliance. She even admired his pajamas (which he was sometimes photographed wearing).

As Roya walked to school with Zari, remembering the incident of Jaleh and the water hose, she wished the polarization and constant political rivalry could end. Politics had seeped into every classroom. Her classmates at school were now divided, much like the country, into pro-king, pro–prime minister, and pro-communist. And she was tired of it.

When Roya and Zari reached the entry gate, Abbas, the door guard, looked stern. It was his job to make sure that no unauthorized person entered the grounds, to protect the sanctity of the institution and the safety of the girls. It was not part of his job description to open the slit in the crotch of his pants and flash his penis tied up in a neat pink ribbon. But he was known for occasionally doing just that.

Zari stiffened as Abbas opened the gate and smiled. Once they were past him and out of earshot, she whispered, "He showed me his *doodool* again last week."

"Was it tied in a ribbon?" Roya asked.

"As ever. How do men even walk with that thing hanging there?"

"It has to hurt."

"It's so big, I'm surprised they don't all have permanent rashes down there."

"Well, you've only seen the doorman's."

"Yes." Zari seemed to reflect on this for a minute.

"Did you tell the headmistress?"

"She said it was very ugly of a girl like me to lie. That Abbas has worked here since before I was even born and that I should be ashamed of myself for making up such vulgar stories."

"I see. Her usual response, then."

"Yup." Zari sighed.

*

Boys had no trouble finding their way from their own schools to the girls' school to linger by the gates at dismissal time. Abbas shouted and shooed them away. "You sons of dogs!" he yelled. "Leave these girls alone, you'll burn in hell!"

Roya ignored the boys who followed them home, but Zari made sure the good-looking ones saw her twirl her thick, dark hair, especially if Yousof was in the mix. Some days the boys appeared at every street corner, round every bend. Slick, sly, clever boys who winked and whistled and flirted. Handsome, smart boys with charming smiles. Quiet, shy boys who sneaked an occasional glance at them, then reddened when caught. Roya got used to them the way one gets used to annoying flies, which meant she never got used to them.

Roya's favorite place in all of Tehran was the Stationery Shop. It was on the corner of Churchill Street and Hafez Avenue, opposite the Russian embassy and right across the street from her school.

Roya loved running her fingers over tablets of smooth pages in that shop. She loved the boxes of pencils that smelled like lead and promised knowledge. She could spend an entire afternoon just looking at fountain pens and ink bottles or flipping through books that spoke of poetry and love and loss. The shop was simply called the Stationery Shop—no fancy name to it—but it was a bookstore as much as a stationery store. As the political divisons deepened that winter and hotheaded people engaged in debates and demonstrations all over the streets, it was the perfect retreat of quiet and learning. It was a sanctuary of calm and quiet: never overlit, never loud.

One particularly windy day in January, when Roya wanted to escape the communist demonstration gathering momentum in the street, she slipped into the shop. She just wanted to read some poetry.

"Rumi today?" Mr. Fakhri asked from behind the counter. He was a calm, kind man in his fifties with salt-and-pepper hair, a bushy mustache, and round wire spectacles. Mr. Fakhri's shoes were always freshly polished. He had owned the shop for as long as Roya could remember and he was an expert on books. Mr. Fakhri kept the shelves stocked with Persian classics and poetry and translations of literature from all over the world.

"Yes, please." Roya had come here so often that Mr. Fakhri knew her reading tastes well. He knew that Roya loved ancient Persian poetry but couldn't stand some of the modern short stories. He knew that she would spend the very last of her allowance on a brand-new tablet of paper and that her favorite stationery products were those imported from Germany because they were the most colorful and modern. Knew that she not only read every word of the ancient poets but that in silence, every now and then, she scribbled words of her own on the tablets she bought from him. Mr. Fakhri knew all these things, and it was his nonjudgmental calm that led her into his shop as much as the piles of pristine books and pencils and paper tablets.

"Here you go." The Rumi poetry book he handed her was printed on shiny new paper and had a dark-green cover with gold lettering. "Some of his best between these covers. Make sure you find yourself a quiet spot and don't let anyone disturb you. He takes some concentrating if you really want to get to the truth of him."

Roya nodded and was reaching into her purse when the bell above the shop door chimed. The door burst open, letting in shouts from the streets and a huge gust of wind. The pages of Rumi ruffled in her hand. A boy her age entered the store in a hurry. He had on a white collared shirt and dark pants; his hair was a thick, black mop, his cheeks red from the wind. He walked in whistling a tune that was wistful and filled with longing. It was unlike anything she had heard and completely out of place with his stride and confident look.

Mr. Fakhri jumped to attention and moved fast. He dove behind the counter, grabbed a pile of papers, bundled them with string, and handed them over to the boy as though he'd been waiting for this special guest all day. The boy stopped whistling, dug into his pockets, and paid. It was a quick, urgent, wordless transaction. The boy was almost out the door when he turned. She thought he'd say thank you to Mr. Fakhri. But he looked right at her. His eyes were joyful and filled with hope. "I am fortunate to meet you," he said. Then he strode out of the store and into the wind.

Mr. Fakhri and Roya stood silently as the store settled back to normal after the effect of the boy's presence, as though they had ridden in a hot-air balloon that was only now landing and deflating.

"Who was that?" Roya asked, feeling, for no reason at all, charged. It was disorienting and confusing to have this excitement surge through her just from the boy's brief visit.

"That, my dear girl," Mr. Fakhri said, "is Bahman Aslan." A look of concern crossed his face. He drummed his fingers on the counter. "That is the boy who wants to change the world."

Roya carefully placed her Rumi book into her satchel. She stared at the doorway. She felt slightly infected, as though she had witnessed something overpowering and surprising but also deeply personal, something of the inevitable beat of hope and life and energy. She said good-bye to Mr. Fakhri in a daze.

❧

For days she looked for him on the streets. Snot-nosed Hossein followed them to and fro; it annoyed her so much. Bold and loud Cyrus insisted on opening doors for her and Zari. Yousof stole a few glances at Zari as they crossed the street and then pretended that he was actually concentrating on the lamppost. It seemed everywhere they went the students from the boys' schools filled the streets. The boys participated in the different demonstrations in groups. But the one boy who had burst into the Stationery Shop and made the world move a little faster, a little more briskly, with a lot more vigor—even if for just a few minutes—was nowhere to be seen.

Roya went to school and back with Zari every day, ate her mother's *khoresh* stews, and listened to Baba tell them all about Prime Minister Mossadegh's plans. He was going to make their country independent of foreign influence once and for all so no one could steal their oil again. He would thrust them into a future of democracy!

Roya studied geometry and scribbled some poetry and smiled

when Baba repeated that she'd be the next Madame Curie, by God she would, forget Helen Keller. But nowhere did she see the boy with the joyful eyes—the one who'd made Mr. Fakhri deliver a pile of papers with swiftness and importance as though he were delivering a weapon to a warrior.

⁓

In the Stationery Shop the following week, Roya picked up a metal pencil sharpener and ran her thumb against the tiny ridges on its sides. Again the wind blew pages of the piled books askew when the door exploded open and in he strode.

This time, he stopped whistling as soon as he saw her. He seemed a little less sure of himself and more shy. "Rumi," he said to Mr. Fakhri, but glanced quickly at her as he said it. His dark mop of hair was combed carefully to the side. His white collared shirt was ironed. His eyes sparkled and he smiled politely.

With the same speed and desire to please, Mr. Fakhri retrieved a copy of the very book that he'd given to Roya the week before. He cleared his throat. "Here you go, Bahman Jan."

This time Bahman thanked Mr. Fakhri, bowed slightly to Roya, then strode back into the street.

"What is his rush? Where is he going? What's so important?" she said, once she'd gathered her wits. She would show Mr. Fakhri that this boy did not render her speechless.

"I told you, Roya Khanom. The boy wants to change the world. That requires rush." Mr. Fakhri picked up a rag and dusted his countertop. "It requires vigilance." He stopped rubbing the surface of the counter. "It requires"—he looked pointedly at her— "severe caution."

Roya sniffed. She put down the sharpener. She straightened her back. "I don't know how he intends on changing the world. He walks too fast. He's not very polite. He whistles for no reason! He barely spoke to you the other time he came in here last Tuesday. He acts like he's so important. His hair is funny. I'm not quite sure how a boy like that will change the world."

"Severe"—Mr. Fakhri put both hands on the counter and leaned toward her—"caution."

She had been warned. A few more times she saw Bahman in that shop—each time he came right after school on a Tuesday as though he knew she'd be there. Each time, Roya pretended to be busy browsing through books or examining new stationery or looking anywhere but at him. Each time, of course, she couldn't help but steal a glance at him, until the fifth Tuesday when she couldn't bear the silence between them any longer.

She pretended that she had a poetry question and addressed it to Mr. Fakhri, who for some reason didn't respond, and so it had to be answered by the boy.

The boy who would change the world managed to say, "Fire," in answer to her question about which word followed in the stanza she'd just quoted from one of Saadi's ancient poems.

Her face grew hot.

"Fire," the boy repeated.

Of course he was right, that was the word that came next in the Saadi stanza. He said it with such surety that Roya half hoped he'd be wrong and half wanted to sit and talk with him for hours. But she had to go; her sister was waiting.

Zari was extra moody when Roya met her across the street. She'd gone deaf listening to all the political demonstrators, she complained, while her sister lingered over pencils and books in that godforsaken shop. She said she needed to go home and lie down with a hot water bottle because she had excruciating menstrual cramps and was starving to death, she'd been waiting so long, and that Roya needed to learn to respect other people's time maybe for a change? Roya listened to Zari grumble all the way home. But she kept looking around wondering when, if ever, she'd see that boy anywhere but in the Stationery Shop.

2013

Roya rested her head against the glass of the car window and watched New England pass by, stoic in its iciness.

She wanted to focus on Walter and how much they'd enjoy dinner together. She would make the fish sticks he loved. She wanted to forget that boy, the visit she'd just had at the center. But the words from his letter wouldn't go away. She had unwittingly memorized them sixty years ago.

I promise you, my love. Meet me at Sepah Square, at the center . . . Wednesday . . . 12 noon. Or a little later, if I can't help it. Meet me there, and once and for all we will be one. The excitement of seeing you will keep me going through these next few days.

"Oh, Walter," she said. And she leaned her forehead against the window and wept.

Chapter Three

Love: How It Tangles

Look at love
How it tangles
With the one fallen in love

Look at spirit
How it fuses with earth
Giving it new life

Roya read Rumi's poem again and waited for Bahman to show up. He hadn't missed a single Tuesday at the Stationery Shop since that first time when he'd burst in. It had made for a winter filled with anticipation, conversation, excitement. *When did you fall in love, Sister? Tell me. He recited a word from a poem and that was it?*

Of course not, Roya told Zari. It wasn't one word, one moment. That kind of thing only happened in American films, didn't she know?

Roya wanted wholeness, she wanted warmth, she wanted escape and comfort. The Stationery Shop and its books gave her that. Then Bahman filled it with his presence. But if she had to determine a day when she actually fell in love beyond repair, it was the seventh Tuesday. That day signaled winter's end. It was the kind of day when the chill and frost and dispirit of the season gave way to the promise of blooms and greenery and new beginnings. It was a day ready to rupture. The whole country was gearing up to celebrate the first day of spring: Persian New Year.

Mr. Fakhri flitted about the shop on that seventh Tuesday with hyper-eagerness and nervous energy, helping mothers buy New Year's gifts for their children, wrapping sets of pens, ringing up customers with an effusive and heartfelt "May you always feel joy and live long!"

"A present for my son," a woman purred, "he did so well on his report card and he loves to read." The pride on her face made Bahman smile—Roya caught him. Another man bought colored pencils that Mr. Fakhri bunched together like flowers in a bouquet and wrapped with green ribbon. Poetry collections were, of course, the hottest item—the thirst for Persian poetry was bottomless, as always. Roya and Bahman steered clear of each other as the crowd in the shop swelled after school. He focused on the political treatise being featured as a pamphlet near the counter; she stayed in the back, by the translations of foreign novels.

And then, as quickly as the crowd had descended, it dissipated. Books bought, presents selected, advice gotten—the customers scattered, and there they were, the two of them, engrossed in their own private browsing but of course each aware of the other, feeling nothing if not the presence of each other. Mr. Fakhri closed his cash register with a loud clang.

"My goodness, they are shopping lots for Nowruz these days. Did all the children in this town get such good report cards to deserve so many presents for the New Year?"

Roya and Bahman remained quiet in their safe parts of the shop.

"Now then!" Mr. Fakhri looked around as if he were speaking to a huge audience. "A shopkeeper can't complain about the sales, but I should get this cash to the bank."

Neither Roya nor Bahman moved.

"I was thinking of stepping out, might have to close the shop, then."

"I'll be here," Bahman said quietly.

"Pardon?"

"I can be here. If a customer comes, I will tell them you'll be right back."

"Oh." Mr. Fakhri looked at Bahman and then uneasily at Roya.

Roya sensed Mr. Fakhri's discomfort. She was petrified at the idea of being alone with Bahman. Of course she couldn't be alone with him. "I need to go home now. Have a good day, Mr. Fakhri!"

"Well, if you are leaving . . . yes, Roya Khanom, have a wonderful day!" Mr. Fakhri looked relieved. He glanced at his watch again. "Bank's about to close. I don't have much time. Thank you, Bahman Jan. I'll take you up on that offer." Mr. Fakhri grabbed his coat and hat and looked pointedly at Roya. "Good-bye, Roya Khanom. Get home safely. Before it's too late." He pressed the black chapeau onto his head. "Bahman Jan, I'll be back soon." He rushed out, and Roya followed him to the door.

"Stay."

Bahman's voice was clear, certain.

"Good-bye." She stopped just short of the door. Her back was to him. She could see Mr. Fakhri disappear down the street.

"Please stay." His voice sounded less certain now.

She turned to tell him why she couldn't possibly stay. But

when she saw him, she could barely breathe. He looked nervous. His face was red, although his expression was kind.

She would leave. She had a lot to do. Maman and Zari needed help getting the house ready for the New Year. All that spring-cleaning. Lots of dusting, endless beating of carpets, vinegar-washing of the windows. There was no possible way she could stay here alone with this boy.

She was alone with him. She was alone with him in this shop, and suddenly the sanctuary held the possibility of absolutely changing everything.

"What's your favorite book?" he asked quickly.

"I don't have one."

"Oh, it's just that . . . I assumed you loved to read."

"I do. I mean I don't have just one. Too many."

He grinned and his face, still red, opened up a little.

"Mr. Fakhri tells me you want to change the world." She walked toward him, aware of jumping off a cliff, surprised that she was putting one foot in front of the other. She stopped when she was just an arm-length's away. His khaki pants, the flop of hair on his head, the continued redness of his face blared.

"Oh, I don't know about that." Bahman looked down at the floor.

"But you're *siasi*, political, no?"

He looked up, surprised. "Is there anyone in this country who isn't?"

"I'm not," she half lied.

"You have to be political. Especially now."

"Well, I don't like it. All the arguments. The demonstrations."

"It's all we have. We have to stay involved. We can't let them oust Prime Minister Mossadegh. . . ."

"You believe those rumors? That he'll be overthrown?"

"I'm worried about it, yes. Foreign powers could do it. Or our own countrymen, traitors in our midst, it's a growing—" He stopped. "I won't bore you with this."

"I'm used to it. My baba says much the same thing."

Bahman smiled. "He does?"

"Oh, yes. I get my fill."

He didn't say anything. His eyes were locked with hers. They just stood facing each other. It unnerved her to be under his gaze and yet it thrilled her. They could not touch. They must not touch.

"You love to read, I know. You love poetry and novels," he said softly.

"How do you know?"

"Every Tuesday, I see you. You love that aisle." He nodded toward the area where Mr. Fakhri kept the translations of foreign novels.

"Oh, you come here every Tuesday? I didn't notice!"

He laughed. And when he did, his face opened up entirely. His eyes carried the laughter; they filled with a kindness that was breathtaking. "I've come here on other days. You're never here. Only on Tuesdays."

"That's the only day I can come," she said.

"What are you doing the rest of the time?"

"Studying."

"Really?"

"Yes." She gazed at him steadily. "My father wants me to become a scientist. Or a published writer . . . like Helen Keller." She mumbled the last part.

"And you?"

"Excuse me?"

"What do you want?"

It was an absurd question. Roya wasn't sure if anyone had ever

asked her that. Wasn't it enough that she had such a supportive father, so progressive in his championing of his daughter? Wouldn't
a pro-Mossadegh activist like him be impressed? "My parents want
me to finish school and go to university to become a scientist,
most likely."

"And what would you do if you could do what you want?"

The audacity of the question threw her. "I would . . . I would
listen to my father. My mother . . ."

He came closer. A mixture of musk and a windy scent made
her feel like she might fall. Then he reached out and took her hand.
She had never felt a boy's hand before. He wrapped his fingers
around hers, and Roya's heart jumped. His touch startled her and
yet was strangely comforting.

"You love novels. I've seen you."

"So?"

"So, read them. As much as you want."

How many times had Maman told her she'd bleed her eyes out
for reading so much? How often had Zari thrown her books off the
bed as she swore she'd never met anyone who burrowed her face
into books like this, it would ruin her posture, by God it would?
How many times had Baba preached the importance of studying
for a serious profession in this world, and if one couldn't be a scientist and chose to read books instead, then one had better produce books like that Keller woman?

"Unless you really want to be a scientist or a writer. In which
case, then of course do that. Do what you want."

The worrying, striving feeling that overpowered her in school
and at home evaporated a bit. She wanted to hear more, talk to
him, not let go.

The bell jangled and Mr. Fakhri swooped in, out of breath, his
hat askew. When he saw them, his face flushed. He looked away,

cleared his throat, and they dropped their hands as though they had been burned, as though they were both holding a ball of fire. It felt like she'd been caught stealing. But even though her hand dropped to her side, even though she looked hard at her shoes, mumbled, "I have to go," and hurried out, she knew that she would come back to this shop forever and ever, despite what Mr. Fakhri or anyone else might think. The contact was irreversible, irreparable, and she did not want to take it back.

Chapter Four

1953

Chained

In the dusty, cool space of that shop filled with books and fountain pens and ink bottles, they continued to meet. The unwanted
boys appeared at every street corner, but the one Roya actually
felt charged by was only to be seen on Tuesday afternoons at the
Stationery Shop. He asked her things like what she thought about
Saadi's *Golestan* poems. Roya was surprised at her own solid answer. Her voice came out a lot more confident and stronger than
she'd thought it would. Before long (because it did not take very
long when Roya was seventeen and in Iran and simply dreaming of
bigger things), she was convinced that he was the most intelligent
boy she had ever met and possibly the best-looking.

He was an activist. He told her that he dispersed pro-
Mossadegh articles at the University of Tehran and at high schools
in the nearby neighborhoods. He delivered National Front news-
letters and pamphlets throughout the city. Where did he get his
political material? From Mr. Fakhri. In the storage room behind
his counter, Mr. Fakhri apparently had a vast collection of more

dangerous political material. Roya panicked when Bahman first told her this. She remembered the day the police had come for Jaleh at school, how Jaleh had jumped in the air to avoid the savage force of the water. How she had landed in the pool of it. The police could just as easily target Bahman and accuse him of spreading anti-Shah propaganda. They could arrest him. And to think Mr. Fakhri was helping him! She never would have guessed Mr. Fakhri to be part of such clandestine political activity. She had underestimated the quiet, calm shopkeeper behind the counter.

Bahman told her not to worry.

Fissures between the political groups grew. Violence at rallies increased. A few protestors were shot by the police, chased and cornered into an alley with bullets. But even though Roya feared for Bahman's safety, it was impossible not to admire his cause. He believed in the prime minister's policies wholeheartedly, with more fervor even than Baba, if that was possible. Things were changing, he said. Iran had a future and it was bright and the prime minister was going to give them everything they needed. Only there were those who would stop Mossadegh, and Bahman was determined not to let them thwart the prime minister.

Roya leaned against the shelves lined with books as Bahman talked, her back digging into the spines of poetry and politics. If he went on too long about representation and taxes and trade, she simply focused on his eyes, lost, but in the best of ways. Mr. Fakhri blended into the background, expressing the need to be in the back storage room more and more frequently. Often they were left alone. But there was always the hazard of other customers walking in, and frequently they did—older men in spectacles with lists of new stationery items they needed to buy, or young communist students asking for more Marx pamphlets, or pro-Mossadegh protesters requesting more books on philosophy and democracy. Some of the Mossadegh supporters recognized Bahman and gave him a nod of solidarity, a look that indicated they appreciated all that he was doing for the cause.

She melted into the spines of the books as he whispered in her ear, his body close to hers, his hand daring to touch hers again whenever they were alone. Before long, there was no place she'd rather be.

⁓

Roya browsed the novels in the foreign translations aisle, waiting. The door flew open. There he was. White shirt, khaki pants, red cheeks, hair puffed up from the wind, breathless. He scanned the shop, and when his eyes landed on her, his face broke into a huge smile.

"Hello, Bahman Jan," Mr. Fakhri said from behind the counter.

"How are you, Mr. Fakhri?" Bahman didn't take his eyes off Roya.

Mr. Fakhri stiffened as Bahman and Roya stared at each other. For a moment Roya thought he would actually tell them off. But then he sighed and said he had to check inventory. His voice was strange as he said it. She heard him march to the back storage room.

"*Chetori?* How are you?" Bahman asked, addressing her in the tense of the Farsi verb used for intimate interactions. He had dropped the formal "you."

Roya swallowed hard. "I'm fine." She bent to put *Anna Karenina* back on the shelf. When she straightened up, he was next to her. He scooped his arm around her waist, and she froze like a statue.

"Come," he said. His arm was strong and solid against the

small of her back. "It's gorgeous. We should be outside on a day like this!"

She mumbled a modest protest, but allowed him to lead her out into the bright light of the street.

He was right. It was a gorgeous day. The city was lush with spring and everything blossomed. Roya blinked at the glory of the world. She couldn't believe they were going out in public. They weren't engaged or married, and she had not told her parents much about Bahman, only that she'd met a studious boy at the Stationery Shop, one from a good family who was very dedicated to the prime minister's cause. She knew this last piece of information would impress Baba. She'd told Zari much more, though, including details about their first Tuesday afternoon meeting, and later the word "fire" after she'd first spoken to him and asked what followed in Saadi's poem. Zari was curious but skeptical. She said politically active boys were overrated, she didn't care how wealthy his dumb family was, he seemed like a silly idealist obsessed with the prime minister, as if anyone but the Shah could change politics in Iran, for God's sake, and that Roya should just grow up and realize that if she was going to net a man, then at least throw the net around a better one. And yet she wanted to know everything about how Roya fell for him.

"Bahman, slow down!" He walked so fast; she had to almost jog to keep up.

He stopped. "I'm sorry. Of course." When he walked again, it was at a much slower pace, and soon their strides were in sync.

"You okay?" he asked.

"Yes. I mean, no. I mean, what will I tell my sister? My parents!"

Bahman looked amused. "You tell them, anyone, that you went for a walk with your beau." He squeezed her hand.

She might explode; her heart could burst. She loved his hand in hers. And his words. Her beau.

As they turned the corner and entered one of the city's main squares, shouts filled the air.

Another rally. Another political demonstration where people screamed. Barricades had been set up at the front of the square. People chanted pro-Mossadegh slogans as a megaphone blared. Roya's hand grew slack in Bahman's and blood throbbed in her ears. Her immediate instinct was to take flight and avoid the raucous crowd.

"Bahman, let's get out of here."

"Don't you want to see what's going on?"

"No. It's dangerous."

"We'll be fine."

"Zari says the police keep track of protestors. They have spies embedded in the crowd. . . ."

"Don't be scared." He held her hand tight and led her not away from the crowd, but right to the center of the action. Cries of *Ya marg ya Mossadegh!* rang through the square. "Give me Mossadegh or give me death!" Her body tensed. Were Mossadegh's supporters really ready to die for him? Was Bahman?

"This," Bahman whispered in her ear as the cacophony of the crowd got louder, "is how it happens. This is how we ensure democracy. We can't just sit at home and say nothing and let the king and foreign companies grab more control. This is where we make ourselves heard."

He pulled her farther in and led her past rows of people to the very front near the barricades. As they pushed through, Roya was surprised at how many people seemed to recognize Bahman. They made way for him. One or two of the young demonstrators clapped him on the back, and an older gentleman winked. Had he gone everywhere delivering the speeches and pamphlets? Despite her fear, she felt a sense of pride being his companion. There was no questioning the respect that others held for him. When they got to the front, Bahman nestled her against the barricade, shielding her as much as possible from the rest of the crowd. His arm was strong against her back.

An electric energy buzzed in the air: a sense of camaraderie, of purpose. She would never have come to a place like this without him. She would have been too shy, too scared. Maybe Bahman was right. Maybe she should stop worrying and allow herself to listen and to speak. Was that even possible? Bahman made it seem possible.

He was in his element here. He was absolutely riveted, lit up. He opened his mouth, and she expected him to say something like "Isn't it amazing?" She was now predicting what he would say—imagine that! As if she even really knew him all that well. But she did know him. He was exciting and unpredictable but also just . . . him.

"We can have everything," Bahman said.

"But the communists are against Mossadegh and might—"

"I mean you. And me. *We* can have the world."

Standing there with him in the crowd, she felt like the future was bigger and more limitless than she'd ever dared to imagine. She leaned into the barricade and joined in the chants. There was something strangely arousing about being there. Every part of her felt a rush, a sense of promise. As her confidence built, she shouted louder and louder. The sun burned her face and her braids bounced against her chest as she pumped her fist. Perspiration ran down her back and eventually soaked her Peter Pan collar. She had been hiding for too long. Why? Bahman was right. None of these people looked scared. They all had to fight, to protest, to march.

So Mossadegh could get his agenda through, so the country could have true freedom. As she leaned against the splintered wood of the barricade with Bahman, everything did seem possible. They were one with each other and with the whole billowing, unified crowd. They would fight. They would *both* change the world.

"You seem to be enjoying this!" Bahman said.

She smiled and continued to chant.

"We don't have to stay long. I just wanted you to see. To feel what it's like out here. I don't want you to think you have to be afraid of it. It's just people. People like us. It's all we have. You know?"

The sound was like the swoosh of a sword. When she replayed it over and over in the coming weeks and months and years, she knew she'd also heard a small clang, like the ring of a mangled bell. Suddenly Bahman was doubled over. He wheezed. She leaned over him as he struggled to breathe. When she looked around, three men behind them smirked. They all wore black pants and white shirts and dark bowler hats. The man in the middle held a baton embellished with a jagged chain. Bahman continued to gasp for air. A large gash at the back of his neck began to bleed. Had the three men been behind them the whole time? Or had they pushed and shoved their way through the crowd to get to Bahman? As blood dripped from the chain at the end of the man's baton, Bahman coughed. For what felt like an eternity Roya rubbed his back and shouted his name, and then finally and with much effort, Bahman straightened up. His face was twisted in pain. A pink-red stain spread through his collar and across the top of his shirt.

"Just a little warning, Mr. Aslan," the man with the baton-chain said. "Don't spread so much nonsense. It's not good for you."

Roya wanted to lunge at him. She wanted to find the police, yell for the men to be arrested, handcuffed, dragged away.

The man in the middle shrugged. "You National Front Mossadeghis are all the same, if you ask me. Every single one of you is worthless. This country would be better off without you." He sounded lazy, almost bored.

Bahman touched the back of his neck. He looked at his blood-soaked hand as if it belonged to someone else. Then he took Roya's hand with his clean one. Without one word, he pushed past the three men and out of the crowd. They made their way onto the streets away from the demonstration, away from the square.

When they were safely on a quiet side street, Bahman stopped. "Are you all right, Roya Joon? Are you okay?"

"You need a doctor, Bahman."

"I am so sorry. I should never have taken you there." The stained shirt stuck to his skin. Blood dripped down his neck.

"I'll come with you to the hospital."

"No. Let me take you home."

"They cut you! You need stitches. We have to tell the police."

Bahman's eyes glazed with tears. "They are the police."

"What?"

"They work for the Shah."

Just then a tall boy about their age ran up to them, breathless. Between gasps and pants, he spoke. "Saw what happened, Bahman Jan. Saw it all. These low-life plebeians. Uneducated vermin. Don't know how those in power can hire these thugs. Well, actually, I do, and so do you. Hello, Khanom, excuse my manners." He lifted his hat to Roya. "I'm Jahangir. Pleased to meet you."

Jahangir wore an expensive-looking fashionable green vest and beige shirt. His mustache was lacquered. He was dressed for a soirée, not a rally.

"I'm Roya. Pleased to meet you," she mumbled.

"*Enchanté.*" Jahangir touched his hat again. Roya had never

Chapter Five

For Nowruz, the Persian New Year, they'd cleaned the house from top to bottom. Maman stayed up late for weeks to sew new dresses for her daughters. On the first day of spring, the family stood around the *Haft Seen* table set with the traditional seven items beginning with the Farsi letter *s*. Roya and Zari wore new clothes down to their underwear. At the exact time of the vernal equinox when winter turned to spring, they all jumped and hugged and kissed. Baba then read a verse from the Quran and a few poetry ghazals from Hafez. It was now the new year.

It was tradition to visit relatives in the thirteen days following the first day of spring. They called upon elders first and worked their way down according to age. All shops and restaurants were closed for the holidays. The scent of Maman's chickpea and pistachio cookies and rosewater rice-flour pastries filled the home.

Two weeks later, on the first Tuesday when the shops had reopened, Roya practically ran to the Stationery Shop. The city had bloomed into a colorful kaleidoscope of flowers. New buds burst forth as she rushed breathlessly through the streets.

When she swung the door open, the bell chimed in its familiar way. And there he was, standing in front of the counter, talking to Mr. Fakhri, who was taking notes on a pad of paper. The sound of his voice gave her a pleasant falling feeling.

"Roya Khanom, *saale no mobarak*. Happy New Year!" Mr. Fakhri saw her first and put down his fountain pen.

"Happy New Year to you. Both."

Bahman looked up and his face exploded into a huge grin. "Hey! How are you? How is your family? Did you have a good new year?"

She walked closer to him and then couldn't help but gasp. What looked like a row of large black ants crossed the back of his neck. Stitches. Those thugs.

"Don't worry," he said. "Jahangir's father doused it with enough antiseptic to sterilize a swamp. I'm fine."

Two other customers came in, and Mr. Fakhri went to them.

Bahman reached for something on the counter and handed her a package wrapped in red paper. "Here," he said. "I got this for you. An *eidy* for the new year."

"You didn't have to get me anything!"

"I wanted to."

She could tell it was a book. She opened the wrapping carefully, as if the paper would be forever kept and stored. When the wrapping came off, she was surprised to see it was a notebook.

"For you to write your own poems in," he said sheepishly.

She opened the notebook. He had written on the first page: *For Roya Joon, my love. May you always be happy and may all your days be filled with beautiful words.* Underneath he had inscribed, in his own hand, a verse from Rumi:

The minute I heard my first love story,
I started looking for you, not knowing how blind that was.

Lovers don't finally meet somewhere.
They're in each other all along.

"I hope you like it?" he asked tentatively.

She wanted to cup his face in her hands and kiss him and show him just how much she liked it, but Mr. Fakhri and his customers were on the other side of the store. "It is perfect. Thank you," she said.

"Do you have time right now? To come with me?" Bahman asked.

"The last time we went out didn't end up too well."

He reddened. "I hate that you had to see that. But no one's demonstrating today. Everyone's still in the Nowruz spirit. I promise to take you somewhere safe. And sweet."

Together they went outside. He walked in stride with her right away this time. With the freshness of the new year, it was easier to forget the political woes. If there was one holiday that made everybody happy, it was Nowruz. Everyone looked plumper and brighter, having benefited from time away from work and school.

They walked through Ferdowsi Square. At the fountain in the middle stood an elderly woman dressed all in red. She was wearing a red dress, even red shoes. She looked around as if waiting for something or someone. Her expression was anticipatory but dejected.

"They say she was to meet her lover here," Bahman said as he took Roya's hand.

"I've seen her here before."

"Yes. But he never showed up. Years and years ago. This boy in my class even wrote a poem about this poor soul."

"How sad," Roya said.

"I can't bear to look at her some days," Bahman said as they walked quickly away.

After a few blocks, Bahman stopped in front of a shop window. White frothy lettering on the glass spelled out CAFÉ GHA-NADI. Roya had passed by this café many times but had never gone inside. It somehow seemed reserved for more sophisticated grown-up types, for people who drank coffee instead of tea, for girls who had fiancés, for chic couples who dressed like American film stars.

Bahman took her inside.

Row after row of pastries in glass cases, small round tables, chairs adorned with pink cushions, blush-colored walls, flowers in thin vases, cream oozing out of éclairs and from the tops of small cakes—it all made her dizzy.

The air smelled of sugar and coffee and cinnamon. Bahman led her to the back. He held on to her arm as if they were a couple, his body pressed against hers as they squeezed past tables. He smelled of musk and something Roya couldn't quite place but which she had noticed that seventh Tuesday in the Stationery Shop when he'd first held her hand. She could only think of it as wind—a fast, cool, exciting gust. She held on to his upper arm, the muscle comforting and strange. Maybe it was the coffee and cinnamon in the air, or maybe it was the fact that she was in a chic café with this handsome Bahman Aslan, but by the time he pulled the chair out for her and she sat down, Roya was sure the whole pink, sugary place was spinning.

"What would you like?"

"Tea, thank you."

"Have you ever had *shir ghahveh*?"

"Sorry?" She could barely hear him. The couples around them

chattered. Fashionable young ladies on pink-cushioned chairs looked like foreign actresses she'd only seen on magazine covers, their hair in perfect waves (waves Zari worked so hard to emulate by setting her hair in newspaper scraps every night). These ladies chatted easily with young men across from them. The surreal world of sophisticated couples was just as intoxicating as the pastries in the glass case. Were these couples engaged? What would Maman and Baba say to see her sitting on a delicate pink-cushioned chair across from a guy?

"Be right back." Bahman disappeared to the front of the pastry shop.

He returned many minutes later with a tray holding steaming cups of coffee with cream and a plate of two pastries. He handed Roya one of the cups, placed the tray on the table, sat down, and watched her take a sip. The coffee burned Roya's lips. It was hot and strong and rich.

"Ear for you, tongue for me."

Roya almost spit out her drink. "Excuse me?" she sputtered.

"The pastries. Elephant's ear for you. Tongue pastry for me." He paused and grinned at her. Roya looked at the plate. One pastry was indeed in the shape of an elephant's ear and the other was an oblong shape: a tongue.

"Do you like your *shir ghaveh*?"

The coffee was intense, unlike anything Roya had tasted before. "It's . . . different."

"Best Italian espresso you can find in Iran!" He tapped the table. "Right here." He leaned across and took her hand. "Maybe this can become our second-favorite hangout. Hmm?"

Roya giggled and nodded.

"I mean, not that I don't love pencil sharpeners and books of Rumi's poetry. And demonstrations. But you know . . ."

She giggled again. It felt like the beginning of everything. She was surprised that he'd led her out of the Stationery Shop again and into the brightness of the world as if it were fate that they should walk together, be seen together, sit and drink and eat together. Would they have sweet cakes and éclairs and *shirini* in the future? Just take bites and dive in? Perch on chairs sipping Italian espresso? Roya was dizzy but suddenly absurdly sure that being with him was her fate for the new year and beyond.

~

"To say you'll marry him is absurd," Zari snorted as they walked home from school later in the week. "You've seen him, what, six times?"

"We've seen each other for months now, thank you. And anyway, time is irrelevant."

"Oh, Sister!" Zari stopped and looked at Roya with pity. "Time is the only thing that *is* relevant. You can't pin your hopes on that boy."

"Why not?"

"Because . . ." Zari paused. "He just can't be trusted. Those political types are not what you think."

"How would you know?"

"I just do. Trust me."

They walked the rest of the way in an uncomfortable silence with Roya wanting to feel that her sister was just jealous and not prescient. Zari had to be overreacting, as always. Zari just didn't like *siasi* types, that was all. Roya tried to swat away the doubt and anxiety that her sister's words made swell inside her. She thought of the notebook Bahman had given her, the poem he'd inscribed inside. *Lovers don't finally meet somewhere. They're in each other all along.*

Zari had to be wrong.

Chapter Six

Bruised Sky

Because it was almost summer, because the bushes and trees were already lush, because it was twilight and they were seventeen and the air was filled with jasmine, their walk on the boulevard was one that would imprint itself onto Roya's heart for years to come.

Earlier, they'd gone to Cinema Metropole on Lalehzar Street. The chic lobby with its circular red sofa, the sparkling chandeliers, everyone dressed up in their most glamorous clothes, the framed portraits of Clark Gable and Sophia Loren, the cigarettes being smoked, the tiny coffee cups in the hands of ladies with hats, the absolute romance of the entire venue made Roya feel like she was in a movie herself. And then, the climb up the steps to the balcony to sit with Bahman on maroon velvet chairs and watch an Italian film directed by Vittorio De Sica: *The Bicycle Thief*.

"I love his work," Bahman had whispered as the film began. "I'm curious to know what you think." Roya was too distracted by the closeness of his mouth to her ear to speak. She swallowed hard and nodded. So much was new and alluring in her world with this boy.

After the film, they left the dazzle of Cinema Metropole's lobby and stepped into a summer twilight that was so beautiful she ached. The sky was an eggplant purple, the clouds the color of bruises.

"The story relates to so much of what is going on in Iran right now," Roya said as they walked down the boulevard. "The poor want a better life. But they're stuck. Our leaders need to help. All that man in the film wanted was a bicycle so that he could go to work. That's all."

"I agree. Our own people are stuck in that same way. Trapped in their class, their fate," Bahman said passionately as he took her hand. "But we can change all of that. With democracy. We're on the right track."

"Zari says it's unrealistic to think we'll ever have full control of our resources. She says the British have too much at stake here," Roya said.

"For someone who doesn't like politics, your sister has good, strong opinions," Bahman said.

Roya laughed.

"Now I just have to convince her that I'm not a horrible person!" Bahman said.

"Don't mind Zari," Roya said. "She's a bit dramatic, that's all."

Toward the end of high school, Roya had started inviting Bahman to regular get-togethers she and Zari hosted after school for their friends. Nothing huge: just cut-up fruit, a few laughs, conversation. And Bahman hadn't been the only boy there. There were others—friends and cousins who were part of their "*équipe*," as Zari liked to call their circle of peers. Bahman had been introduced to Maman and to Baba, and it was amazing to think he could be in her home, chatting with her friends, just one of the group.

Bahman suddenly stopped and went quiet.

"What's wrong?"

"I've been wanting to know . . ." He looked nervous. "For a while now. I've just been wanting to ask, Roya . . ." His voice broke off at her name, cracking like a thirteen-year-old's. From the middle of the sidewalk, he gently pulled her to the side near a shrub so large that its greenery and flowers spilled out and made a nook. Suddenly they were blanketed by the sweeping scent of blossoming jasmine, heady and full.

He looked at her, and she was surprised at how vulnerable he seemed, standing there.

She didn't let him get the words out, there was no need; she didn't play games. In the fog of jasmine, she kissed him. It was like landing somewhere she should have been all along, a different plane, soft and unbelievably seductive—a place completely theirs but one she'd never dared explore.

The taste of him, his arms around her, his body against hers as she continued to kiss felt boundless. When she finally drew back, he looked flushed, overwhelmed.

"I think that's a yes." He looked like he could fall.

"Yes. It is." Her new feeling of authority was liberating and surprising. She'd had no idea until that moment about the power she held over him.

"I'll go to your parents, of course."

She'd assumed he'd been kissed before. But then again, maybe he never had. She certainly hadn't kissed anyone before this, and she was astonished at how natural it felt, as if she had been doing this all along.

"If your parents give me their permission, we can be married by the end of summer. I just want to get closer to you. I want nothing more than that. For our worlds to be one."

This had to be the fate written on their foreheads in invisible ink all along. She'd said yes . . . to what? To the kiss, to marriage? Her heart raced, and then he leaned in and kissed her. What had been strong and startling the first time morphed into something so tender even the flowers on the shrub could have carried it in their exquisite stamens, borne it in their tiny translucent petals. She melted into him. This was not supposed to happen before marriage. But here they were. My God, good girls did not do this. But Roya didn't care. She could eat him up right there. If they did this for the rest of their lives, it would never be enough.

⁓

"You like his VOICE? You said you would marry this person because his voice cracked?"

"I like his everything," Roya said. "We are in love."

Zari and Roya lay in their room later that night whispering after the lights had been turned off. Roya kept replaying every moment of the evening in her head. How Bahman's voice had cracked when he asked her, the kiss near the bushes—all of it. She had shared some of the details with Zari but was regretting it now.

"So his voice cracked and it was so adorable that you're considering marrying someone who could be imprisoned for his activist work any day now? Whose parents you've barely met?"

"Stop catastrophizing everything, Zari. He is passionate about the future of this country and is helping a very worthwhile cause. That's to be admired."

"And his mother? You said she was rude to you when you first met her."

"She wasn't rude, exactly. She hasn't been feeling well. Bahman said she's been a bit sick. She'll get better."

"I can't believe you said yes!"

"Look, Zari, being in love is difficult to explain. When you know it's right, you just know. There's no avoiding it. It's like . . . it's like a tree has fallen on your head."

"Sounds delightful."

"What I mean is, it's impossible to miss. That's just how life is. Bahman is my fate. Together we will . . ." It was impossible to capture in words the tender web in which Roya and Bahman had been suspended earlier that night and every time they were together. Even trying to describe it to her sister felt like cheapening it.

"Good night, Sister," Zari sighed.

Roya snuggled next to her, grateful that the conversation was over.

"I will pray for you!" Zari added, and squeezed her sister's hand.

⁂

When Bahman came to ask her parents' permission, everyone was nervous. Even though he'd been over a few times at the end of spring and beginning of summer, it had always been when their other friends were also there. This time he came alone. Tradition called for the boy to attend with his parents when asking for a girl's hand, but Bahman told them that his mother was quite unwell and his father had to stay to take care of her and so he'd had to come by himself.

At those small gatherings with friends, when Bahman spoke of his passion for the prime minister's policies, Baba had been like a man struck by a match. They agreed on politics, which already put Bahman in Baba's good graces and was a huge advantage. But it was different to request formal permission to marry their daughter and they all knew it.

Roya was so anxious; she spilled the tea as she served it to Baba, Maman, and Bahman. Bahman sat across from her parents in the living room, chewed on his lip, and shuffled his feet. Roya felt bad for him, wanted to help him; all of this was supremely unconventional. His being there without his own parents made it so much harder. They should have been there! As was custom, Roya left the room after serving the tea so that Bahman could speak to her parents without her present. But she left the door a tiny bit ajar and immediately joined Zari, who was waiting outside the living room. The two of them watched through the crack in the door.

"Bahman Jan, welcome to our home," Baba said quite formally.

"*Noghl* for your tea?" From the door crack, Roya saw Maman hold up a silver bowl filled with the almond candy.

"May your hands not ache, Khanom Kayhani, thank you." Bahman used the common Persian *tarof* expressions for exaggerated polite talk and dutifully took the *noghl*.

A few more niceties were exchanged. Baba remarked about the weather. Maman said something about fruit, would he like it, please take this plate, the cucumbers are so fresh. Bahman knew better than to decline. Then there was silence. Roya held her breath and Zari chewed on her thumb.

Bahman coughed. "For the past seven months, as you know, Agha and Khanom Kayhani, since this past winter, I have had the pleasure of getting to know your daughter. This has made me an extremely lucky and fortunate person."

Zari stifled a giggle.

Maman and Baba didn't say a word. Bahman went on: "I want you to know that I have worked very hard in high school and will be graduating, thankfully, as a *shagerd aval*, at the top of my class."

"Well, from a high school like yours, that would practically guarantee a position in the professional class!" Baba said.

"Thank you. Yes. But"—Bahman cleared his throat—"I think you should know that I would like to start working at a progressive pro-Mossadegh newspaper in the fall."

Zari hit her forehead with her palm.

Maman shifted uncomfortably. Roya knew that working at a political newspaper was not what she'd had in mind for a future son-in-law. Roya held her breath as though the sound of her exhalation could ruin everything.

"It would be temporary. Just till things settle down in this country. We have to do what we can. To help the National Front. I have friends at the paper," Bahman went on. "It would be a good starting position. I hope you know that I am devoted to your daughter and I would do everything in my power to make sure we have a secure and happy life together. Everything. She would want for nothing. It would be a privilege . . . it would be my good fortune to be able to start a life with her. My parents couldn't be here today, I know they should be here, but I will be sure to bring them if—if a match could go ahead. If I could be given the opportunity to have the honor of making your daughter . . ."

"Is a tree falling on your head right now?" Zari whispered.

Roya wanted to run out into the living room and just sit next to Bahman. How long had he practiced this speech? How nervous must he be right now? She knew Maman would not like the continued political activism. But it was hard not to be besotted by Bahman's charm, not to want to inhale the air he breathed, not to wish that half of his good cheer and optimism could infect them all. Surely Maman and Baba would approve.

"What I am trying to say, Agha Kayhani, Khanom Kayhani, is that I would very much like, well, I would very much appreciate the honor of . . . I would like to ask permission to marry your daughter," Bahman finally said.

"My dear boy! Please. My boy, my boy!" Baba's voice boomed. "*Albateh!* Yes, of course."

Roya let out a long, deep breath. Zari stood still and was silent.

Maman dabbed her eyes with her fingers. "May you live a long happy life together," she said. She smiled when Bahman pumped Baba's hand up and down far too many times.

And Roya leaned into the door feeling a surge of relief and nerves. Her parents had approved. Now his parents just had to come and meet with hers officially.

⌘

A few days later, Roya drank strong coffee with Bahman as they sat on the pink-cushioned chairs in Café Ghanadi.

Suddenly she had the strange feeling of being watched. Her body tightened at the thought of thugs on the prowl for political dissidents again. She looked around the café with dread. But there were no men with batons. Then she noticed a tall young woman sitting a few tables away, wearing a green feathered hat with a large pin in it. The woman stared directly at her. She was beautiful, with olive skin, large dark eyes, pouty lips colored a deep crimson, and hair that fell in perfect waves beneath her hat. Roya could even make out a dark mole above her upper lip, like a movie star's. The woman continued to stare at Roya with an expression bordering on disgust.

"Bahman," Roya whispered. "Don't look now, but this woman at that table keeps staring at us."

"Who?" Bahman swiveled around.

"Don't look now!" Roya muttered under her breath.

But it was too late. Bahman had seen the woman. He turned around to face Roya again. His face and ears were red.

"She keeps staring, right?"

"Oh, that's just . . ." Bahman mumbled. "Don't worry."

"You know her?"

"That's Shahla."

"Who?"

He sighed. "My mother thinks she's my destiny."

Roya couldn't speak.

He leaned into the table and took her hand. "What matters is what I think. What *we* think," he quickly added. "I don't subscribe to that old-fashioned nonsense of arranged marriages. You know that."

Roya's head throbbed. "You never once mentioned her. You didn't tell me there was someone planned for you."

"Look, my mother, like most mamans, has—correction, *had*—a girl in mind for me. She picked Shahla out a while ago. Trust me, it's not what I want in the slightest. It's not what's going to happen."

"Why didn't you tell me? You should have told me. I would have liked to know!"

"Well, because. Look, Roya, my mother has some . . . issues. Sometimes she is not well. Emotionally. In her mind. You may have noticed."

Roya had first met Bahman's parents back in the spring when they were courting and they had gone to his house with a group of friends after school. Bahman's father was kind and quiet, but his mother intimidated her. The first time she'd met Mrs. Aslan (and each time since), it was as if she was being evaluated from head to toe. When she spoke in Mrs. Aslan's presence, Roya felt awkward and childish. It was obvious that Bahman's mother did not like her. She had been against their engagement. But in the end, Bahman's father, quiet and unassuming, had the last word because he was a man.

"You should have told me." Roya pushed away her coffee cup and got up. "No wonder your mother can't stand me. She had someone else in mind for you. How could you not tell me something so important? Did you think I wouldn't find out? In this city? Where students like us know the same people, when boys from your school date girls from mine, did you really think that I wouldn't find out?"

"Please, Roya. I feel nothing for her. Less than nothing. My mother has her own ideas about everything. She's . . . she's struggling."

Roya sat again because she didn't want to give the girl in the hat the satisfaction of seeing her quarrel with Bahman. She wanted to leave, but she couldn't. Even though she was furious with Bahman, she was already trying to save face on his account. This was the societal web of niceties and formalities and expected good female behavior that often suffocated her. But she had no choice but to bear it, to try to navigate within it. That much she knew.

"Don't worry, my mother will come around. Give her a little time to get to know you better. How could she not see in you all the goodness that the rest of the world sees?"

"Please. She thinks you can do better."

"That's actually impossible, so she's wrong. Look, it's her nerves. My mother's not entirely in control of her emotions. She has her dark days. But she will come around, you'll see."

Of course there would be other contenders; Mrs. Aslan would have had other girls in mind for Bahman. In Mr. Fakhri's shop, among the bookshelves and in the dark, musty corners, it seemed that Bahman was hers alone. The boy in the white shirt and khaki pants was hardly ever there with other friends. Their conversations, private jokes, jaunts to Café Ghanadi seemed encased in a separate sphere. Because he was politically active, she'd at first as-

sumed his circle of friends consisted of wonkish nationalists obsessed with Prime Minister Mossadegh. When she'd thought of
Bahman socializing, she'd imagined political debates held over
espresso with intellectual young men in cafés. But Jahangir was his
close friend, and she had already seen that Jahangir ran in very elite
circles. He was known for giving the best parties. Bahman was a
part of all of that—she was learning. Of course there would have
been other women planned for him, wanting him.

He leaned in and kissed her on the cheek. His mouth smelled
of burnt coffee. The Shahla girl could not have missed it. In public,
at the café, Bahman drew her in as if they were alone in the world,
as if they had nothing to hide.

Roya should have pushed his face away, but instead she allowed
the kiss to land. They were engaged, for God's sake. Their fate was
bound. No mother's prearranged plans could thwart them.

From the corner of her eye, Roya saw the girl called Shahla get
up and bump her way through the tables as she scurried out.

Chapter Seven

Mrs. Aslan

Against her will, Mrs. Aslan had to approve of the engagement because, as she often said if only people would listen, in this hellish world all it took was for the man to give his go-ahead, what did the woman's opinion matter? Apparently her feckless husband had to just approve of the match, and lo! It was done, stamped with a seal of legitimacy. As if she, the mother, hadn't been the one to push that boy out of her flailing, frail body, as if she hadn't held him to her breast month after month as he sucked her dry, as if she wasn't the one who held his hand and walked him all over the city to show him the world, as if she hadn't sat with him night after night encouraging him to tackle the poems and math problems in his notebooks. As if she hadn't done everything in her power so her son could do better, rise in this life! From the very beginning she had seen in this baby the potential for greatness. He would shuck the yoke of class and stagnancy; in this new, modern Iran, he could get to better social circles. Wasn't the country changing? Wasn't that what everyone said? Hadn't she managed through sheer determination and God's will to escape a destiny of poverty? She had been a little girl in torn slippers with a shabby headscarf tied at her neck, a girl who should have been nothing more than a destitute man's daughter, a peasant, a servant perhaps. A girl who had suffered un-utterable losses. But she had Bahman now.

She had married Mr. Aslan (it did no good to wallow in the grievances of a broken heart; whatever it was, it had happened this way) and through this marriage, she had defied the trappings of class. She'd married an engineer! She had raised their boy; did any-one in the entire city doubt the energy and intelligence and abso-lute talents of her son? Was he not the sun and the stars? She wanted that Roya girl gone from her son's life. Instead she had to stomach the girl giggling on her living room sofa. (Yes, they had a sofa. That was *it*; they had a sofa, Western-style furniture. In the tiny room of her childhood, there had been no chairs, no table, no fancy sofas. They had sat on the floor. They ate their meals cross-legged, from dishes arranged on the *sofreh* cloth on the floor.) Now this girl sat on *her* sofa. It made her livid. It made her sick-ness, a monster that was unpredictable and unforgiving enough, bear down even stronger. A tsunami of this horrible nervous ill-ness sometimes drowned her with little warning. She'd go down beyond reach, and when that happened not even her boy could haul her out of those moods. Though he did try.

It was during a particularly bad down-cycle of her sickness that Bahman boldly announced his desire to propose to Roya, and her husband, weak and ineffectual as he was, had suc-cumbed! Encouraged him, even. In her low moods, Mrs. Aslan had little power; she could barely get through the day, even the hour, didn't they know that? How could they pounce this news on her then? Maybe that's exactly why they *did* pounce it on her then, the sons of dogs. She would attend the god-awful engagement party only because, as ever, a woman ultimately had to give in to her husband. Even a weak, pathetic husband like hers. She wanted to prevent this catastrophe of a match. Her gorgeous son, who had so much to offer, who could do fabulous things with his life! Marrying some bookish, average girl who thought reading novels translated from Russian or English was something worthwhile, who was pretty but not astoundingly so, whose father struggled to maintain his stagnant clerkship. Whose father, worst of all, exhibited the same obsession with nationalism and the prime minister that had lately infected her own son. She didn't need her boy embroiled further in useless political activism. She wanted Bahman to succeed. Join the oil company, make money—there was so much to be made—so much potential for these young people!

"How are you, Mrs. Aslan?" that Roya girl dared to ask her now as she sat on her sofa. "Bahman said you had a difficult evening sleeping. Are you feeling any better?"

Limp and snotty and rude, that's what this girl was.

"How do you expect me to be?" Mrs. Aslan said. "You just wait, my girl. Life will slap you down too. It'll push you down when you least expect it. You'll see. This world lacks justice. Did you know babies die?"

The girl looked stunned, absolutely flummoxed and shocked. She couldn't even say anything.

"That's right. Did anyone tell you that when you seduced my son? When you lured him into that stuffy bookshop?" Her heart tightened as she spoke, her stomach lurched. Suddenly her body raged with heat; she wanted to tear her clothes off, to stand naked near the window, to feel wind on her skin, to feel anything but this suffocating descent into loss.

"Mother, please. Please." Bahman's voice sounded like it was coming from a mountaintop away. She had sunk into a sweaty panic attack.

"Love," Mr. Aslan began in a sonorous voice. "As our poet Omar Khayyam says, love is—"

"Enough!" Mrs. Aslan said. "Shut up." She couldn't bear it. Her husband was always pretending nothing was wrong. He was a wimp, a coward, a fool. He wouldn't even talk about the losses. She got up and walked out of the room to get away from his platitudes of poetry and that snot-girl Roya.

~✑~

The door slammed.

Roya only looked at her hands as she sat on the sofa. Her whole body shook. Bahman had warned her, he had told her about his mother's illness—how she descended into rages, how she could not control her moods. She would have to please this mother-in-law for decades to come, but even now it seemed she could do nothing right in Mrs. Aslan's eyes. Mr. Aslan looked like he had been kicked by a horse. They had pretended for a while to be normal and to have tea and to visit in the traditional way. But Mrs. Aslan had made zero pretense of liking Roya, and now she had rushed out in panic and anger. What was this illness, this "mood monster that takes her over," as Bahman had once described it? Mr. Aslan was constantly trying to make up for his wife's rudeness. Now he offered Roya another glass of tea, another piece of baklava. When Roya said no thank you, Mr. Aslan closed his eyes and leaned back, assuming the pose many Iranians took when they were about to recite the ancient Persian poets.

For a minute, Mr. Aslan remained in this position, breathing deeply. Then he got up too. "Excuse me," he said with a slight bow. His eyes were teary. "I'll be right back."

Roya watched him shuffle out of the room. She stayed seated on the couch next to Bahman, next to the son of these parents who were so different from any other couple she had met, who seemed so very far-gone and alone.

When his mother acted this way, when her rage took over and she abandoned the niceties of social etiquette, Bahman changed. He became quiet, deflated.

The sound of Mrs. Aslan's sobs landed like bullets against the closed bedroom door.

Roya squeezed his hand. "It doesn't bother me," she lied. "It cannot be helped."

The muffled sound of Mr. Aslan comforting and cajoling his wife came through.

Bahman didn't say anything. He just looked straight ahead. After a few minutes that felt endless, he quietly rested his head on Roya's shoulder. She felt his cheek even through the tiny stitches on the seam of the blouse that Maman had sewn. He burrowed his face into her. It was as though he wanted to disappear.

Roya kissed his head, stroked his hair. She would save him from this.

When Mr. Aslan finally came back, he looked depleted. "Now!" he said in a tone of forced cheer. "Who would like another tea?"

Babies die rang in Roya's ears.

Bahman stood up and went to the kitchen to bring more tea. It was all for her sake, this charade of holding the edges together. Of keeping the door shut to Mrs. Aslan's room, of pretending that her sobs did not continue. Bahman came back with fresh tea from the samovar, the glasses balanced on a silver tray. He was used to this, to getting tea, navigating the kitchen, serving, possibly even cooking. Women's work. He and his father did more of it than any men

Roya had ever seen. The woman in their house was ill. Father and son picked up the pieces, picked up the slack. They made sure the house functioned. Bahman had told her that any servant who was hired to help was eventually fired by his mother—she could not take their gall, their presence. She did not get along with the help. It was better this way, he said. They were a private family; better for others not to be exposed to her moods anyway. As he stood with the tray of tea now, it was clear he would have preferred to protect Roya from this embarrassment of emotion, this lack of control.

Bahman carefully placed the tray on the table.

It would be worth it. She would accept his mother, do her best to get along with her. For this boy, she would do anything.

Chapter Eight

Engagement Party

Their engagement party was on a summer evening in July, several weeks after Roya and Bahman had both graduated from high school. Maman and Baba had invited family and close friends to their home for the celebration. Maman and the girls worked for hours in the kitchen, cooking and preparing. On the day of the party, Kazeb, a woman they sometimes hired to help with the housework, came over to go shopping with Zari for last-minute items while Roya and Maman focused on the star main dish: jeweled rice.

By the kitchen sink, her brown hair up in a bun, her kind, round face damp from exertion, sleeves rolled up so her chubby arms were visible, Maman cleaned the *zereshk*. These small dried barberries would be nestled into the basmati rice when the dish was done. Roya stood next to her mother and inhaled her familiar lemony scent. She helped her pick out any pieces of dirt or tiny stones from the barberries and then watched her put the dried berries in a small sieve and rinse them.

"Do you think it will be different, Maman?" Roya asked.

Maman put the sieve in a bowl of cold water to soak.

"What will?"

"Us. You and me." Much as Roya yearned for a new life with Bahman, it was strange to think of the changes ahead. Would this house with its white lace curtains and kitchen so meticulously organized still feel like her home? Would everything change? Would she still be able to joke with Zari and be one of the family like before?

Maman sighed. "This is what was intended, Roya Joon. Girls grow up. They marry and move out." She pulled the sieve of barberries out of the bowl of water and shook it several times over the sink. "Would I want you to be living in this house with me till the day I die? I cannot lie. There are selfish moments when the idea of my children never leaving my side seems fine by me! But of course you need to start your own life. You have your own future. May you and Bahman have a long and happy life together, *inshallah*, God willing."

A long and happy life together. The ground would shift in so many exciting and scary ways when she and Bahman got married at the end of the summer. Maman handed the sieve to Roya and Roya laid the barberries on a kitchen towel, patted them dry, and scattered them onto a big plate—all movements she'd mastered with Maman's guidance over the years. But this time she was keenly aware that though she was cooking with Maman like always, it was for an event that would take her further away from her mother.

"We'll still be close. You'll only be forty minutes away, Roya Joon!" Maman laughed as if she could read her mind. "We can see each other every day, if you like. If you don't get tired of your maman."

Roya and Bahman had decided to lease a few rooms in a house with levels for rent conveniently located near his parents' home. That way Bahman could still keep an eye on his mother in her volatile state. The new rooms were a bit far from the newspaper office where Bahman would start working in the fall, but he could take the bus to work. Eventually they would get a bigger place of their own, of course, but this would be a good stepping-stone. Roya was so relieved that Bahman had said no to their staying at his parents' home; it was a common custom for newlyweds to start married life in the groom's parents' house. But Bahman insisted that he didn't want Roya to feel like a caretaker to his mother, and that he and his father could handle it all as long as they lived close by.

Maman wiped her forehead with the back of her hand. "In this new stage of life, with your husband's blessing, of course, you can decide your next steps. Many will expect you to stay home and have babies, and that is a fine path too. Or if you like, you can try pursuing at least for a bit the science studies your father so cherishes?" Maman slit open a sack of rice and poured the grains into a large bowl. The grains clinked against the sides and landed in a mound inside.

Baba and his lectures. *Madame Curie!* Roya took the rice and filled the bowl with water to get the extra starch out. "I know he was so excited and proud of us for even having the option to study science. But it was never what I . . ."

"Wanted to solely study?" Maman finished the sentence for her. Maman's hair shone in the sunlight that came through the kitchen window. A few strands of gray were visible in the light. "My daughter who loves her novels. Who loves to read. You will figure it all out, Roya Joon. Baba is so happy for you, as you know. He loves Bahman." She stroked Roya's cheek. "You will always be my baby. Forty minutes is nothing."

Roya finished washing the rice and set down the bowl. Together they would slightly sauté the barberries in a pan. They would
take chicken pieces and sprinkle them with salt, pepper, and turmeric and roast them till they were golden brown. They would boil
the rice and drain it and pour it back in the pot with a cloth under
the lid to catch the steam. Together she and Maman would drizzle
lime juice and dissolved saffron over the roasted chicken pieces and
arrange them on platters. They would chop up pistachios and sliver
almonds with a knife and add the pistachios and almonds to the
cooked rice. They would fold in a few curly orange rinds that
Maman had dried in the sun. For her engagement party, they would
serve a dish actually worthy of a wedding. It was a time of joy. Of
new beginnings. Maman was right. Roya could come by anytime to
say hello, ask for advice, sit with her in the kitchen and drink tea.

Zari and Kazeb came in, talking loudly as they carried large
pink boxes of pastries.

"These are so heavy; my back won't recover for a while!" Zari
plopped the boxes onto the kitchen table. She took a look at Roya.
"What's wrong with you? Why the serious face? Aren't you excited?" Zari's tone was slightly taunting but also concerned.

"Of course I am. Why wouldn't I be?"

"You aren't nervous?"

"A little. But a mother will still—" She meant to tell Zari that
Maman had reassured her they would still remain close.

That was all Zari needed to take the baton and run. "It's his
mother getting you down, isn't it? She thinks we're not good
enough, I know! She thinks her son can do better. She's just one of
those greedy women who want to climb the social ladder. She
wants even more money, higher status. Right? She's thinks Baba's
job as a government clerk is beneath their family. She looks *down*
on us!"

"Zari, enough!" Maman said.

"No, really. How will you put up with her?" Zari asked Roya.

"I love him."

"She was against your engagement! Doesn't that tell you something? Is that really what you want? To be married to someone whose mother hates you?"

"Enough with the dramatics, Zari. Please," Maman said.

Zari sucked in her lips but went on: "How naïve you are sometimes, Sister! His mother has done nothing but try to sabotage you. Sons are putty in their mothers' hands. This son more than most. 'Oh, what can I get you, Mother? Oh, do you want another tea, Mother? Oh, let me get that for you, Mother!'"

"That's what good sons do!" Maman said.

"To this extent?"

"Yes!" Roya said. "And anyway, she finally agreed, didn't she? So it's not as if she's against us marrying now."

"Just be careful, *basheh*, okay?"

"Zari." Roya lowered her voice and looked around as if about to divulge a difficult secret. "She is not well."

It was only when Roya had met Mrs. Aslan a few times that she realized Bahman compensated for his mother's fragile state by trying to be everything to her and the family. It was as though his competence and kindness and generosity were in direct response to his mother's lack of those qualities. He met his mother's pit of nerves with steadiness. Where she was unkind and rude, he was generous and forgiving. His mother's fragility seemed to create in him the need to suck everything he could from life and to be strong. Was that why Mr. Fakhri said he was the boy who would change the world? Roya had always thought it was because of his activism for Prime Minister Mossadegh. But maybe it was because seeing his mother trapped by the whims of her illness, isolated in her house most of the time, unable to converse well with others or navigate social situations effectively, drew from Bahman an ever-stronger desire to stamp his mark on life. To steer his own ship, right wrongs, "change the world," as Mr. Fakhri put it.

"Look, Zari. There are things about Mrs. Aslan that you just don't know. So maybe you can be a little more considerate. Just leave it be. You don't know the whole story," Roya whispered in the kitchen.

"I know about her crazy moods. Who doesn't! That's no secret!"

Roya put down her spatula, defeated.

⁓

Roya, Maman, and Baba stood in a row near the entrance, smiling and greeting each guest as they arrived. Aunts and uncles, close friends and relatives came in with flowers and pastries, congratulated Roya and her parents, and made themselves comfortable around the living room. The women sat, chatted, and drank tea on one side while the men stood in groups on the other, tea glasses in hand. Roya had expected Bahman and his parents to be the first to get there, but they were late. Where was he?

Finally the door opened and a worn-looking Bahman came in, leading his mother by the arm. His father looked ravaged as he shuffled in behind them.

"Sorry to be so late," Bahman greeted Maman and Baba, then kissed Roya on the cheek. Roya was shocked by the gesture. They were engaged, yes, but it still felt forward and bold. Displays of affection like this in front of elders were disrespectful. But her body grew warm from the kiss and she softened.

"Is everything all right?" she whispered.

"We just had some . . . trouble," Bahman mumbled.

Trouble meant his mother. Mrs. Aslan must have been in one of her moods. "Fragile and forceful" was how Bahman had described her once.

Roya stiffened as her future mother-in-law approached her in a black blouse, black skirt, and thick black stockings. On a beautiful summer evening! Most of the other women were dressed in light colors: Maman shone in an elegant turquoise dress. Zari wore pink, just like the Hollywood movie stars she so admired. Roya had slipped on the green dress that Maman had sewn for the occasion. But Mrs. Aslan looked like she was attending a funeral. She even clutched a dark knit shawl around her shoulders. Two circles of rouge stood out on her cheeks. She smelled of a cloying, flowery perfume.

Maman did not approve of makeup. She derided women who needed "war paint" to prove their beauty. As Zari toiled in front of the mirror putting newspaper strips in her hair to create perfect waves, Maman would lecture, saying, "Beauty should speak for itself. No need to edit God's work."

"Some of us need to edit, Mother," Zari would retort. "Some of us have to help him out."

"Oh dear, Mrs. Aslan, aren't you hot in that shawl?" Maman asked gingerly, and nudged Roya. "Roya Joon, take Mrs. Aslan's shawl for her."

Before Roya could take it, Mrs. Aslan tilted one rouged cheek, then the other, for Roya to kiss.

The pasty rouge on her future mother-in-law's face tasted like withered roses. Roya withdrew her face and reached for the shawl. But her hand was met by a dry and brittle slap. "Don't!" Mrs. Aslan snapped.

"Oh, I'm so sorry." Roya's face grew hot.

Bahman quickly grabbed his mother's arm. "Let's sit you

down, Mother. You need to take a breath." Bahman led Mrs. Aslan to the far corner of the room and placed a chair against the wall, away from the other guests.

"So odd!" Zari whispered as she sidled up to Roya holding a tray filled with nuts she'd been offering to the guests. "It's boiling outside! Who wears *that*?"

"She's probably just . . . never mind! Just pass around the nuts!"

Zari raised her eyebrows, shook her head, and trotted away.

"My girl, don't worry. Mrs. Aslan had some difficulties getting ready for the festive occasion tonight, that is all," Mr. Aslan said, walking up to her. "Some days are better than others. You must forgive. Seeing you young people fills our hearts with joy. It is the best thing."

He looked like he meant it. Roya felt sorry for him. Mr. Aslan smiled at her now, his eyes kind. They both turned their gazes to the far corner of the room where Bahman had seated his mother.

He hovered over her, holding her bag in one hand and adjusting her chair with the other. Mrs. Aslan was talking nonstop. Bahman shook his head adamantly in response to what she was saying. But Mrs. Aslan didn't stop; she looked like she was pleading. Bahman stared at the floor, quiet. Mrs. Aslan fumed, pointing to her bag. Finally Bahman opened the bag and took something out. Roya's eyes widened. It was a rectangular bamboo flag, the kind used to fan flames when grilling kebab. Balancing himself on his haunches, Bahman slowly fanned his mother's face with the bamboo flag. Mrs. Aslan stopped talking, closed her eyes, and leaned back in the chair.

Roya looked away.

"If only," Mr. Aslan said in a voice tinged with sadness, "she would take off the shawl. She won't listen, Roya Khanom. She will not budge from her ways. Please, forgive. It's just not in her hands."

In the kitchen, pink boxes from Café Ghanadi covered the counters. Kazeb and Zari took out the elephant ear and tongue-shaped pastries they had bought earlier that day and Maman arranged them onto platters with care, as if not one crumb could be out of place. She looked up, her face flushed from working in the hot kitchen. "What are you doing here, Roya Joon? Go back to the living room and mingle with the guests. You should be talking to everyone. Go on!"

"I want to help."

"No, you're the future bride! Please, go and talk to the guests. Especially Mrs. Aslan. You mustn't be rude now. If you're going to have a happy marriage, you need to please your mother-in-law. That is what every woman knows as God's indisputable truth!"

"Khanom, that's why if I ever get married, my hope is to find a decent orphan as my groom," Kazeb chimed in.

Zari burst out with an approving laugh. "Good plan!"

Maman shook her head. "Roya Joon, you need to be respectful. Go and talk to Mrs. Aslan, you can't ignore her."

Roya wanted to stay in the familiar coziness of the kitchen with her mother and sister and Kazeb, enveloped in the scent of basmati rice and saffron, arranging elephant ear and tongue-shaped pastries onto plates and discussing the crispiness of the bottom-of-the-pot crunchy *tahdig* rice. It was strange to be in the role of soon-to-be-bride. As her mother arranged the pastries, Roya wondered how things had happened so fast. She and Bahman had danced their way out of the Stationery Shop and into

Café Ghanadi and met each other's families and gotten engaged al-most in fast-forward motion, like the old Charlie Chaplin films shown on repeat at the cinema.

"Off you go!" Maman shooed her out.

Roya reluctantly walked back into the living room.

Bahman no longer fanned his mother. He now stood with a group of men including Baba, holding court. It was good to see him back to his old bold self. The subservient boy fanning his mother's face had been hard to watch. Above the din of voices, Ba-ba's laughter rang out. He was clearly enchanted by his future son-in-law. Roya felt a surge of gratitude for Bahman: his energy, his kindness, his ability to delight his audience. Surely she could talk to his mother.

She made her way between the groups of guests to the far cor-ner where Mrs. Aslan sat. She would be polite, she wouldn't argue, she would dutifully listen to Mrs. Aslan complain about how hot it was in the room even as she sat there in a winter shawl.

As she approached Mrs. Aslan's chair, Roya was surprised to see a man leaning over her. She couldn't tell who it was; she could only see his back. He wore a crisp linen suit. Was he a relative? Bahman had told her how part of the reason his mother had such a hard time was that she was so alone. Her relatives were all down south and she did not see them much. Mrs. Aslan was isolated in Tehran, counting on only a few neighbors and a social network that, due to Mr. Aslan's timidity and her own difficult personality, was scant.

Roya drew closer to Mrs. Aslan and the unidentified man. This time it looked like Mrs. Aslan's complaint was about much more than the temperature of the room. She talked rapidly to the man, clutching her shawl with one hand and gesticulating with the other. She stopped when she caught sight of Roya and pursed her lips and motioned to the man. He turned around. "If it isn't the young bride!"

Roya recognized the voice before the face. "Mr. Fakhri?"

She'd never seen him so sharply put-together. At his shop, he usually wore a simple shirt and comfortable pants and had a professorial look, but tonight he was all dressed up. He cleaned up well.

"Oh, girl, don't look so surprised!" Mrs. Aslan sounded annoyed.

Roya blushed. The engagement party was for family and close friends. It wasn't a big affair; it was in their home and was simply an opportunity to share pastries and tea with their closest circle. But Maman, in typical fashion, hadn't been able to resist cooking a feast. To the traditional menu of pastries and tea, she had added her famous *jujeh* kebab chicken dish. Of course, she'd then had to make rice too, and white rice alone wasn't enough, she'd said, she couldn't *not* make the rice adorned with barberries, slivered almonds, pistachios, and orange rinds. "Manijeh Joon, it's not a wedding, it's just an engagement party!" Baba had protested. "I'm just making a little something!" Maman promised as she rushed around getting everything ready. "We don't want to overdo it now, we may jinx it!" Baba had appealed to Maman's superstition. "Don't worry!" Maman had said, and Baba rubbed his face the way he did when he worried. Roya knew he was tallying up the cost of everything. He was always thinking of how they could make their budget: pay Kazeb, buy chicken and meat, purchase the fabric so their dresses could be on par with the other girls'. *She thinks we're not good enough, I know! She thinks her son can do better. She's just one of those greedy women who want to climb the social ladder! She wants even more money, higher status.*

"Come, girl, all the color has jumped from your face!" Mrs. Aslan had the irritated tone of one addressing an inferior.

"I just . . ." Roya stammered. She turned to Mr. Fakhri. "I'm just surprised to see you here."

"*I* invited him. It is my son's engagement party, after all. Or don't I have the right to invite old friends?"

"You know each other?"

Mr. Fakhri laughed nervously. "My dear, it was in my shop, on my watch, under my bookshelves, with my pages surrounding you, that your romance began. You know that. That is all Mrs. Aslan means."

Roya remembered how Mr. Fakhri had told her to exercise "severe caution" with Bahman that second time he'd come into the shop. Had he meant because of Bahman's mother? This difficult woman who made her feel unwanted and second-best? Did Mr. Fakhri know that Shahla had been planned for Bahman? How did he even know Bahman's mother?

"What a masterpiece you've conducted, indeed. Brought my son and this girl together, now didn't you, Mr. Fakhri? Bravo! What a miracle-maker you are." Mrs. Aslan snorted.

Beads of sweat formed on Mr. Fakhri's forehead. "You give me far too much credit, Mrs. Aslan," he said quietly. "I don't have the miracle-making powers you claim."

"Oh, aren't you just so humble. Such a perfect gentleman! The kind who would harm no one, not one soul. Not . . . one . . . child," Mrs. Aslan said slowly.

The scent of saffron rice wafted from the kitchen. They would eat soon. The guests would eventually leave. The engagement party would be over. She and Bahman would marry at the end of the summer. Mrs. Aslan would come around. She would get well. She had to get well.

"Take a bow!" Mrs. Aslan said shrilly. "Take your bow, Mr. Fakhri. Look at what you did!" She whirled her arm in a huge circle above her head. "You brought two young lovers together! How absolutely magical of you!"

Roya felt weak and sick. She was embarrassed to see Mr. Fakhri look so uncomfortable and defensive. And Mrs. Aslan's sarcastic tone was off-putting and unsettling.

Then a slight breeze, like a fresh gust of wind. The particles of air around her shifted. Bahman was next to her. He had strode toward them, like a captain recognizing the warning signs of a sinking vessel. He put his arm around her waist, and suddenly Roya was on safer ground. Right in front of Mr. Fakhri and his mother, he pulled her close to him. She could smell the soap on his skin. She could feel the crispness of his white shirt against her arm.

"Is everything good here?" Bahman asked pointedly. "Mother? Everything all right?"

It was a warning as much as a question. Roya knew that Bahman did not want his mother to spoil this evening. His torso touched hers as they stood as a unit in front of Mrs. Aslan and Mr. Fakhri, protectively, daringly.

Mrs. Aslan slumped in her chair. The rouged cheeks looked more ridiculous than ever against her wan skin.

"I was just congratulating Mr. Fakhri, Bahman Jan. He changed the course of your life, he surely did! You could have had your pick of any number of beautiful, wealthy young women. You know I've had my eye on one in particular for so very long—she is the perfect match for you! But Mr. Fakhri and his books and papers came to the rescue and provided *love*. How quaint! The two of you, just like the characters in those books you read, the novels from the West. Artificial romance—"

"Mother, can I get you anything?" Bahman interrupted. His voice was strained. "Mother, can I please ask you to stop?"

"I am simply thanking Mr. Fakhri," Mrs. Aslan continued, "for his services. He is so good at finding the right match for love. For him, love is what matters above all else. Mr. Fakhri would do anything for it. He is just *so* pure of heart."

Mr. Fakhri stared at his shoes. He didn't say a word.

"It is hard for me . . ." Mrs. Aslan's voice faltered. ". . . to tolerate this. I cannot tolerate . . ." She gazed off into the distance. "Tolerate is all I've done." Her voice choked up.

Bahman's arm slipped from Roya's waist. Something in the texture of the air had changed again. Bahman stepped away from Roya and knelt by his mother. When he spoke, his voice was soft. "Perhaps I can get you more tea. Let me get you more tea."

Mrs. Aslan tilted her head and brought her knitted black shawl to her face. She sobbed.

"Mother." Bahman took her hand. "Oh, Mother."

Most of the other guests were deep in conversation. The room was filled with their laughter. Roya envied them for their obliviousness to the scene in the corner. They did not have to bear Mrs. Aslan's anger, the drama created by her presence. On this sinking ship, she, Bahman, and Mr. Fakhri were alone.

Bahman knelt in front of his mother and pulled her head to his chest. Roya and Mr. Fakhri stood frozen, spectators to a painfully private moment, as the mother sobbed into her son's chest.

When Bahman got up, his white shirt was stained crimson. The red rouge his mother wore sat in splotches near his heart.

Roya wanted to take Bahman's shirt and scrub it clean, scour off his mother's stains. But she was paralyzed, numb.

"I'll get more tea," Mr. Fakhri finally said.

"Don't forget what I told you," Mrs. Aslan murmured.

"I won't," Mr. Fakhri said quietly. "You like your tea strong."

With small, nervous steps, he moved away.

Mrs. Aslan tightened her shawl around her shoulders and looked at Bahman. "This place is too cold and the lights are all wrong."

"I am sorry, Mother," Bahman said softly. "I am just so sorry."

Everyone went home, and the engagement party ended. Afterward, Maman burned incense to get rid of any jealous energy. She waved the fumes of incense over Roya's head and muttered for the jealous eye to be blinded.

"Oh, don't let them *cheshm* you, Roya Joon, give you the evil eye," Zari said, even though she'd been quite vocal that she didn't like the idea of Roya with Bahman from the very beginning. "There is nothing worse than the power of the evil eye. Jealous fools see that you're happy and successful now with that boy, and then *zap*! They jinx it all. Watch out!"

Chapter Nine

1953

Tangled Tango Troubles

Roya's life kept getting bigger, deliriously exhilarating. Just when she thought she had reached the cusp of something (for example, after she'd finished all the translations of Russian novels that Mr. Fakhri stocked in his shop), another exciting frontier came along. The country was awakening artistically with a new class of intelligentsia. The city blossomed with publishing, cinema, theater, literature, and art.

Now that they were engaged, she and Bahman could mix without chaperones and go out openly, even in the evenings, without worry.

Bahman's friend Jahangir had a bona fide gramophone. He owned records from the East and the West. They started attending his social gatherings as a couple. At his parties, Roya heard songs in a foreign tongue that was so sexy it was sinister. So smooth, it softened hardship.

Jahangir's dance soirees were on Thursday nights, the eve of the Friday holiday. His parents had access to all the latest gadgets, such as the gramophone. Bahman said that when his mother first found out that Jahangir's family dripped with wealth, she'd greedily encouraged his friendship with him. Roya grimaced at this; Mrs. Aslan no doubt had been excited about the sophisticated, rich young ladies like Shahla who could be prospects for Bahman at Jahangir's house.

"*Bah bah*, come in, come on *in*!" Jahangir hugged Roya and Bahman when they arrived. "Look!" he shouted to the other guests. "It's the Perfect Couple! Do we know two more good-looking people? Just look at them! *Tabrik*! Congrats!"

Roya and Bahman's engagement was shiny and fresh, their couplehood something to be celebrated. And based on the expressions of a few women in the crowd, something definitely to be envied.

"What's on the menu for tonight?" Bahman asked.

"Tango, my friend!"

Roya couldn't even make it to the table laid with goblets of crushed melon and ice. She and Bahman were surrounded. Bahman glowed with his usual charm as everyone jostled around him. Though Jahangir owned the gramophone and the music and the dance know-how, it was Bahman everyone wanted. With him, they practiced their first steps. For him, they flirted. Bahman had memorized the lyrics, in a language he did not speak, of Sinatra songs and Rosemary Clooney ballads. From being with him at other get-togethers since their engagement, Roya knew that if a part of the room grew quiet, if for a minute the conversation went stale, Bahman's presence lit everything up again. It was hard not to be glued to his movements as he danced. Roya was well aware that she wasn't alone in being enchanted by him. The girls laughed in high staccato near him, swooned when he told jokes.

"Come with me." Bahman took Roya's arm and pushed past

everyone. He led her to the middle of the living room. A song for a
waltz had just started. This she could do—it was one of the first
dances Bahman had taught her, and she'd practiced with Zari for
weeks. Zari had pulled Roya back and forth in their bedroom,
scolding her when she made a mistake. *Roya, remember. This isn't
our twirling hands/swaying hips Persian dance. This is serious. Concentrate!* With Bahman's instruction week after week and Zari's
forced practice, Roya's confidence grew. Now she glided with Bahman across the room, inhaling his familiar scent.

"I need a drink," she said when they finished.

He let her go.

At the refreshments table, Roya picked up a goblet of crushed
melon-ice and a spoon. The sweet melon-ice filled her parched
mouth. Suddenly there was a sharp tap on her shoulder.

She expected to see Bahman, but instead a tall, wavy-haired
woman with olive skin and a movie-star mole above her lip (real or
drawn on? If Zari were here, she would know) stared down at her.
Shahla, the girl from the café.

"Thirsty?" she asked. Her voice was husky, coarse.

"Yes," was all Roya could think to say. No hello, no introduc-
tion, no niceties.

"Well, you cast your net and caught him. Hoorah! He's always
been a slippery one. But somehow"—the girl studied Roya's hair,
her green dress—"somehow *you* did it. It's mind-boggling."

The melon and ice stayed in Roya's cheek, frozen.

"To think, Jahangir didn't want me to come tonight because
he was worried it would upset Bahman or . . . *you*. Jahangir and I
have been friends almost all our lives. Why should I not show up
to his party? Besides, I had to see for myself up close what made
Bahman such a lover boy. And now"—she looked Roya up and
down again—"I get to see what the fuss is about." Shahla looked

down at Roya's shoes. They weren't the baby-doll shoes of her high
school uniform. They were mules that had belonged to Maman:
green suede with a small brass buckle on the side. "Please God,
look!" Shahla shook her head, snorted, and then walked away.

"Everything good?" Bahman came over, face flushed from
dancing. Roya hadn't even noticed who he'd danced with after
their waltz. She couldn't stop people from being lured to his side.
Men and women would always flock to him.

"Hey, what's wrong?" he asked.

Roya cracked down hard with her teeth on the ice. "Nothing."

Bahman glanced in the direction of the wavy-haired movie
star look-alike, who had slinked to the other side of the room.
"Please. Don't worry about her. I saw her talk to you. I can't believe
she had the audacity to show up tonight. What did she say?"

Roya couldn't speak.

He took the goblet from her hand and rested it on the table.
He pulled her close and touched her neck. "Hey, Roya, come on.
She's nothing to me." He kissed her forehead, right where Maman
would claim her destiny was written in invisible ink. Shahla, wavy-
haired and pouting from across the room, could not have missed
this kiss either.

"She can see you. Stop. Everyone can see you."

"Good. Let them. I want"—he kissed her again—"to kiss you
in front of the whole damn world."

"*Basseh*, enough," Roya said. But after the fourth kiss, after he
was so close that she could feel the perspiration on his shirt, she
had almost forgotten about Shahla.

The soirees and the dancing, the music and the women
mixed with men, the songs from America and the dances, the
crushed melon in ice-cold goblets sometimes spritzed with what
she was sure must have been alcohol—all of this was an unex-

pected secret scene for her. Who knew that the boy who would change the world even knew how to dance? That he had this group of friends? That he was so close to the ever-popular wealthy playboy Jahangir?

"I hope they all writhe with jealousy," Bahman said, and nuzzled his face into her neck.

"I think you just want to writhe." Roya giggled.

"With you? Always. How much longer till we get married?" He gently kissed her throat.

"Now, you behave, mister. I am a virtuous girl," she teased. But she let him feel the contours of her neck with his mouth.

He looked up then with his dark eyes twinkling—the eyes that had struck her as filled with joy that first day at the Stationery Shop. "I'm counting down the days till we can be together. Roya, I love you so much."

They stood like that, face-to-face. His breath was warm. Her heart pounded against his chest.

"Well, you're stuck with me!" she finally said.

"I want to be stuck so badly," he groaned, and laughed.

She picked a piece of lint from his collar. "Now then. As the boy who would change the world, can you please be a role model in front of all these people?"

"*Bacheha!* Kids!" Jahangir lifted his arms into the air and wiggled his waist. "The time has come to taaaango!"

He put on a new record, and sultry guitar chords filled the room. "Bahman, get over here!" Jahangir motioned from across the room. "I'd like to demonstrate with you."

Bahman walked over and they stood face-to-face, cheek-to-cheek, Jahangir's arm around Bahman's waist, his other arm extended with his hand clasping Bahman's. Jahangir drew Bahman in tight and slowly they moved. The song was sensual, almost alarming. It made Roya long for something she couldn't even define, something forbidden and inviting. Watching Jahangir and Bahman dance felt like watching two strangers. Like watching what she'd never known she yearned for.

After the tutorial, after giggles and titters from the girls and the end of the song, Bahman dropped Jahangir's hand and took Roya to the center of the room. They were joined by a few brave couples game enough to give it a go. When Jahangir started the song again, Bahman and Roya clasped each other. At first they got it wrong; they wobbled, and she almost fell over. The stubble on Bahman's chin dug into her cheek. Being so close to him filled her with a desire so strong she had to force herself to focus on the steps. Her movements were wrong, but it just didn't matter. Her body was flush against Bahman's, her arm extended as one with his, her hand in his. Bahman stayed in character, imitating Jahangir's serious and sexy look from the tutorial. It made Roya smile, and he frowned as if to chide her, so she quickly imitated his mock-serious expression. They tried and tried again until they were able to get across the room without looking like they'd collapse.

If she believed in fate, she would know that they were meant to meet, to fall in love like this, to want only to be together. Her body fit so well into his, it was as though she'd found her home. She was meant to have been in that Stationery Shop when he strode in whistling; she was meant to share Rumi's poetry with him, to feel this connection with him. These things were meant to happen—it was impossible to think of a life without him now. She was his. It was that simple. It was more than destiny. It was reality, a practicality almost. It wasn't a dream. It was simple fact.

"Hey, what are you thinking?" Bahman asked her as they glided across the floor.

"What?"

"Never have I seen anyone think so hard while dancing. You're doing great, don't be scared."

"Oh," Roya said. "Thanks."

The sensual guitar music practically vibrated through them. He was right. Why worry? None of it mattered. They were together and that was all that mattered and would ever matter.

"Where are you? You're so far away." He kissed her neck.

"Could I be any closer to you? We're practically stuck to each other! Your dream come true!"

"I'm not complaining." He smiled. "But your thoughts. You look like you're trying to figure out the world."

"I know better than to try."

"You had the same deep look of concentration when I first met you."

"You whistled like a fool. You didn't even look at me."

She thought the dance was over, but the song just blended into another one. Bahman clearly had no intention of letting her go. Together they continued. Whether the other couples had stopped dancing she did not know. Her face was so close to his he must have tasted the melon on her breath.

"Last winter. The politics, the rallies. You saved me," he said.

"Hardly."

"You did, you have no idea."

She wondered what he meant. Saved him from being sucked even deeper into politics? Saved him from being wedded eventually to Shahla? Saved him from the force of his mother? She wanted to ask, but she also didn't want to get into it. That winter galvanized by politics had melted into a spring so soft, so sweet; it would forever be ingrained in Roya's memory with the taste of *shirini*, the buttery pastries, and the bitter, intense, creamy coffee.

"You're less political now," she admitted.

"It matters less to me now. But I'm worried."

"About us?"

"They want to oust Mossadegh."

When she heard the prime minister's name, her hand grew slack. "Of course. I thought it all mattered less to you now, you just said—"

"No such thing as no politics for us, Roya Joon. Politics drives every single thing in this country whether we like it or not. All of this: the dancing, the gramophone, these girls dressed like they're in an American movie, do you think any of it could exist without the efforts of those who are political?"

She wanted another crushed melon-ice drink. She wanted to sit down. They were stuck together in an embrace that was sexy but also suddenly stultifying. If she even tried to peel her body away from his in the middle of this dance, it would probably be impossible, against the laws of nature, against fate.

"You're worried," she sighed. "About the prime minister. I see."

"There are rumors that they want to overthrow him."

"Who's they?"

"The Shah's forces. The English. The Americans. All of them together. I've heard that—"

"He's crazy about you!" Jahangir suddenly tangoed past them with Shahla. Shahla, stiff in Jahangir's arms, kept her gaze on the ceiling, looking stoically at the chandelier. "All I hear is Roya, Roya, ROYA!" Jahangir sang out.

Bahman held her even closer as Jahangir and Shahla spun by in a fury. Shahla's glare could have extinguished the lights of the chandelier.

Bahman leaned into her and whispered, "Did you know that Shahla's family works for the Shah? Her father is allied with his police."

"Oh God. Please don't tell me you think she's a spy for the Shah."

"I'm just saying. I don't put anything past anyone." His belt dug into her.

"Does she know you're spreading Mossadegh's speeches all through town? Would she . . . get revenge on you for not fulfilling your mother's pact of arranged marriage?"

Bahman pressed his cheek into hers and was quiet. They didn't talk about the prime minister anymore, they just danced, hanging on to each other tighter, as though they could lose each other right there in the middle of Jahangir's living room. The Perfect Couple!

"Will Shahla and all the rest of these fancy friends *cheshm* us, give us the evil eye?" Roya asked as they danced across the room. "Sometimes their envy feels palpable. Like you can even touch it."

"Oh, come on! Don't believe in that evil-eye stuff. It's superstitious junk. I wish our culture could move past it. What we have? No one can touch it. Anyway, *this* is meant to be."

"I thought you didn't believe in superstition."

"I don't."

"Isn't *meant to be* another way of saying *destiny*?"

He smiled. "Nothing can come between us. We can't be jinxed. By anyone."

"Your mother," she dared to whisper.

He didn't say a word.

She looked down at their feet, ashamed. "Sorry."

"Look." He was suddenly serious. "She'll come around. You'll see." The music swelled into a crescendo, dramatic notes hitting a climax. Without warning, he dipped her. The blood rushed to her head, the room swam, everything was upside down.

"You can't get rid of me," he said as he pulled her back up. "I'm not going anywhere. Ever."

Chapter Ten

1953

Letters in Books

The following Tuesday, Bahman disappeared. When she called his house, no one answered. When she knocked on the door, no one came out. Not a tired, wan Mrs. Aslan with rouge on her cheeks. Not a pleasing, generous Mr. Aslan asking her if she wanted tea. No one. Neighbors shrugged. One of them suggested they'd maybe gone to the North? To the sea? To escape the heat. That must be it. Just innuendos, just guesses, nothing clear.

After three days of no news from Bahman, Roya was weak with worry. Finally she broke down and went to the one place that had been at the center of it all: the Stationery Shop. She was afraid of what she might discover there—what Mr. Fakhri might know about political arrests. She had avoided going there at first, but now she had to know.

"My dear girl, are you not aware? Prime Minister Mossadegh has a lot of enemies. He wants to take our country forward, but foreign powers and our own two-faced traitors are trying to topple him. At any cost."

"Mr. Fakhri, please. Where is he?"

"He can't be with you right now."

"We're *engaged*. Look, Mr. Fakhri, your kindness is not overlooked—we'll always be grateful for how you helped us, how you let us . . . meet. But it was one thing when we came here before in secret. Now we're getting married. At the end of the summer! Please, just tell me what you know. One of his neighbors told me he might have gone up north to be by the sea. But why wouldn't he tell me? He would tell me, right?"

She was embarrassed to be so open and desperate with Mr. Fakhri. It was completely unbecoming. Zari would have a fit if she knew Roya was pleading so intently, practically begging for information. Roya had finally told her family that Bahman was missing. Baba, convinced that the Shah's thugs had arrested Bahman, couldn't sleep. Maman prayed for his safety holding the prayer beads of her *tasbih*, muttering Quran verses under her breath as she slid each bead to the other side.

"Just leave it be, my girl," Mr. Fakhri said.

"They're rounding them up left and right, I know. Please tell me what you've heard."

"Don't worry yourself, my dear. These things are just quite complicated. You need to rest. Don't worry—"

"Rest? He's missing! Tell me, in a city like this where everyone is in everyone else's business all the time, how is there no word about him or even about his father or his mother—"

Mr. Fakhri stiffened. "His mother?"

"Everyone I talk to knows nothing! How could no one know a thing?" It wasn't how a young woman should behave in front of an older man, raising her voice and making demands. But it nauseated her to think of Bahman in jail.

"His . . . family." Mr. Fakhri's face was pale. He quickly cleared his throat. "Are they all right? What have you heard?"

"Nothing! That's why I'm asking you!" Roya had the sudden urge to hurl the nearest book at him. Why was he giving her the runaround, acting like he had no idea what she was asking about? She spoke again in a deliberate, calm voice. "I know a lot of the political activists come through here, Mr. Fakhri. We all know that your shop is a safe haven for the pro-Mossadegh people. That you disseminate the information from here for the National Front and even for some of the communist *Tudehi* groups. Please tell me what you know. I can take it. I can be discreet."

"Okay then, young lady." Mr. Fakhri was silent for a moment. His expression was hard to read. "Fine. Did you know the government police come here too? That not everything is easily said?" He raised his eyebrows. "I'm telling you that you shouldn't worry. Just . . . trust in God. God is big."

Of course. She had been so blinded by her worry for Bahman that she'd completely overlooked the danger for Mr. Fakhri. She looked behind her, making sure no one else was present for this conversation. Spies could be anywhere. Was Mr. Fakhri on a watch list now? Had he been interrogated?

Mr. Fakhri leaned forward as though he was about to say something of great importance. Roya remembered her second encounter with Bahman—how Mr. Fakhri had leaned in and told her to practice "severe caution." She forced herself to remain calm. She couldn't lose his trust.

"My dear girl," Mr. Fakhri whispered, "Bahman is . . . busy. That is all. And he cannot be seen romancing right now."

"I'm his fiancée," she said through gritted teeth.

Mr. Fakhri sniffed. "Regardless. You understand, I'm sure?"

"No, actually, I don't."

Something changed in his composure; his intensity gave way. Mr. Fakhri looked around the shop with fear. Finally he sighed. "Bahman told me that anything you'd like to say to him can be said through letters."

"He did?" Roya's heart beat fast.

"Yes."

Her mind raced; she tried to think of all the possibilities that could warrant an exchange of letters. Why couldn't they talk? He had to be in hiding to avoid arrest.

"Of course. I'll write to him, then. "

Mr. Fakhri readjusted his glasses but said nothing.

"Mr. Fakhri? Can I please have his address?"

"His address?"

"You must know how to reach him?" She was walking on eggshells; she didn't want to sound too forward. If he were to renege on his offer . . .

"You give the letters to me. I'll make sure he gets them."

"Excuse me?"

"Please, young lady."

"But how?"

"The way it's done for others. I have my ways."

She couldn't stop herself from saying, "What ways?"

"Roya Khanom, how do you think a lot of young people who can't call each other or see each other in this city get their messages across?"

"Telegrams?"

"My young lady. It's in the books. They give me their notes

and I place them between the pages of the books. And when the next person comes to 'buy' a book, they receive the volume with the note inside it."

Roya glanced around the shop, at the bookshelves filled with the volumes she loved so much. She'd had no idea that these books were used as vehicles of communication. That people placed notes inside them using Mr. Fakhri as a conduit. The shop she had loved, where she had spent so many afternoons in study and sanctuary, suddenly seemed slightly sinister. So it was not only a place where political material was secretly disseminated, but a hub of letter exchange as well?

Not wanting to lose her only potential strand of communication with Bahman, she took in a deep breath. "Of course. I appreciate it. I'll have a letter for you tomorrow."

When she walked out into the harsh sunlight, the city reeked of heat and worry. Talk of a coup had been circulating for a while; Bahman's fear that the Shah's forces could team up with foreign powers and overthrow the prime minister was now shared by many others. Wherever he was, Bahman had to be involved with activists trying to stop a coup. Maybe that meant he hadn't been arrested; maybe he was just hiding. Surely Mr. Fakhri couldn't transfer letters to him if Bahman was actually in prison. Of course, Mr. Fakhri knew more than he was letting on. It was absolutely clear. But for some reason he was holding back. Fine. At least she could write to him. At least she had that.

❦

She composed her letter on a tablet of paper she'd bought in Mr. Fakhri's shop, blue ink from her fountain pen filling the page with words of longing. She had endless questions. Sometimes she couldn't help but write in a certain rhythm, a rhythm that someone kind (unlike her senior-year literature teacher, Mrs. Dashti) might call poetry.

The next day, when she gave the letter sealed in an envelope to Mr. Fakhri, he promised he'd get it into Bahman's hands. He said it with a worried sigh, as if he was doing all of this against his will.

"He will write back, yes?" she couldn't help but ask.

Mr. Fakhri shook his head and mumbled something about young love and "flagrant acts of hope." But he took her envelope.

When she went back to the shop a few days later, a few men in bowler hats and black pants lingered inside. She worried that they could be undercover hired spies for the Shah's forces. Mr. Fakhri handed her a copy of Rumi's book of poetry with a formal smile. She took it, exited, and walked for a few blocks with a heart that felt like it would explode; then and only then did she dare open the book.

In its pages, nestled tightly inside, was an envelope. She held on to it so hard that her knuckles hurt. Then she placed it back inside the book, not daring to open it in the street and read its contents in public, as if doing so were somehow illegal. She would have to wait until she was alone.

She clutched the book to her heart all the way home. But of course, the minute she got home, Zari complained that her fingers were tired from peeling all the eggplants as Roya gallivanted in the streets. That Roya never did her fair share of the work. Kazeb, the housemaid, eyed Roya suspiciously, her headscarf askew, her face sweaty from the eggplant-peeling, which apparently was the chore for the afternoon. Maman motioned for Roya to sit on an overturned bucket in the kitchen, and together they all finished peeling the eggplants, slicing them, salting them, rinsing them, drying them, frying them. Baba loved this dish, and at dinner that night he marveled at what cooks they all were. The more he talked about the eggplants and only the eggplants, the more Roya knew he was worried about Bahman and trying to cover up his anxiety. And she could not wait for dinner to be over so she could go to the room she shared with Zari, wait for her sister to fall asleep, and finally open and read Bahman's letter.

When they were in their nightgowns, after Zari had wrapped sections of her hair with newspaper strips, Roya itched for her sister to snore away. But Zari was in a talkative mood. "All this eggplant peeling is ruining my hands. Look at my skin, Roya. Just look at it. It's all raw and getting coarse. I can't stand it."

"Your hands are fine," Roya mumbled. Please, just let Zari sleep so she could read the letter.

"No thanks to you, Roya! Where were you this afternoon anyway? Kazeb and I had to do almost all the peeling. It's not fair. Just because you're a bride-to-be—" Zari stopped herself. "I'm sorry. I know you're worried about him. You were so quiet at dinner tonight. I know that all you do is think about Bahman. But you have to admit . . . you just have to agree that—"

"That what, Zari?" Roya asked under her breath.

"That maybe it's fate that Bahman skedaddled. Maybe you just can't expect much more from someone so obsessed with the prime minister. He is probably planning some political intrigue in hiding. Who knows? Perhaps we were all dumb to think he'd go against his mother and just marry you." Zari crossed her arms. "It could be he just couldn't do it, Roya. I hate to say it. But it could be. Roya?"

Roya didn't say much; she just listened as her sister droned on. When Zari got on one of her rants, it was best to ignore her. She didn't want to prolong the conversation. She just wanted to read the letter. Zari didn't know that Bahman had written to her!

"Change the world, my foot! It was foolishness supreme to think he'd stand up to his mother like that. But don't worry, Sister! At least now you won't have Mrs. Aslan chipping away at your soul for the rest of your life. Right?"

"Good night, Zari."

Finally, when her sister's breathing had relaxed and Roya was sure she was asleep, she got out of bed, and sat down by the window to read Bahman's letter by moonlight. She opened the envelope with great care, as though the words inside could break or tumble out of order if she didn't handle the letter correctly.

My dearest Roya,

When I got your letter, I thought I'd die of happiness. God, I miss you so much. I can't think, I can barely eat. I've wanted to crawl out of my skin these past few days. It feels like I haven't seen you for years. I am sorry that I had to leave so suddenly. I wish I could tell you why—I will one day. For now, please know that I am fine, that you need not worry. I'll be back as soon as I possibly can. It's just complicated right now and I have to figure it all out, to find a way. I can't wait till you're in my arms again.

I was so relieved to get your letter! Tell your parents not to worry about me. I'm fine, I promise. I hope Zari isn't torturing you too much.

You are in everything I see. In every moment, you are with me, Roya Joon.

In the hopes of seeing you again—the sooner the better.

You are my love.
Bahman

She ran her fingers across the letter, willing his scent to rise from the paper, wanting part of him to sink through the pads of her fingers. She had only seen his handwriting once before, the inscription he'd written inside the notebook he'd given her as a gift for the new year. Seeing his handwriting again felt like holding a piece of him. In each stroke, with each curve and dip of the letters on the page, she could feel him. And when she read the letter over and over and over again, his voice was inside her.

Naturally her response was effusive and filled with longing. She tended to be more reserved in what she said even when they were alone together. But somehow on paper, she was able to say what she'd had trouble saying in person. She could be just as loving. But she also could be direct; she could ask him difficult questions. *Where are you?* she wrote. *Why can't I see you?*

When she handed the letter to Mr. Fakhri the next day, she felt naked. But the envelope was sealed. Besides, surely Mr. Fakhri had better things to do than read the sweet nothings of two teenagers. She thought of her words being placed inside the pages of a Persian poetry book, hugged by the verses of the ancients. Their love was safe there. In a way, it belonged there. She tried to imagine one of Bahman's friends or a fellow activist coming into the shop, picking up the book, then delivering it to Bahman, wherever he was.

Until his next letter arrived, she was restless, distracted, preoccupied. She walked into walls, stared into space; nothing could shake her thoughts of him. Only when she received a reply was she temporarily at peace. To read his words, to see the strong script of his hand, the way he made his Farsi *n* so confident and intense, the way his lines sloped slightly upward at the end . . . It felt like hearing him, to hold that thin sheet of paper in her hand.

More and more frequently, the government police came to the Stationery Shop. Unlike just a few months ago, it was no longer a haven of privacy. A policeman or two lingered by the stacks of books—at first randomly, and then, it seemed, consistently. They watched who bought whose speeches. They took note of customers asking for pro-Mossadegh works, and they especially paid attention when anyone wanted anything Marxist. Mr. Fakhri looked beleaguered and tired. Like anyone being watched by government agents, his movements were self-conscious, his words robotic. He would still select for Roya works by the best writers and would still make sure that she got her weekly dose of poetry. But he was distracted and preoccupied now. Roya no longer lingered in the shop. She took her book from Mr. Fakhri in as natural a way as possible, careful not to show that she knew the volume contained not just the author's words, but Bahman's. Then she ran outside and waited for a time to be completely alone to read his words.

My dearest Roya,

I think of you all the time—every single day, every night. Truth is there are no times when you are not on my mind, and I wouldn't want it any other way. One day we'll look back on this separation and laugh. I can't wait till it's all behind us. Everywhere I see your beautiful face. If you are worried about me, please know I am safe, healthy, I only lack you, which means that I lack everything, of course. I am counting down the days, Roya Joon. Things are just a little difficult now. And the prime minister, his administration, it's all in jeopardy, but we will be the ones who'll look back on this time in history with pride. We are cementing our future in democracy. And here I go again, I know you don't like it when I speak too much of politics. Well, then, let me tell you that I can't wait to be married.

I dare to dream of our children.

I have it all planned out. I should be back in a few weeks.

In the hopes of seeing you again—the sooner the better.

You are my love.
Bahman

Chapter Eleven

1953

Sour Plums

"Sister, put that rubbish away and come to bed, my God!"

Roya stayed seated by the foot of the bed. "Have you *read* them? Tell me you haven't read them."

"Actually, I'd rather peel ten kilos of eggplants with Kazeb than read the sugary effusions of your activist lover."

"Then how do you know?"

"Come *on*, Roya. We have no secrets. Sisters have to trust each other, right? Just come to bed. You read the letters every night. You think I can't hear you drag the box out from under the bed, the paper rustling, you sniffling like a buffoon? It's a little silly, if you ask me." She paused, then asked, "Why did he leave? Where is he?"

Roya was embarrassed that Zari had known about the letters this whole time, and mortified that after so many letters from Bahman, she still couldn't answer the question of where he was and why he'd left. "It doesn't matter," she mumbled.

"Has he been arrested? Is he in a prison?" Zari suddenly sat up in the dark. Though it was hard to make out the expression on her sister's face in the sliver of moonlight, Roya sensed a certain thrill in Zari at the thought of Bahman in jail.

"Go back to sleep, Zari. It's not something I'd expect you to understand anyway."

"Why?"

"It's hard to describe the power of it to you. No offense, but you have no idea what it's like to be in love."

The minute she said it, she regretted it. A small sound came from the bed. A tiny squeak. Was it a swallowed sob? But of course Zari was probably laughing at her—it was likely a suppressed chuckle at Bahman's expense. Roya put the letters back in the box and slid them into their place. She climbed into the bed they shared. "Good night, Zari." She turned her back.

"You're thinking about him, aren't you?" Zari's voice wasn't even sleepy.

"What?"

"You think about him all the time. Right? He's the first person you think about when you wake up in the morning. He's in your dreams. You wish you didn't think about him all the time, but you can't help it. It can't be stopped. It's like he's always with you. No?"

"Have you been reading foreign novels too?" Roya propped herself on her elbow and faced Zari's side. How could Zari know so much about what it felt like? Her self-absorbed sister couldn't possibly have a love of her own. Could she?

Zari's figure under the soft cotton sheet was a small bundle. She was quiet. Then she said, "Good night, Sister."

Roya turned again and they lay back-to-back, each curved into the fetal position, only their bottoms touching. This was how they had slept ever since Zari had been old enough to leave Maman and Baba's room as a baby.

"Good night, Zari."

The phrases in his letters became as familiar to Roya as lyrics of famous poems, or the words of popular songs. They became permanently stored in her memory. She recited them in her mind that summer, as she waited for him to come back. *I think of you all the time—every single day, every night. . . . Everywhere I see your beautiful face.* She'd remember a line from one of his letters as she helped Maman in the kitchen, as she sewed small flowers onto a blouse with Zari, as she drank crushed melon-ice to chase away the heat. She remembered his words as the rallies outside grew in number and the political factions divided further.

She'd picked a small tin box to store Bahman's letters because he'd be back any day now and she didn't think they'd need to exchange too many. But surprisingly, the pile in the box grew. He didn't come back as soon as she'd hoped. With his absence, she felt smaller. With him gone, she was lost. Each letter she received gave her nourishment, a reason to keep moving forward. But her worry did not subside. She was sick with questions, sick with loneliness, and sick with longing.

Was it possible that through the letters her love for him grew? It did. It strengthened, solidified. The more she read his words and traced his handwriting on the page, the closer she felt to him. Food didn't taste quite the same since he'd left; the sun was listless; a pall hung over everything. But his letters sustained her and alleviated the feeling of emptiness, at least temporarily. His voice was in every syllable—she convinced herself his musky scent was in the fiber of the paper he used to write to her.

If only I didn't have to be away right now. I wish I was with you. We'll have the rest of our lives together, I will make it

up to you, Roya Joon. You will see and you will understand
soon enough.

Though she desperately wanted to know why he'd had to go,
she trusted him. It was impossible not to finish reading one of his
letters without being convinced that no man had ever loved anyone as strongly as Bahman loved her. He had to have his reasons,
he would tell her later; she believed him. Anytime she felt the tug
of doubt, anytime she felt too lost, she pulled the box of letters out
from under her bed and his words were the antidote. The letters
were exciting and comforting at the same time. They convinced
her that a sweeter, more romantic man had not existed.

I want nothing more than to get closer to you, Roya Joon. I
want nothing else.

‿✑

Bahman always wrote back. He never kept her waiting. The second-
to-last letter was inserted at the page of the Rumi love poem she'd
been reading that spring day when Mr. Fakhri had rushed to the
bank and she and Bahman were alone for the first time. Roya was
moved by this gesture. Had Mr. Fakhri seen her read that poem?
Had he paid such close attention and now placed the envelope
there for her? She sniffed the paper as she always did for the scent
of Bahman. His letter started with how much he missed seeing her.
But then it devolved into paragraphs about his fear of Prime Minister Mossadegh being overthrown and the dangers of foreign influence. Having oil was their curse, he wrote—imagine how different
it would be if others weren't always greedy for their oil. He wrote
about how the British and the Russians competed for influence

in their country. *The threat of a coup, of invasion and war—it is all there, Roya Joon. But we will fight!*

He signed the letter *Ya marg ya Mossadegh!* Give me Mossadegh or give me death!

Later that night, Roya sat at the foot of the bed in the dark with the letter on her lap until Zari finally yelled, "By God, come to bed, you lovesick fool!"

⌇

The spring of sweet pastry shop outings and walks together and the early summer of their engagement and dancing soirees turned into a midsummer composed of just the letters, hidden in books. But Bahman's most recent letter sounded like a political speech as well as an ode of love. As Tehran teemed with demonstrations and political tension, Roya felt more and more alone. Amidst the turmoil, she worried more than ever for his safety. Was he participating in covert anti-Shah activities? Was he actually in prison? His last letter had expressed his devotion to her and the prime minister almost in the same breath.

To escape the heat, Roya and Zari often went to the rooftop of their house in the evenings and at night. Maman had arranged rugs on the flat surface, and some nights they even slept there. One afternoon after a long nap and after the rest of the household, including Kazeb, were all up and about, the two sisters went to the rooftop even though it was hot up there. It felt like getting away to go there in the middle of the day. They sat on a rug up on the rooftop, a bowl of tart green plums between them. The sun beat down on them as street peddlers yelled about their wares in the street below.

"Sister, you have to cheer up. Come on. It's been weeks since he left, and you just have the long face all the time. You have his letters, right? I thought that made you feel better."

Roya didn't know how much she could confide in Zari, but her sister was all she had. "His last letter was a bit strange," she finally confessed.

"Oh?" Zari picked up a green plum and bit into it.

"It was all about his worry that Prime Minister Mossadegh would be overthrown in a coup."

"How very romantic."

Roya lay down on the rug and put her hands behind her head. The sun felt good on her face, though Maman would hate that she was exposing her skin to the rays. Maman's nemesis was the sun: she worried about freckles and a tan. She believed her daughters should remain as light-skinned as possible. It drove Roya crazy that Iranians were considered more beautiful if their skin was lighter. Tears crammed her eyes. She wanted to be with Bahman. Whether it was biology or foolishness or youth that was at the root of it, nothing could make this all-encompassing desire go away.

Suddenly Zari's plum-juice soaked fingers were stroking her cheek, wiping the tears. "Come on. Enough. I'm sure he's fine. He's probably just away for . . . a good reason. I bet they are up north by the sea, that's all. Lord knows his mother couldn't stop showing off about their *villa* there, rubbing our faces in it. Come on, Sister. I'm sure he is fine."

"He would have told me," Roya said, as Zari's sticky, plummy fingers continued to wipe her face. "He's probably arrested. Or else in hiding for a bad reason. He would have told me if he was just going up north to the villa."

The shouts of the melon seller pushing his cart in the streets below sounded like a voice of mourning, almost like a call to prayer. In the hot, relentless summer heat, it sounded like grief.

"Get yourself up, Sister. Pull it together. Go to the shop. I bet there's a letter waiting for you."

When Roya arrived at the Stationery Shop, Mr. Fakhri was attending to other customers. She waited patiently for him to be done with the transactions and eyed the other customers warily. No one knew anymore who could be an anti-Mossadegh spy.

"I apologize, Roya Khanom, but I have orders to fill. It's inventory time. I have calculations to make," Mr. Fakhri said after the last customer left.

"Of course." She was taken aback by how direct he was, but maybe he was just busy. "I just wondered if you have . . . anything for me?"

The bell rang and they both looked at the door. A woman swiftly turned around so her back was to them. Roya couldn't make out her face.

Mr. Fakhri looked dumbstruck. "Give me a minute," he said distractedly to Roya.

He disappeared into the back for longer than usual and returned with an envelope. She was alarmed that he hadn't tucked it away between the pages of a book. The envelope looked vulnerable and dangerous in Mr. Fakhri's hands. She wished he would hide it.

As though he'd read her mind, he said, "When there's no one around, of course I can just give you the letter. No need to hide it right now."

Roya looked around. The woman was nowhere to be seen.

"Oh," she said. "I just thought that . . . well, never mind. Thank you."

She reached for the envelope, but Mr. Fakhri held on to it. For a second, it looked like he'd changed his mind, and Roya wondered if a policeman, or perhaps the woman she'd seen moments earlier, had entered the shop again without her hearing the bell, or if someone suspect had suddenly emerged from the shelves.

"Mr. Fakhri?"

He looked at her with great worry. Then he loosened his grasp on the envelope. "There you go, young lady. There you go. Just . . ." He sucked in his breath. "Please be careful."

"Of course," Roya said, puzzled at his tone.

⁓

The letter was short, but it was everything.

I can't bear this any longer. I'm coming back. I will explain everything. Please forgive me, Roya Joon. I know this can't have been easy on you. I don't ever want us to have to go through being apart again. I can't wait to be with you, to really be with you. I know the wedding is planned for the end of summer; I know your mother has her preparations. But I have an idea. Will you come with me to the Office of Marriage and Divorce? We can participate in a short official ceremony there, we can be legally wed. It would mean the world to me. If you agree, please write back, and give your letter to Mr. F. as soon as possible, and we can do it. I promise you, my love. Meet me at Sepah Square, at the center, a week from today. Wednesday, the 28th of Mordad. 12 noon. Or a little later, if I can't help it. Meet me there, and once and for all we will be one. The excitement of seeing you will keep me going through these next few days.

In the hopes of seeing you again—soon!

You are my love.
Bahman

Chapter Twelve

August 19, 1953

Coup d'État

On the night of August 15, 1953, a Colonel Nassiri and his men went to Prime Minister Mossadegh's house with a decree from the Shah demanding that the prime minister step down. But, as Roya later learned, Mossadegh had caught wind of the attempted coup and was ready when Colonel Nassiri's forces arrived. Colonel Nassiri was arrested and declared a traitor. The next morning, Baba, who always listened to Radio Tehran at exactly 6 a.m., slapped the radio repeatedly because it was stunningly silent. Finally, about an hour later, military music exploded into the house. Baba must have turned up the volume to its highest hoping to get any news. The announcer updated the country on the treasonous ousting attempt. Prime Minister Mossadegh came on the air; the Shah and foreign forces had attempted a coup, he explained, but it had been averted. All was fine. Baba couldn't move for a good fifteen minutes.

"It's all right, Baba. They failed," Roya reassured him.

"I cannot believe they actually tried," Baba said. His face was drained.

"But they didn't succeed. Mossadegh is safe. Everything will go back to normal," Roya said. She wanted to reassure him as well as herself. She was to meet Bahman in just a few days and nothing could go wrong.

They listened to the news that the Shah had grabbed his wife and a few belongings and flown a plane himself to escape to Baghdad in the middle of the night.

Baba was livid. "Shame on him," he said. "To try to oust the good prime minister and then to flee when it didn't work out! That's what happens when you allow greedy imperialist countries to influence you. The British are behind it all, mark my words. And quite possibly the Americans."

"The Americans? They'd never do such a thing. They're not crafty like that," Maman said.

Roya was filled both with relief and fear. Bahman had been right: people had plotted against Mossadegh, and the Shah's decree had even chosen a General Zahedi as a replacement for the prime minister. But thank goodness Mossadegh had stopped it. Over the next few days, as more and more coup conspirators were arrested, Roya counted the days and then the hours. She could hardly wait for Wednesday to arrive. She wanted to see Bahman again more than anything. Was he still safe? Had he had anything to do with all of this? If not and he was simply in hiding, what must he be thinking about these crazy events?

On the day after the coup attempt, Roya and Zari walked outside but didn't venture far. Extra police stood everywhere. Photocopies of the Shah's decree saying that Prime Minister Mossadegh must be replaced by General Zahedi were all over the streets.

"How do they even make so many copies of one sheet of paper so fast?" Zari asked.

Roya shrugged. "Machines in America can make copies like this."

"You believe in the conspiracy theory too?" Zari asked.

"Jaleh Tabatabayi said—"

"Jaleh Tabatabayi is a Russian-loving communist and you know it. America has nothing to do with this."

Roya wanted her sister to be right. From the films at Cinema Metropole, and translated novels at Mr. Fakhri's shop, and Sinatra songs on Jahangir's gramophone, Roya knew an America that was sparkling and filled with glamorous people who kissed a lot. She wanted that America, not the one that could plot to overthrow her country's government.

When Baba came home from work on Monday, he said demonstrators had marched from the south of the city to Baharestan Square and toppled a statue of Reza Shah. They had looted buildings and ransacked offices, even setting things on fire.

"Why are the Mossadeghis so violent right now?" Maman asked. "Their National Front won. Why instigate things for no good reason?"

Baba rubbed his face. "I don't even know if these are real Mossadegh supporters. They could be paid protestors."

"Who would pay them? The Shah's out of the country—his crowd is dejected. Who would pay them to destroy things and riot?" Maman's voice was skeptical.

Baba didn't answer. But Roya knew that he was thinking about foreign forces being behind it all. She knew that he was thinking of America. But he had to be wrong. She wanted to believe in the America of the romantic movies, not in the one of Baba's horror.

At the end of the third day of disruptive demonstrations after the attempted coup, Prime Minister Mossadegh demanded that his supporters stay at home. Enough was enough, he said. No more pouring into the streets. No more demonstrations.

When Roya walked to the local *hammam* baths on Wednesday morning, the streets were calmer than they had been in days. Thank God. People had listened to Mossadegh and stayed home. Even the *hammam* was almost empty. Five hours. In just five hours she would see Bahman again. Hold him, fold into him, talk to him. Each day of his absence over the past weeks had been excruciating. Without him she had felt weighed down and untethered at the same time. Only the phrases from his letters had kept her going. His words propelled her to put one foot in front of the other even in the large bath hall now.

She took off her clothes in the locker room. Inside the steamy main domed hall, she slipped into one of the warm tubs. While a middle-aged attendant washed her hair and slowly massaged her scalp, Roya closed her eyes and breathed in deeply. After a few blissful silent moments, the attendant blurted out, "Miss, let me tell you. If only Prime Minister Mossadegh hadn't dissolved Parliament a few weeks ago, he wouldn't have had trouble in the first place. Would he? He was trying to grab too much power, is what he was doing. Mossadegh was pushing the monarchy aside. But we have thousands of years of shahs, don't we now? We are a country of kings. Mossadegh shouldn't mess with that."

"Do you think we could just—"

"With all due respect, Khanom, the Shah has done so much good for this country that the prime minister should thank his lucky stars we even have a Shah like him. Ingratitude for the Shah will be the death of this country, I'm telling you."

Roya squeezed her eyes shut and said nothing.

At the next station in the baths, a young girl who looked to be about Roya's age exfoliated her skin with a rough *keeseh* cloth. Dead skin cells unfurled from Roya's limbs like shreds from an eraser bought at Mr. Fakhri's shop. It felt good to get rid of the unwanted toxins and stress of the past few weeks. It was an unburdening, a lightening of the load. But then the girl said that Russia was our friend and Iran was best served by following in its footsteps with a political system that ended class disparity, endless slavery of the masses, and a leftover feudal system that poisoned people. Mossadegh needed to make Iran communist, didn't he? The girl continued to scrub hard and said she knew she could tell Roya all this without getting into trouble because Roya didn't look like a tattletale double-faced spy for the Shah. By the time she was finished, Roya's skin was raw and pink. Roya did not reply with any of Baba's likely retorts about how Mossadegh wanted democracy, not communism.

At the final station in the bath hall, an older woman lathered every inch of Roya's body with soap, then rinsed her with hot, steamy water. This attendant, thank goodness, was quiet. After the cleansing, Roya lay down while the woman rubbed an essential oil that smelled like jasmine onto her legs, stomach, arms. With each deep stroke of the woman's hands, Roya became more and more aroused, awake. Two and a half hours now. In two and a half hours, she would see Bahman. Every part of her was alive. She couldn't wait.

⌘

"*Vay*! Why did you walk home with that wet hair?" Maman cried when Roya sauntered into the house. "Do you want to catch a cold?"

"It's so hot, how would I catch a cold in the height of summer?" Roya's wet hair had soaked into the top of her blouse, spreading a stain around her shoulders. It had actually cooled her off in the heat.

Maman looked worried. "I hope it's safe out there today."

After much deliberation, Roya had decided to tell her family that Bahman was coming back and that they were to meet at the square. For weeks Baba had been so worried about Bahman's safety. Maman had prayed for his return with her *tasbih* beads every night. It was only fair that she let them know that he was fine and on his way back.

"I was just out there, Maman. The streets are quiet. People are listening. They're staying home. It's probably safer today than any day."

Maman did not look convinced.

"I have to get ready." Roya left before Maman could say anything else.

In the bedroom, Roya set her hair in barrettes to give her waves a boost. She had stopped wearing her hair in braids a few weeks ago, and now it felt liberating, not strange. On her wrists and neck she dabbed rosewater. She slipped on the rose-colored skirt she'd carefully selected to wear today and then tucked in her blouse. As she ran her finger over the nub of embroidered flowers on the collar, she remembered how she and Zari had stitched these tiny flowers for days, their heads bent together. Finally, she picked up the white ankle socks. Victory! After searching in all the fancy shops uptown, she'd found the coveted ankle socks at the stall of a merchant in the Old Bazaar. "From Amrika!" the wrinkled shopkeeper had declared, smiling toothlessly. "Lady! From Amrika!"

The socks, soft and snowy white, were perfect for today. She slipped them on.

"Please at least eat something before you go!" Maman shouted from the living room.

"I'm not hungry!" She was far too excited and nervous to eat.

When she entered the living room, Baba, Maman, and Zari were all sitting in a row as though waiting to inspect her. Or stop her.

"Are you sure you don't want to eat?" Maman looked more worried than ever.

"All of a sudden he's back in town?" Zari asked suspiciously.

"I'm not hungry, really, Maman Joon," Roya said.

"Why didn't he say to meet here? Or at your beloved Stationery Shop?" Zari asked.

Imagine if she'd actually told them everything! That Bahman had written in the last letter that they should not only meet at Sepah Square but then go to the Office of Marriage and Divorce to get their marriage license. Maman could prepare the wedding for early September to her heart's content, and relatives and friends could come and celebrate then. But for a few delicious weeks, she and Bahman would be husband and wife in sweet secret. It would be a secret so verifiably luscious and dangerous that she could barely even believe it herself. He'd probably picked Sepah Square because it was close to the Office of Marriage and Divorce and they could quickly go there before the lunchtime siesta hour if they met at noon. Bahman would never put her in danger. Then again, he had written the letter before the attempted coup had even happened. But who knew if anyone was following him? Maybe he didn't want to expose her family by coming to her home. Maybe a public square was safer. The truth was that at this point, she would walk through fire to meet him.

Baba got up, went to the coatrack, and reached for his hat. "I'll just walk with you to the square. You shouldn't go alone. There could be demonstrations again, for all we know."

"She shouldn't *go* at all," Zari said.

"No, Baba Jan! Thank you, but really it's not necessary. It's as safe as anything out there today. I'll be fine."

Baba looked down at his hat. Then he rubbed his face repeatedly as if trying to figure out a difficult math problem.

"I will give him your regards!" Roya kissed him and Maman and Zari on the cheeks and rushed out.

But Zari ran after her from the *andarun* to the outer rooms of the house and into the garden. "Look, Sister. *I'll* come with you."

"Don't be silly!"

"It's crazy to go out there today with everything that's going on. This week of all weeks! They tried to have a coup three days ago. What timing the two of you have, I must say!"

"The coup was stopped. The prime minister couldn't be knocked out. He's still in power; we're fine!" Roya cried.

"You sound just like *him*," Zari said.

Roya waved to her sister and passed through the garden door.

As she walked into the alleyway, her heart beat so fast she hoped it wouldn't give out before she even reached the square. She couldn't get to Bahman fast enough. Of course she'd be fine. All her family did was worry! And what did her little sister know about true love anyway? She couldn't understand that Roya was empowered, filled with strength and purpose at just the idea of seeing Bahman again. That she would walk through burning buildings to get to him.

More people were out than earlier in the morning. But of course they would be. People had to go about some of their business in the city, after all. As long as they weren't demonstrating.

It started with chants and the sound of chains and thumping. All of a sudden, the ground beneath her throbbed. Roya turned and saw a group of what must have been several hundred men approach from the bottom of the sloping street, marching and shouting. As they got closer, she recognized their chants as phrases from the *zurkhaneh* gyms where devotees practiced the traditional physical fitness and training rituals. Baba sometimes imitated these phrases in jest when he lifted something heavy or did stretches. Hundreds of weight lifters and athletes in their tight exercise gear made up the crowd. A few hefted cone-shaped wooden blocks and barbells above their heads. A mustached man with oiled hair juggled pins in the air. Eventually the strange mob took complete control of the street. Cars had to swerve out of their way.

To Roya's amazement, smaller clusters of men and women joined the almost comical group of athletes and weight lifters and jugglers. And as they did, and the marching crowd grew, the chants became more political.

"*Zendeh bad Shah!* Long live the Shah!"

With her heart pounding, Roya moved northward in the same direction as the massive crowd because she had to get to Sepah Square. *Who paid these yobs to come out today?*—she could just hear Baba ask the question. What kind of crazy new joke was this? Maybe Bahman knew of some foolhardy attempt that had been resurrected out of desperation. She couldn't wait to share this spectacle with him. They would laugh about it when they were reunited. They had to.

She walked just outside the edge of the crowd, sticking near a small group of women who had not joined the mob. "*Faghat eeno kam dashteem.* We only lacked this," one of the women said sarcastically, and the others laughed. It was comforting to hear the women's banter.

But as they all walked toward the city center, a nervous energy belied even the women's lighthearted jabs. Maybe it was just Roya's own anticipation feeding her fears. More men joined the crowd, some arm in arm.

"*Marg bar Mossadegh!*"

Roya suddenly stopped. This wasn't a slogan shouting, "Give

me Mossadegh or give me death"; it was saying "Death *to* Mossa-degh." The groups of anti-Mossadegh men who kept streaming in to join the original motley crew of athletes and jugglers filled the streets and sidewalks so completely that it became impossible to walk without being part of the mob.

For a second, she considered going back. No, she'd be fine, she told herself. Bahman was waiting. She put one foot in front of the other, the way she always did when stuck, and forged ahead. She just had to soldier on, to get to the square.

When she finally arrived at Sepah Square, it teemed with an even bigger mass of demonstrators that made the crowd of athletes look small. Roya couldn't move without pushing through people. It was a struggle to get to the spot in the center where she and Bah-man had arranged to meet. It was hot, but a breeze blew her rose-colored skirt tight against her thighs. Three men leered at her and one of them whistled. She remembered the thugs who had hit Bahman with a chain and baton. Heat rushed to her face, and she pulled down hard on her skirt.

The anti-Mossadegh contingent shouted louder. She hated being near them. She just wanted Bahman to arrive so they could grab each other and get away. She tried to focus on what it would feel like to see him at last, be near him again.

Twenty minutes later, the crowd had almost doubled. The chants were louder and more aggressive. Perspiration soaked her armpits. She craned her neck, searching for him. He was not there—but of course, how could he be; he would have to force his own way through this mob, to cleave through protestors to get to her; it was completely understandable that he was late. No one could have foreseen this mess. *This week of all weeks! They tried to have a coup three days ago. What timing the two of you have, I must say!* Zari's words drilled through Roya's head. But if the prime minister had successfully warded off a coup just a few days ago, surely no one would be foolish enough to try anything again so soon?

"*Marg bar Tudeh!* Death to the communists!"

"*Marg bar Mossadegh!*"

More and more people poured into the square, and soon the sharp smell of sweat and anger was suffocating. The crowd was on a mission; they were not simply gathering, they were trying to move, to march to a destination, and it was definitely not the square that was their end goal. As she fought a wave of nausea, Roya realized that they were moving in the direction of the prime minister's house. Their shouts for his demise continued. Bahman would be heartbroken at this turnout of anti-Mossadegh bullies. Where was he?

Time dragged on, and still she couldn't see him. She was parched and weak and dizzy. Her blouse stuck to her chest; the square spun. Maman was right. She should have eaten. She could barely move now that there were so many people around her and in the entire square. She was trapped.

Finally the armed police arrived, and Roya felt a wave of relief. Thank God. But to her surprise, they didn't even try to disband the mob. They just joined it. Every ounce of energy drained from her as she realized the police units were in on it. Everything Bahman had feared was coming true. The police were colluding with anti-Mossadegh protesters to attempt another coup, to try to finally oust the prime minister. The prime minister whom Bahman and Baba and so many others loved. The prime minister they believed was their democratic leader, who had the courage to stand up to foreign powers wanting their oil, whom the people had elected with the hope of achieving democracy. Bahman would be sick to see this scene. Where was he? She hoped to God that he was safe.

Time ticked on. No sign of Bahman. She had to move from her spot in the center; she couldn't just stay here hemmed in by the mob. Maybe she could go to the side where the crowd was thinner. Maybe Bahman had just arrived and was stuck there, unable to get to her. She wanted to make her way out, but the throng of people kept her trapped. She pushed and shoved, moving inch by inch, but not making any genuine progress. Panic welled inside her. She wanted to scream, to run away.

Suddenly someone grabbed her shoulder. "Roya!"

She turned to see who had called her name. His hair was stuck to his head with sweat. He panted and was wrung out with anxiety. Her vision blurred, but when it cleared, she realized it was Mr. Fakhri. His eyes were raw with a desperation Roya had never seen before.

"Oh, thank God! Mr. Fakhri! Have you seen—"

"Roya Khanom, please listen to me. . . ." He clutched her shoulders with both hands now, wild with an urgency that frightened her. She had never seen him outside of his cool, clean shop except for the night of their engagement party, when they'd both witnessed Mrs. Aslan's sad meltdown. Here, under the burning sun and amidst the crowd, he seemed almost feral, a mad version of the quiet man who had handed her poetry books and abetted her correspondence with the lover whom she sorely needed to see right now.

"I just need to find Bahman," she shouted above the noise.

"Roya Khanom, I need for you to please know something—"

His voice was drowned out by gunshots. Shouts filled the air. The smell of sulfur stung her nostrils. From her peripheral vision, she saw two tanks at the edge of the square. It couldn't be. She shook off Mr. Fakhri and swerved to see better. The bastards. Soldiers stood on the tanks aiming rifles. And a few people stood with them on the tanks waving pieces of paper that looked like money.

Did her body swivel slowly? Or swiftly? Did she stare at the soldiers just one second too long? What made her shake him off and twist around to see the young, uniformed soldiers on top of their tanks surrounded by men and women waving money? Why did she loosen herself from Mr. Fakhri's hold? Why did she turn? Why did she let go of him?

Why did she get away?

Next to her she felt something shift, slump, sink to the ground.

"Mr. Fakhri!" He lay on the ground, writhing. Blood spread across his chest. She squatted down and grabbed his arms and screamed, "He's been shot, he's been shot!"

A few people formed a circle around her and Mr. Fakhri. She was watching a girl kneel by a man shot in the crowd. It was happening to someone else. It couldn't be happening to them.

Shouts and warnings and noise all around. Two rivulets of blood streamed from Mr. Fakhri's eyes and ran down his face. She touched his soaked shirt, his bloody torso.

Suddenly she was shoved aside. A man straddled Mr. Fakhri's body and pumped his heart with both hands while other men and women hovered and bustled and tried to help. In the midst of the din—so loud it swallowed all noise and grew into a kind of silence—she heard only one sound clearly, crisply. The tear of cloth. A melon-colored piece of someone's clothing was wrapped around Mr. Fakhri's upper chest, around his heart. Soon it was soaked red.

Only Mr. Fakhri's eyes moved. Even with blood streaming, he looked over. Not at her, not at the man bent over him trying to save his life, not at the group of people holding on to him, chanting prayers for him. Mr. Fakhri's eyes looked to the left of the square, toward the embassies, toward the street that held his shop.

Roya followed his gaze. Maybe it was gunpowder or her own blurred vision from tears, but she thought she saw a cloud of smoke rise from that direction. Before she could be sure, the man pumping Mr. Fakhri's chest collapsed over him. "He's gone!" he cried. An older man near them rocked back and forth and chanted prayers.

After several minutes, a few men quietly lifted Mr. Fakhri, hoisted him up into the air, and carried him above their heads.

In this way, Roya and a small group carrying Mr. Fakhri with his heart wrapped in melon-colored cloth left the crowd. In shock and silence, people made way for them. At other spots in the square, the mob was parting for others who were carried out in the same way. What had started as something of a joke, a game, a boisterous show, a performance with jugglers, had ended in this: a demonstration, a riot. It had brought out police and soldiers. And it had killed the stationer.

"Take him to the hospital!" a woman yelled as Roya followed the small procession out of the crowd. "Every single one of these unjust deaths needs to be recorded."

To be recorded. With a pencil and a pad. On clean sheets of paper.

She tried not to throw up.

Sirens wailed and police shoved their way through. The core of the crowd moved northward despite the chaos.

When their small group exited the square and turned right to head toward the hospital, Roya stopped. She had already given Mr. Fakhri's name and occupation to the man who'd tried to save his life. The others had insisted that she go home. They had told her this was no place for a young girl. *Thank you for the information, we will make sure to have it rightfully recorded. The family will be notified. We'll make sure of it. Now, you, young girl, go home. This is no place for a young lady. You've seen enough.*

Trash cans set on fire dotted the side streets as she made her way to the corner of Churchill Street and Hafez Avenue. Broken windows in office buildings, shards of glass on the ground were a kaleidoscopic horror. Nauseated, Roya forced herself to go in the direction of Mr. Fakhri's gaze during those last minutes of his life.

When she got to the street that held the Stationery Shop, the windows of the small market nearby—near where the beet seller would sometimes drop his mat to pray at noon—were black holes. The roof of a newspaper kiosk near the shop was bathed in smoke. And the building that housed the shop itself danced in flames so high that they looked like they could swallow the sky.

Roya stood in front of the shop, numbed by fire. The licking flames danced and soared. She was drained of movement, energy, feeling. It was too late. They could do nothing. From a distance she heard the wail of a firetruck. They'd come. They'd try.

But flames consumed the walls, the windows, the roof, the beams of support.

Crinkled, blackened pages of books fluttered out of the flames. They floated in the air, suspended for a minute, and then dissolved as black ash when they hit the ground.

One day she might forget the helplessness of standing there while words burned. One day she might be far away from this terror. But the smell of charred paper would always be part of her, embedded in her skin. As she stood in front of the burning shop, she remembered the traditional bonfires lit before Persian New Year, how she and Zari jumped over the flames squealing with joy, their faces flushed from the heat, their hearts soaring.

Soon there would be nothing.

The words she had loved, the poetry books in which her letters had been exchanged, the tablets of notepaper and bottles of ink and fountain pens and pencil sharpeners, scorched to nothing.

The hidden political pamphlets in the back storage room, the colored pencils tied into bouquets with ribbon, the sanctuary and the secrets inside—Mr. Fakhri's life sizzled into nothing.

She wondered if the bell above the door would withstand the fire. If she were to find it, lift it, shake it, would it still ring?

∽

Through the gate into the courtyard, past the koi pond, and into the cool sanctuary of her house she went.

Inside, her family was still deep in their afternoon nap. Maman's big bowl lay in the kitchen sink, the one in which she always served the chicken and prune *khoresh* stew. Zari lay wrapped in her *shamad* cotton sheet in bed. In the next room, Baba snored and Maman lay next to him. Her slippers were lined up neatly on the floor. Everyone was accounted for, safe. Her family had no idea what was happening in the squares of Tehran, the force making its way north, the danger of the crowd. They did not know Mr. Fakhri's fate; they could not smell the smoke from the Stationery Shop. They had had their chicken and prune stew with rice and taken their afternoon nap as if it were any other day. And Bahman was nowhere to be found. Had she really gone to the square expecting to see him, with a rose in his hand, wearing his crisp white shirt, ready to whisk her away so they could get their marriage papers? It seemed vaguely amusing now to think she could have had those expectations.

When her family woke and turned on the radio, they would learn that the mob had made its way all the way to the home of Prime Minister Mossadegh. People had scaled the walls and entered his house. Mossadegh had managed to escape through a window and climb a ladder to his neighbor's. When her family woke up from their afternoon nap, when Zari popped open her eyes and stretched, when Maman went into the kitchen to put the tea on the samovar, when Baba turned on the radio at 2 p.m., they would learn that the coup conspirators had overtaken the broadcasting station in Shemiran Avenue and that the crowd had attacked the prime minister's house, looted it, burned some of its contents, run off with the rest. Destroyed it.

This time the coup had succeeded. This time the world had changed forever.

But first, while her family still slept, Roya padded around the house in her ankle socks. Alone, she wept for Mr. Fakhri, for Bahman, for her new country. She did not even notice, nor would she have cared, that the white ankle socks, the ones she had bought to meet Bahman again so they could get their marriage papers and be husband and wife, were now splattered red and blackened by smoke—stained with the blood of a man who had died at her feet as she tried to find the man she loved.

Chapter Thirteen

Dream Destiny

Zari brought her hot tea mixed with *nabat,* the rock sugar that was supposed to cure most ailments: an upset stomach, the flu, menstrual cramps, possibly heartbreak, never grief. She sat at the edge of the bed and pressed the glass into Roya's hand. "Drink."

Roya lifted her chin to indicate "no." She did not want tea, she did not need Zari. But even the small movement of her chin made her head feel like it would burst.

"Come on. Sit up. You've been in bed all day. Look, yesterday was the worst day in the history of time to meet at a square in the middle of Tehran. He's probably just derailed. I'm sure he's fine. And Mr. Fakhri—" Zari stopped. Then she whispered, "God bless his soul. He was . . . in the wrong place at the wrong time."

They sat in silence for what felt like hours. Roya couldn't tell or feel time anymore.

"Now drink," Zari finally said.

Roya reluctantly took the glass and sipped. A nerve throbbed above her right eye. Did Bahman even know Mr. Fakhri had died?

Had he been involved in trying to stop the coup? Was he with a bunch of pro-Mossadegh activists in prison now?

"Bahman's probably been arrested. Maybe killed too," Roya said.

"You have no idea if that's true."

Roya had called and called—again—but there was still no answer at his house.

"Not to be a pest, but, Sister, he probably never planned on meeting you. I mean, where the hell has he been for the past few weeks anyway? And who writes a letter saying 'meet me at a square in the center of the city' when all this ridiculous political stuff is going on? I knew it was a bad idea, I told you."

"He couldn't have known there'd be another coup attempt when he wrote the letter. He just wanted to see me," was all Roya could manage to say.

"If he's such an activist, such a protective gentleman—he was supposed to have enough brains not to ask a seventeen-year-old girl to stand in the middle of the square at times like this, for God's sake! With people being shot! I cannot believe Baba even let you go!" Zari looked down at her hands. "Sometimes Baba tries too hard to be all modern and progressive, if you ask me. Sometimes women do need protection."

Even in her heightened state, Roya could see that Zari was speaking out of worry and a grief for Mr. Fakhri that she wasn't even equipped to express. Roya let her sister fume and vent about Bahman and say that the worst thing in the world was to fall in love with someone who was in love with politics.

◦∾◦

Roya waited all that day to hear from him. Hours stretched out, and still nothing. Everyone she asked was shell-shocked from the coup. When she got in touch with Bahman's friends, each one said something different. His old classmates told her they still hadn't heard from him, but they insisted that Bahman would not have been involved in anything on the streets. Another friend said that maybe Bahman had gone to a square during the coup and was actually arrested and that they should contact every prison to find him. When asked, Jahangir only cursed and said that a man nobler than Mr. Fakhri did not exist, for God's sake, and how could the soldiers just randomly shoot into the crowd, and he hoped Bahman was fighting every day to bring Prime Minister Mossadegh back to power. Roya had no idea whom she could trust. She had always assumed that Bahman's friends were on his side, that they had his back. But when Jahangir ranted about the Shah, Roya began to feel a seed of doubt. Could Jahangir be egging her on so she'd reveal something anti-Shah to him? Maybe he was a spy. It revolted her to think that she was now suspicious of everyone. She couldn't even fully trust Jahangir.

The rumor of foreign agents being involved in displacing the prime minister was already being discussed in bazaar stalls and in cafés over espressos and in living rooms everywhere. Zari countered every conspiracy theory with: *Okay, what if they did pay them with foreign money? What about our own people? We have spineless thugs who are only too happy to take to the streets to repeat whatever the slogan of the day is. And to take money from the Americans to do their bidding!*

Roya couldn't sleep. When she did, it was in fits and spurts but with vivid, detailed dreams.

In the dream that haunted her the most, she entered Mr. Fakhri's shop, the bell above the door ringing like always. Inside, it smelled of ink and books; the familiar comforting coolness enveloped her. At first she didn't see Mr. Fakhri, but then there he was, behind the counter, writing in his inventory book, the fountain pen gliding across the page. He looked like himself again: clean and calm, his glasses on straight. He had nothing of the wild look that she remembered from that fateful day in the square.

He looked up and for just a second panic crossed his face. Then he broke into his usual smile. In the polite voice to which Roya was accustomed, he asked how her parents were doing, how her sister, Zari Khanom, was, how all of the extended family fared, if all was going well in their neighborhood, may they all be healthy and live long lives. He added extra heapings of Persian *tarof*—the formal niceties required in every social interaction.

"Have you heard from Bahman?" she asked.

"Roya Khanom, no."

"Nothing at all?"

"Not one word."

"But he was delivering his letters to you till just a few days ago. Right?"

Mr. Fakhri sighed and looked up at the ceiling. "My advice to you, young lady, is to forget about that young man. Move on with your life. Get married. Have children. Be good."

"I'm sorry?" Roya's heart banged against her chest. "Get married is exactly what I am going to do. I'm engaged to him."

"Yes, well, sometimes engagements don't work out. Did you know that?" He said the words delicately, as if they could break her if he said them carelessly.

"I want to know if he's all right. No one has heard from him. I just thought maybe you had, since—"

Mr. Fakhri held up his hand. "We do not always get what we want, Roya Khanom. Things do not always work out the way we planned. Those who are young tend to think that life's tragedies and miseries and its bullets will somehow miss them. That they can buoy themselves with naïve hope and energy. They think, wrongly, that somehow youth or desire or even love can outmatch the hand of fate." He took a breath. "The truth is, my young lady, that fate has written the script for your destiny on your forehead from the very beginning. We can't see it. But it's there. And the young, who love so passionately, have no idea how ugly this world is." He rested both hands on the counter. "This world is without compassion."

Roya felt like she had suddenly been soaked in ice.

"You would do well to remember that," Mr. Fakhri said. A low, grating whistle passed between his teeth. He took off his glasses, rubbed his eyes, and finally said, "It seems to me that he never loved you. It was all a game for him."

Roya would wake up with a start then, soaked with cold sweat.

Even awake, she could *feel* Mr. Fakhri in the Stationery Shop as it used to be, taking inventory of his stock, organizing the translations of authors from all over the world. She could see him dust the table that carried volumes of poetry, including the ones in which she and Bahman had passed their notes. He had opened up a world of possibilities for her, offering a place where her dreams had formed into a viable path, where she had escaped the tumult of politics and found refuge. Where she had fallen in love.

She could still feel the shelves digging against her back where she had leaned as Bahman pressed into her, whispering to her.

But in her dream, Mr. Fakhri always said that Bahman had never loved her. He told her to start a new chapter of her life. Even if so many unanswered questions remained in this one.

He had been their ally, their encouraging chaperone. A middle-aged man dusting books and arranging school stationery in a shop, talking to the young and helping them secretly get access to political material and exchange love notes.

He was gone. He was gone, and but for the grace of God, it could have been her. Quite possibly should have been her. It was something she would always carry, like a scar, like a cold truth, like the sizzling embers of the shop's remains embedded in her skin, like the body of Mr. Fakhri carried invisible above her extended arms forever.

Now that Mr. Fakhri was gone, she thought about him more than ever. What personal pain he had carried inside, she did not know.

Part Two

Chapter Fourteen

The Melon Seller's Daughter

A young man meanders through winding alleys of the bazaar downtown. Since his birth, his marriage has been arranged to his second cousin, Atieh. Atieh means "future," but she is not the future he wants. He is in love with a young girl who works at the bazaar, who heaps melons onto crates every morning and stands haughtily next to her father as he haggles with the customers. Ali can't stop thinking about this poor girl. He goes to the bazaar just to see her seed the melons, to catch any glimpse of her.

Amidst the cacophony and chaos of the stalls, he watches. She always wears a small headscarf. Her clothes are shabby, but her face is like the moon. She is young, too young perhaps, but stunning. With a knife that looks like a sword, the girl's father magically whisks out the inner soft flesh of the fruit and sells slices and chunks to his thirsty customers. Some customers take a whole melon and drop it into their baskets; others want the immediate sweetness, the cool relief of melon cut and iced. The ice is just as special as the fruit, and the melon seller comes to the bazaar every morning carrying a coveted block of it. The girl guards the ice vigilantly, standing next to it with her hands on her hips.

Ali's mother plans the items for his wedding *sofreh*. "Wasn't I patient to wait till she's older?" she says. "Your cousin is sixteen now and ripe and ready for you. You two were destined from birth. We all knew it."

His mother chuckles, as though she is gaining something uniquely valuable. She tells the maids to make sure there is enough cinnamon to decorate the *sholeh zard* dessert on the wedding day. "At the end of summer, Ali Jan. Can you think of a better present for your eighteenth birthday?"

Ali thinks that Atieh looks like watery yogurt; he imagines her to be just as bland and tasteless. In his dreams, the shabbily dressed girl at the bazaar feeds him slivers of melon, the juice soaking his mouth.

One Friday, he walks downtown as usual to spy on her. He stands half-concealed behind a post at the spice stall as the girl arranges whole melons into pyramid-shaped heaps. He watches her slice the fruit into uneven pieces.

"Badri, *bia,* come!" Her father is toothless, skin leathered from too much time in the unforgiving sun.

Badri. Badri. Badri. Ali repeats the name under his breath as if he could possibly ever forget it. As if he won't ache for years whenever he hears it.

Shoppers push and shove, women in chadors carry their baskets of greens and eggplants, babies cry, and peddlers moan about their wares. *Badri, Badri, Badri.* Ali, as the son of one of Tehran's most esteemed scholars, will be sent off to Qom to study religion and the classics soon. This girl is not a thing that should enter his mind. She works with her father in the market. She is a *dahati,* a villager. A girl with nothing, from the same class as the servant who washes Ali's clothes.

When the noontime call to prayer floats through the alleys of the bazaar, stalls are left and prayer mats picked up. The market methodically empties out; buyers and sellers disperse. One by one the men leave their stations and walk out. In the courtyard of the mosque at the end of the bazaar, they'll make their midday ablutions. There they'll wet their elbows and wrists with water from the concrete basins. For the prayer, they'll kneel and touch their foreheads to the ground and lose themselves in meditation. They will rise and bend as one.

Is Badri going to pray? Ali feels a sting of disappointment as she leaves the stall. Of course he won't be able to follow her into the female section of the mosque. The most he can do is see her take off her shoes at the entrance (they are slippers really, made of cloth, torn and ragged). She'll then be swallowed up by the women's entryway, inaccessible.

After she leaves, Ali lingers alone in the bazaar. He suddenly feels naked at his post near the spice stall. He's conspicuous now that the crowd has left, vulnerable and uncomfortable without the shield of people covering his lookout point.

Footsteps. The slow scuff of slippers against the dirt. He looks up and can barely believe it. She's back. He watches, hoping he's unseen, as Badri moves a few things around her father's melon stall. She lifts a large tin tub. For a moment she struggles with its weight, then hoists it on her hip. Soon it's balanced there perfectly as though it's a part of her anatomy, as though it was always perched there.

She walks out of the stall, and after he's sure he can't be seen, he follows her. There is something strangely alluring about her; she has such confidence and sway even though she's young and poor. Instead of turning right toward the mosque, Badri turns left. Ali follows her down a small path to the back of the bazaar where a square yard shielded by trees serves as an unloading and garbage dock. It must be here that every morning donkeys carrying wares are unloaded and men unpack their crates of goods. The dock is lined with big bins where the garbage of the day is deposited in heaps. Flies swarm over the receptacles. The girl calmly navigates her way through the smelly, gorged bins until she reaches one that isn't overflowing. The tub remains balanced on her hip as she walks. Ali marvels at how she carries the heavy tub as though she's been doing this all her life. Then again, he thinks, she probably *has* been doing this kind of thing her whole life. For isn't that how it is with this kind? They work. Manual labor all the time, Ali sniffs to himself, even the females out in the fields and in the markets from their earliest days. They are hardy, they are tough. Ali thinks of Atieh and her paper-white skin. He thinks of Atieh's long fingers, her lips that seem transparent (when they are married, the excited relatives will profess joy at the thought of him grazing the perfection that is Atieh). He has seen Atieh without her veil; as children they were told to play together. Now Atieh's face is always shielded from the sun to save her skin from going dark, to keep her pale and pure.

Badri stands on tiptoe next to the bin, hoists the tub higher on her hip, and then in one swift move, neatly and expertly tips it over and empties its contents. Rinds of melon and slippery seeds fall in an arc and the air is filled with the sweet smell of melon. The scent catches in Ali's throat. He can almost taste the sugary fruit in his mouth, can almost feel the cool melon flesh between his fingers. Badri shakes the tub a few times to get out the last remnants. Then she whips around.

"Why are you following me?"

Her voice is a lot more adult and bossy than he'd expected. She addresses him with the informal singular "you," not the plural "you" that should be used by a peasant girl when addressing a young man so obviously of a much higher class. Is she so uneducated that she doesn't know any better? Something about her haughty look makes Ali doubt this. The girl looks like she knows exactly what she's doing.

"You can speak, can't you? Or are you mute?" She hoists the empty tub back onto her hip and plants a hand on the other hip. Her feet are wide apart, a pose that Atieh and girls of her class would not dare in the company of strange men. "Hey!" the girl calls out. "I asked you, why are you following me?"

"I'm not." His voice is a whisper. Here she is, a melon seller's daughter, a child, really, and for some reason Ali is weak in the knees. It's her round face, the eyes that dare to look right at his, the rosebud lips.

"I'll tell my baba to cut your throat! Don't you come near me. I don't care if you're a highfalutin posh man or whatever you are. I know what your kind thinks about girls like me. Well, you come near me and I'll scream so loud your ears will rupture. I will kick you! Hard!" She lifts the tub with both hands high above her head. "I'll bash your head in with this tub. I'm sick of men like you. Thinking that just because I'm poor, you get to have a taste. Well, you don't. My baba will slit your throat with his knife if you come near me. Understand?"

Ali is speechless. No one has ever spoken to him this way. At home, his mother defers to him; he is the prince of the house. The maids don't dare even address him; the male servants only do to say what he'd like to hear. His father is the only person who is honest and forthright with him. No girl has ever spoken to him like this. He is at once amused by her pluck and mortified. He must look like a pervert. Like nothing more than an entitled lout lurking around a peasant girl.

"No, no, I'm afraid you're mistaken. I am not here for unto-ward reasons. Please, I don't mean to scare you."

A wave of heat permeates the air, and it's as though someone has sprayed every particle of dust with the suffocating melon smell. Despite himself, Ali walks closer to the girl. He must reas-sure her. He wants to prove her wrong—he feels a strange need to show that he is not after that kind of thing at all. The closer he gets to her, the more the sweet scent fills his lungs. Every scrap of fabric on her body, every strand of hair peeking out from the headscarf, even the tassels on her torn slippers must be infused with that mel-ony scent. Her face, now that he is closer, is tan and remarkably healthy, as though she's received a dose of nutrition inaccessible to the girls he knows, the ones whose mothers have warned them to avoid the sun, the ones who are taught to embroider and study reading and writing, the rich young women who are trained to ar-range roses immaculately in crystal vases. Badri glares as he nears her, the tub still balanced above her head.

"Put the tub down." Ali finds his voice again, the steady and calm one, the one used to talking to servants, the one accustomed to giving orders and being obeyed.

"His melon knife!" Her voice is higher and less confident as he nears. "He will cut you with it!"

Now she sounds like the young girl that she is, vulnerable even though she's trying so hard to be tough. Ali is drawn to her more than ever, to her wide stance, her rude speech, the rosebud lips, the round moon face with its quivering chin raised up. And the sweet melon smell that will forever be associated with her.

"Put the tub down," Ali repeats, more calmly this time.

She drops the tub and it bounces on the dirt a few times, with a muted noise that is almost comical. It should have landed with a loud crash, there should have been a huge sound, but the tub bounces softly and lands a few feet away from them, settling quietly on its side. No one could have heard it fall from afar. In fact, Ali realizes, the girl has reason to be scared. This square dock is shielded by trees; they are unseen, no one knows they are here. Everyone is at the mosque praying, holding their palms in front of their faces, whispering verses of faith.

He will tell her again that he's not here to hurt her. He will reassure her that he is simply . . . what exactly is he simply doing? Following her. Of course he cannot help but be attracted to her, but he'll explain and reassure her. She needs to realize he's a gentleman. Ali is confused, and angry that this girl can make him confused. She is nothing. She is below him. He will let her know he is to study religion and the classics in Qom after he is married—

Before he can decide how best to word all this, the sweet flavor of melon envelops him. In the noon sun, Ali is momentarily blinded, he must be hallucinating. Something sticky and warm has landed on his cheek, and for a minute he is unable to identify it. Then he realizes the girl is next to him, she has walked right up to him and kissed him. She stands there, balanced on her toes, for what seems like a snatch of time separate from all the rest. For a few seconds—seconds that will be suspended in Ali's memory until the day he dies—for a moment encased in a sphere, sealed off from the rest of his life, her lips are warm and sticky on his face. She feels like a burst of fire.

After she lands back on her heels and almost tips over, after her lips are no longer on his skin, Ali cannot move. He is transfixed. Transformed. The nerve of this girl. The warm, bursting touch of her. Her kiss has rendered him mute, frozen.

"There!" Her voice is soft now. "You got what you wanted."

He doesn't dare look at her.

"Didn't you?"

He touches the imprint of the melony kiss on his cheek and, without thinking, takes his fingers to his nose. He is inhaling her. Never will he forget this taste, not when he marries Atieh, not when he is the father of four children, not when he introduces great works of classics and foreign writers to the young people who will frequent the stationery shop he will one day own. How disappointed his father will be in his choice not to pursue anything more prestigious. "You have the means to become a religious scholar," his father will plead. "You want to own a *shop*? Like a *bazaari*? Like a merchant?"

"Now," Badri says as he stands in the sun, unable to move, afraid of the reaction to her kiss, obvious in the way he is breathing, "I told you that if my father ever finds out that you tried to kiss me, he will cut your neck with his knife. People think it's a knife, but it's really a sword. His grandfather's sword. His grandfather was a bandit. Who killed men who bothered him." She stops, her eyes boring into Ali's. "With that sword."

Ali stands in the sun, and forces himself to look away from her.

"Just killed them. If Baba were to know that you followed me back here behind the bazaar to grab a kiss—"

"I didn't," Ali interrupts, finally facing her again.

"He would swoop off your head. He's good with that knife of his. You've seen him slice the melons, haven't you? Don't think I don't see you standing there day after day, spying on me in the market. Doesn't someone hoity like you have school to attend or something?"

"It's summer," Ali mumbles.

"Of course! I know schools close in the summer!" A look of embarrassment crosses her face. "You think I'm uneducated and easy, don't you? Just because my father sells melons at the market, and your father . . . what? Runs the country? Takes our money? Smokes cigars? I don't know. But I'm telling you that if my baba finds out about this, he will cut your throat."

Ali nods.

"So, if you want"—she walks over to the tub on the ground, picks it up, and hoists it back onto her hip—"you know where to find me. I empty the tub quite regularly. When Baba goes to pray at noon."

"Excuse me?" Ali whispers.

"They all go to pray, don't they? It's so quiet here then." She looks up at the sky and smiles. "It's nice and quiet and peaceful here. Just us and the flies."

"At noon?"

"Yes."

Ali presses the toe of his polished shoe into the dirt, his heart beating fast. He watches her walk away, the tub bouncing on her hip.

What happened on other days at the garbage bins under the summer sun were things that should not have happened between an educated, rich young man and a girl whose father sliced melons at the market. Her melony sweetness stuck to his trousers, to his throat; she was everywhere with him and all over him.

Atieh got fitted for her dress. Tiny jewels were sewn onto the hem of her wedding veil. Ali inhaled Badri by the bins at noon, he tasted more parts of her than he should have; he walked home dizzy and drained.

At what point did his lust become love? Was it when Badri whispered in his ear as he tried very hard not to explode (explode he did, each and every time)? Was it when nothing but images of her occupied his thoughts before sleep? Was it when the possibility of not being with her made him feel empty, even sick? At what point did Ali stop inhaling the scents and sounds of a beautiful fourteen-year-old peasant girl and start wanting this girl to be his? Rightfully his, ridiculously his, impossibly his. These things shouldn't happen. They shouldn't ever, not when lives are planned, not when mothers have made arrangements, not when destinies have been ordained, not when a match is perfect. Futures are organized, thought through, carefully planned. Atieh was his future. Badri was his melon girl by the garbage heap.

Badri was his heart. Badri permeated his skin; he walked around smelling of her, tasting like her, wanting her. Wanting her. And even though she miraculously, absurdly, dangerously, carelessly let him take her—it wasn't enough. Once he had a taste, he wanted more. And she gave him more. Once he had more, he wanted it more often. And she showed up more often. Once he had more often, he wanted it consistently. And she started to give herself to him every day. Once he had every day, he wanted forever. His desire for her was insatiable. To the point that it didn't matter whether it was lust or love. There was no demarcation anymore. Not for Ali. He just had to have her always, all the time. And he did not want to imagine a time or a future without her.

Plans are made for reasons. Financial, logical, social reasons. His parents navigated their lives with reason and power and care. Atieh was right for Ali. The two families had always wanted that wedding. His class of people followed optimal paths, creating more wealth and pursuing good sense. His class of people did not pine for grubby girls who worked at the bazaar—and if they did, they took their due, stole their kisses, groped and fondled and then moved along. No harm done.

But Ali does not want the powdered, pristine bride his mother chose for him at birth. His home is filled with books; his living room floor is covered with the best Persian rugs. A *dahati* peasant girl would be a joke in his family's eyes. When he enters his father's study and dares to tell him that he doesn't want to marry Atieh, his father simply asks, "Why?" in a manner conveying that Ali's statement is a nuisance. When Ali, with much throat-clearing and fidgeting and difficulty, mentions a girl who is sweet, who is beautiful, so gorgeous, her face like the moon's—Ali's father says impatiently, "Well, who is it?" Upon hearing that the girl is the melon seller's daughter, his father's face freezes for an instant, and then he doubles over in a throaty, loud, coughing laugh that Ali realizes with creeping disgust is the deepest laugh he's ever heard from his father. Ali leaves the room as his father continues to clear phlegm with his laugh.

He and Atieh marry at the end of that summer. Ali thinks of the girl at the bazaar: her beauty, her scrappiness, nothing about her leaves him. He climbs on top of Atieh, the girl he has married, with the melon scent of Badri in his mind. The following year, their son is born. Celebrations are held in their community, in their part of town, in their rich inner circles. Atieh is enchanted with her child. Three more children follow in quick succession and none of them dies. Everyone marvels at how blessed he and Atieh are. All the children healthy. Atieh embraces motherhood and the domestic life. She embroiders on linen and knits perfectly patterned sweaters. She raises their children to be obedient and considerate. She ignores Ali's aloofness and his burrowing in books and simply brings tea to his study every night. She does not complain when he pours his energy into opening a shop, does not express embarrassment and disappointment at his becoming a mere merchant, not the scholar he was meant to be. Atieh remains devoted to him. She ages beautifully. Her skin remains undamaged by the sun.

The melon girl is always scrappy and feisty in his dreams; she kisses him by the bins at the back of the bazaar, she smells sweet and heady. He wakes up craving her. Over the years, every now and then, Ali looks for the melon seller's daughter when he is downtown. She must have married some *dahati* peasant boy; she must have twelve children by now. Sometimes he sees poor women walking down the street in the outskirts of the city, clasping their flowered chadors with their teeth, their baskets filled with wilting vegetables and the worst cuts of meat (if they're lucky). He looks among them for that melon seller's daughter, all grown up, but does not see her.

When he opens the Stationery Shop on the corner of Hafez Avenue, he is one of the first to import foreign books. The young students are crazy about reading these days. Obsessed with novels and stories from abroad as well as reading all the ancient and modern Persian literature.

One day, while Ali Fakhri is at his shop, taking newly printed Farsi translations of Dostoyevsky and Dickens out of a crate and arranging them with their spines aligned, the bell above the door rings and someone steps into the shop. A rich perfume fills the room.

She is tall and elegant, dressed like a Western movie star. She has clearly embraced Reza Shah's reforms in dress. Some women resisted and found the removal of the veil traumatic. When Reza Shah's police ripped the veils off women's heads to force them to modernize, religious women resisted. But others welcomed their new Western ways of no covering. This woman is clearly not one who misses the veil. She even has rouge on her cheeks, and her face is like the moon. A resplendent, round, beautiful moon.

For a moment Ali is confused. He knows that he cannot be

staring at the melon seller's daughter. This woman standing in front of him cannot be that poor girl who emptied her father's melon rinds into the garbage bin.

"Good morning, Ali Agha." Her voice is confident and clear. "What a lovely shop you have."

Behind the counter, Ali Fakhri remains frozen.

"You didn't think I'd find you? It's not that hard. Don't look so scared. Did you think you'd find me on the side of the street getting by? I am an engineer's wife now, didn't you know? My husband taught me how to read and how to write. He took the time. And now, here I am. In this lovely shop of books!"

Before Ali can answer, the bell rings again, and in comes a boy, about fifteen, his cheeks red, his dark hair in a thick mop on his head, his eyes joyful and filled with hope.

"This is my son," the woman says. "I thought you'd like to meet him. He loves to read. I brought him here because I have heard that you have the latest books, the best ones. They say you're quite a bookseller."

Ali clears his throat and tries to say something.

"Good morning." The boy walks over, nods at Ali, and smiles. His confidence takes Ali Fakhri by surprise. "My mother has told me so much about you. She says you even have the Americans like Henry David Thoreau? I would love to read books like that."

At this, his mother rolls her eyes. "Always with the politics and philosophy! I tell him the future of this country is with oil. Study hard. Learn how to manage economics. Learn finance. I tell him do something useful! But what *can* you do?" She ruffles the boy's head with a mixture of frustration and pride. She pushes his head slightly, and the boy cringes. "Always with the politics! The youth of today! He wants the fancy books, Ali Agha." Her manner of speaking is slightly false, the strained tone of a poor woman who is now rich. For a minute, her eyes lock with the bookseller's, and Ali Fakhri's body grows weak. He is the father of four healthy children. People say his wife, Atieh, is a wonderful woman, an angel. He has opened a shop selling books and stationery that is respected throughout the city as a haven for the intelligentsia. He has guided students to their intellectual matches on the shelf. He has imported works and products from all over the world; he is admired and successful, even if his father always remained disappointed that he didn't become a religious scholar. A melon seller's peasant girl does not deserve his attention, his mind, his energy. Years ago, she might have been forward and brash with him at the bazaar. Today he is a man above it all.

And yet. When she stands before him, it is hard for Ali not to remember the sweet, sticky encounters they stole in hiding. It is hard not to remember every detail. She had been entirely his. He remembers her impossibly smooth skin, her confident laugh. He promised her they would marry. Badri had sobbed as though her heart would fall out when he told her his father's reaction, how it would actually be impossible, quite unthinkable.

For years, he's carried her with him. Now, as she stares at him, Ali feels that all the pages of all the books in his carefully curated haven of a shop could fly in the wind and float as scraps of paper in the sky and he would not care. When she stands before him, he is again filled with desire. He is again lost for her. Her voice has not changed. It was always too grown-up and confident for a girl. Her voice finally matches her build.

Behind the bins in the bazaar, Ali had done things he would not have dared with a girl from his own class; he would not have dishonored a girl from a respectable family. But with her, his teenage passions got the better of him. She hadn't resisted. She'd surprised him. He had told her he would marry her. He had even meant it.

Part of him had hoped it could happen, even though of course he knew it was impossible. He didn't want Atieh, he wanted *her*, could it be possible that his parents' choices were negotiable? No, of course not. A girl who helped her father sell melons in the bazaar was not marriage material. He could never have children with her.

"My husband," Badri now says with emphasis, "is an engineer. His family, the Aslans of Isfahan, you may have heard of them? Top-class. Descendants of royalty. We have been married," she continues, "for over twenty-five years. Oh, what a wedding we had. And now my son. He loves to read, as I said. You know how it is now with these bright students. Everybody wants the latest on philosophy. In our part of town—" She drops the name of the street where she lives. It is in a neighborhood up north where the new bourgeois class has moved, building big houses and filling them with fancy newfangled furniture and lace curtains and gold-rimmed dishes. She is rubbing her address in his face, stinging him with news of her engineer husband, pushing her handsome, polite young son in front of him. He files away the street in his mind. He knows he will be unable to resist walking by there, to look for her house, for her window, for her silhouette.

"Show my son the brave philosophers. He wants to read men with spines. He wants to learn from those who have courage, from men who make their own destinies. Those, you see, are the real men. Not the ones who adhere to outdated rules about class and marriage. Wouldn't you agree?" Her words pierce him like darts. She keeps her eyes on him for an extra minute after she says this, not blinking.

Yes, he acquiesced. Gave in to the demands of his parents. It would have been absurd, a joke—to marry a *dahati* girl. People of his class did not do that. It was not done. For her to harbor bitterness over it is ridiculous.

Ali Fakhri will take the boy to the philosophy bookshelf. He will show him the very new edition of *Walden* by Henry David Thoreau that has arrived. A brand-new translation in Farsi. He will shepherd the boy through the giants on his shelves, help his young mind discover and grow. How many students has he helped in this very shop? He is the city's encyclopedia, the de facto reference librarian, the knowledgeable resource, filled with expertise about literature and philosophy and poetry. This is what he does. This is what he is good at. He will take the boy's hand and help him. He will make it up to his mother. He will shepherd the boy and hope that Badri forgives him.

He will do anything for Badri to forgive him.

She stands still, challenging him, taunting him in her tight dress, her hand on her hip, rouge on her cheeks, how dare she? Isn't she nothing more than a melon seller's daughter who has magically landed an engineer husband, exhibiting everything Ali Fakhri hates about new money?

"I know that street well," he says, referencing her address. "I go there often."

"We are the house at the very end of the street. With the big sycamore tree in the front. Such a beautiful view of the Alborz Mountains that we have! Now, Bahman!" She turns to her son and pushes him toward Mr. Fakhri. "Bahman Jan, go see what you can find in these books."

Ali Fakhri takes the young Bahman to the corner of the shop that houses the philosophy books and shows him the contents of his collection as Badri puffs up her hair. He will teach this boy what he knows. He will show him what he has learned. He will help guide him to whatever it is his heart desires, whatever is his destiny. It's the least he can do.

Chapter Fifteen

1953

Fate on the Forehead

Zari came into the house holding an envelope. "This was in the mail today," she said.

Roya's heart jumped. She grabbed the envelope. It was his writing! Would she finally know why he hadn't come to the square, if he was okay, where he had been this whole time? She had been so heartsick for so long. All she'd wanted was to hear from him just to know he was safe. She clutched the envelope with all her might and felt delirious just to see his writing again.

She pulled out the onionskin letter paper she knew so well. And read for her life.

Roya Khanom,
  I hope that you and your family are all well and healthy. For the worry and sadness that I have caused you, I apologize. I know that we spoke of marriage and all that, but please know that my priority now is in helping this nation. I will do everything within my capabilities to make sure this

happens. If I deceived you with words of love, I apologize. If I made you think that we stood a chance for a future together, I was wrong—I see that now. We had a love because we had a hope for a good future together. But we were naïve. I was naïve. I'm not ready. We rushed into it. We were too rash. I need time. I need space. Please don't contact me. It's actually dangerous to do so—you would be putting me in a harmful place. I must pursue the cause in secret. I must help the National Front. I got swept up in teenage love this summer. Now there are bigger concerns for me, you have to trust in that. You are a smart, beautiful young woman who will find many men knocking on her door. I wish you a prosperous future. I wish you joy and good health.

Sincerely,
Bahman

Her fingers shook. The letter was in Bahman's handwriting. It was on the same paper on which he'd written all his previous letters. But the words were garbage. Bahman would never write this.

Roya put down the letter. What *chart o part,* what utter nonsense. She could make no sense of it. "Where did you find this, Zari?"

"I told you. It came in the post."

"But he never mailed his letters to me. They all came to me through the Stationery Shop."

Zari crossed her arms and stared at her. "And how would he deliver them now?"

"But this letter makes absolutely no sense. For it to arrive today, it must have been mailed a few days ago—before the coup, before the shop was destroyed. . . ."

"Did any of his letters make sense, Sister? Now that you think about it?"

"You read them?"

Zari reddened. "Of course not." She answered in an extra-high voice, "So tell me, Sister. What does he have to say for himself?"

Roya just shook her head. "He never says why he didn't come to the square. Not once."

"Well, for the letter to reach us today, it must have been mailed before the day of your meeting, right? So how could it address that?"

Roya knew Zari was right even though it made her sick that the horrible letter couldn't even answer where he had been when they were supposed to meet at the square. Roya gave in and showed her sister the letter from Bahman. She wanted confirmation that it had to be a joke, a prank.

Zari read it quickly. She sucked in her breath and said, "A snake. I told you he was a snake. A political donkey!"

"He would never write something like this."

"Sister, he is *siasi*—these political types are crazy. He's telling you in pure Farsi what he is. Why can't you just believe it?"

Roya tossed and turned again that night. The letter had been written under duress. It must have been. When she finally fell asleep, she dreamt that Bahman was held captive somewhere, guards breathing down on him, clutching his hair as they forced him to write those nonsensical, insensitive words.

⁂

"It's for you, Roya!"

When Roya went into the living room, Maman handed her the telephone with a worried whisper: "Bahman's mother."

Roya was so shocked she could barely lift the heavy black receiver to her ear. "*Salaam*, Khanom Aslan."

"Roya?"

She hoped her pounding heart couldn't be heard over the phone. Out of habit, out of deference, out of the social code that demanded respect for one's elders, she said, "How are you, Khanom Aslan? I am so happy to hear your voice."

Mrs. Aslan spoke in a rush without taking a breath. "*Azizam*, dear, I want to say one thing—it is difficult. Bahman is back, by the way. We were all up north. . . ."

"Is he all right?" Roya was dizzy.

"Very. Anyway, never mind the details, I don't want to worry or mislead you. The truth is, Roya Jan, that Bahman was just fine this whole time. We have a villa up there, you know, as people do. Well, you don't, but you know that we love our beach house. He was up there with us and, well, he is back now. The fact is, Roya Jan, the fact is that I am calling you because . . . I'm not quite sure how to say this. The wedding is in two months. Bahman is getting married."

Roya wasn't sure if she'd heard Mrs. Aslan correctly.

"My dear, I know how difficult this is for you. Of course it would be. My goodness, I didn't have enough heart to tell your mother, forgive me! Your poor mother, who has been nothing but kind. You are good people. Don't take this the wrong way. You are good people and your father is a decent man and his clerkship at the government has nothing to do with this. Bahman understands that your father needs to stay on and work for the Shah despite all that's happened."

"Excuse me?"

"In any case, darling, these things are difficult—don't get me wrong. We've all been through the tunnels of young love, and I can attest, quite personally, I know well its twists and turns, its fickleness." She paused and then said, "Its losses. So, my apologies to you for this bad news, but he is happy now, Roya Jan, you understand. And you are young. Life is just this. Our destiny isn't in our hands. We can't change it. God willing, you'll be successful."

Roya could not form words. Her hand was clammy and the receiver felt like it might slip from her fingers.

"I must go now, there is so much to plan! I'm sure you can understand why an invitation to the wedding isn't being extended to you and your family. He is happy now and he is healthy, and may you be too, my girl. May God protect you."

For a long time after the phone call, Roya sat on the floor staring at the wall. Her mother came and fussed over her and said words that Roya could not hear. Time must have passed because Baba was back from work and talking to her and Roya could see his mouth move but she had no idea what he was saying. Finally, Zari's shrill voice broke through her daze. "I told you so," she heard her sister say, and "son of a dog," and "lying lunatic." Zari dragged Roya to bed and put a cold washcloth on her head. Roya heard occasional phrases like "wimp of a man" and "nutcase mother." But she was underwater. Everything happened around her without happening at all. She kept hearing Mrs. Aslan's words on the phone. The matter-of-fact, bold voice. He had been at a summer villa this whole time? Telling her about Bahman getting married. As though she were discussing the price of cucumbers. Or upcoming rain. Or just simple fate.

Zari didn't arrange her hair in newspaper scraps that night. She repeated how much she hated that lying dog, Bahman Aslan, and his opportunistic, money-obsessed wack job of a mother.

And with shame and a heart pulverized, Roya just said, "Sister, you were right."

Chapter Sixteen

1953–1954

Pioneers

"You'll get accepted, *inshallah*," Baba said at breakfast. "How long can a father stand to see his child heartbroken? You can't just sit around, Roya Joon. You too, Zari. Both of you. In a country that's lost hope and its youth . . . Well, you can't lose your future. I won't let it happen. God gave us two beautiful and intelligent daughters, full of promise, didn't he, Manijeh Joon? God gave us just these two children; it wasn't in our destiny to have more. He hasn't allowed our country to be democratic, why? All we wanted was a say. For the people to have the say. Right, Manijeh Joon?"

Maman crossed her arms and looked out the window.

"See, despite the heartbreak and Mossadegh's ousting and the loss of life, we have to go on, no?"

Baba had insisted that Roya start English lessons so that she could consider applying to an American university. He even suggested that Zari sign up and start learning English as well. After initially resisting, Roya agreed. It became her one distraction from heartbreak and grief.

"This is an unprecedented opportunity," Baba continued.

"It is impossible to even think these things. Girls going abroad? To study? I know of boys. Rich boys. From wealthy families. We're just . . . we're in the middle. What even are we doing to ourselves?" Maman looked like she might cry.

"But it's the modern age. Women can go to study abroad just like men. Europeans do it. Americans do it. What are we, backward? We are not. And why should it be just the rich ladies? There is a special program now. My boss is willing to help. He has already helped so much. His son did this program. You would be pioneers, girls! Think what this would mean. What an opportunity. An unprecedented opportunity. When your mother and I were your age, if someone had told us that young Iranian women could go study in American universities, do you know what we would have said?"

"That they were stark raving mad," Maman mumbled.

"Yes! I mean, no. We would have been astounded. Proud, I think."

Zari sighed. Kazeb came and took away some dishes. Roya sat still.

"Say what you want about the Shah, but he is making this kind of thing actually possible. He is helping women so much, I have to give him that. Do you know what you would be if you went to America?" Baba asked.

"Mad," Maman said.

"No, not mad! I said it: pioneers! Your generation is the first that even allows Iranian women to have this kind of opportunity. It's mind-boggling." Baba rubbed his face. "Relatives are saying things about me. That it is dishonorable to send one's daughters abroad. 'How can you even consider sending your unmarried daughters to a foreign land?' they say. . . ."

Unmarried. Roya winced at the term. An unwanted image of

Bahman marrying Shahla in a garden in northern Tehran played in her head. Bahman had been married for two months now. According to Jahangir, the wedding had been quite glamorous. Shahla looked like a movie star. Mrs. Aslan had outdone herself.

"All I'm saying is that we have to do something! Sitting here and sulking will only pave the path to becoming a pickled old spinster. You would waste away. Or you could go and study in an American university. Just think of that. Getting on an airplane to fly in the sky?"

"We are not rich," Maman said.

"We are richer than many. It can be done."

Roya had told her parents that she would never marry nor go near another boy. In the four months since she'd stood in that square, waiting for Bahman, seeing Mr. Fakhri die, she had mostly stayed home. Cried in her room with the door shut, barely ate, felt empty. High school was done anyway, and her plan had been to start a new life with Bahman, so without that, she actually had nothing.

Eventually she'd ventured out with Zari and sometimes walked with her to the grocer's. She always dreaded the possibility of seeing Bahman or any of his friends in the city. Shame filled her, shame and regret at her own lack of judgment, her stupidity and naïveté. Dances at Jahangir's felt as distant and alien now as the foreign films she'd seen at Cinema Metropole. Had she even gone to those dances? Had she once done the tango in Bahman's arms? Had any of it really happened? Now it was all she could do to study English and to help Zari practice the new words. Roya found some relief in studying together. As always, work of the mind came to the rescue.

She thought of the days spent in Mr. Fakhri's stationery shop. She avoided that street entirely now. She couldn't bear to go near it, not with all the memories it held, not after she'd seen it scorched. She still had the dream where she went to the shop and saw Mr. Fakhri again. Who was the girl who had run into his shop so full of hope, wanting to give or receive a letter? What a fool that girl had been.

". . . which is why I want to preserve them," Baba was saying. Roya had lost track of his words and didn't know if he was talking about his daughters or pickles. "Even if that means my daughters have to leave me to get a university education on the other side of the world. Don't look at me like that, Manijeh Joon. For the children, we make the sacrifice."

For the children. Roya knew that academics had always been tough for Zari. Did she still have a thing for Yousof? He was studying medicine at the university now. It seemed that Zari had had more than a passing flirtation with Yousof. Would she really want to leave Iran?

"Do you know how hard it was to learn how to apply to university in America? I had to put my own doubts aside. My heart is still filled with salt! It's nerve-racking enough, let me tell you."

Maman shifted in her seat.

"If my boss hadn't offered to help with the applications and information about the scholarship, I don't know how I could have done it."

"Let Zari stay," Maman said. "Why does she have to go? Let Zari stay."

"Manijeh Joon, it's safer if they're together."

"Safer? How on earth is it any safer? You are sending our daughters to America, where they know no one. Modernity has limits. Is it the new bourgeois fashion to send our children abroad?"

"The Shah's sister went to—"

"We are not the Shah's sister!"

Though the four of them sat at the table and Kazeb floated in and out with more butter and more tea, the discussion was a private battle between Maman and Baba, and Roya and Zari knew it.

"Manijeh Joon, I had to jump through hoops! Just getting the girls to consider it was hard enough. And figuring out the whole process hasn't been easy. Don't you know I had to use every connection I had, practically beg to learn how to do all this?"

"Who *does* this?" Maman was close to tears. "They are so young."

"We need to join the modern way of thought. If my boss is willing to help, if they have this opportunity, why not try? They will come back. They will get an education that is beyond anything we ever dreamed. And then they'll come back to us." Baba motioned to Roya. "For months she's done nothing but cry. She is becoming depressed and bitter here."

Roya felt herself grow small. Her role had become that of the jilted lover, the object of pity and shrugs. It was beyond humiliating.

"And you saw what happened with the coup," Baba went on. "The stationer is gone! So many died. For what? Iran just isn't stable right now. I want it to be, you want it to be, it almost happened. Maybe it's just not the fate of this country to be a democracy. God knows we've tried. My father was fighting for the Constitutional Revolution back in 1906. He was the same age these girls are now. His generation gave us the Persian parliament. But where are we now? It's always two steps forward, three steps back with this country. Just when we have a prime minister who is decent, he is knocked aside. Now the Shah has solidified his grip. He is nothing but a lackey for the West. He is their puppet."

"So the girls should go to the West? You make no sense!"

"We can't count on democracy here. That dream is dead now.

At least in the West, they won't have to worry about coups or dictatorships! It's an insurance policy, Manijeh Joon. We just need to be prudent right now. They cracked down on so many pro-Mossadegh people. Maybe we're next. Roya was out there in the streets. She could have been shot!"

Maman dropped her face into her hands when he said this and was quiet.

"I'll go," Zari suddenly said. She sat up very straight. "Yes, Baba Jan. Let's apply, let's try. I'll go. With Roya. And then we'll come back. We'll come back and be near you and Maman for the rest of our lives but with an American education that no one can take away from us."

Baba looked like he could faint. "Zari!" he simply said. "Yes, yes. That's what I'm saying. No one can take that education away from you once you have it. Do you know? You can take your degree from the university and put it in your pocket and it will be there for the rest of your life. That is all that I am saying."

Dust motes floated in a band of sunshine from the window. The tea smelled of bergamot. Kazeb's sounds in the kitchen were comforting, familiar. Outside a peddler moaned about his beets. Roya wanted to leave the humiliation, but she did not want to leave all of this: Maman's soft presence, her city, her home. She did not want to say good-bye to her father.

"They can study here. They can apply here. Get that degree here," Maman said.

Baba just shook his head. He didn't have to say anything else. They all knew that *here* meant the city of the coup. The city where people were shot for no reason. And also the city of Roya's betrayal by her fiancé. She still had a hard time going around town, in case she ran into Bahman. Or Shahla. Or worse, the two of them together.

Zari sipped her tea, and Roya wanted to tell her: *You don't have to come with me. You have a life here. I think you're in love with Yousof. Of course you are. You stay. Just because one of us had her life derailed doesn't mean both of us have to change course. You stay here with Maman and Baba. Live the life you were meant to live. My life is up in the air; yours doesn't have to be.*

She knew she should say all this to her younger sister. It was what a good older sister would do. But no matter how modern their family was, Roya did not have the power to override Baba. Or maybe she could not bear to go without Zari and was secretly relieved at the package deal that Baba had dreamed up.

In another neighborhood in that very city, Bahman was sitting with his new wife. According to Jahangir, Bahman had put off getting a job as a journalist for the progressive newspaper to work for a while in the oil industry. Just as his mother wanted. The boy who would change the world had simply listened to his mother. Roya imagined him waking up next to Shahla, getting dressed in front of her, going to work to learn how to maximize the profits of oil. This was the life he had chosen. The life his mother had chosen for him. And he had said yes to it all. Prime Minister Mossadegh was gone now anyway. Bahman and Shahla had a life together.

She hadn't heard one word from him since that last letter. He hadn't called, hadn't written. She had to hear his news from Jahangir. And she was far too proud to contact him. Why would she, after how he'd treated her? After he'd specifically stated in his last letter that he didn't want her to contact him? She wasn't desperate. She wasn't going to grovel. Who did he think he was anyway? How wrong she'd been about him. How stupid. How young. To think he had actually married Shahla! Roya hated the look of sympathy that followed her wherever she went about town: *The poor thing! They had been such the perfect couple! Now look at her. What a destiny! Did*

*you know she pushed the stationer away from her at the last minute?
He died! That poor stationer. . . .*

It was impossible in this city to continue as before. Maybe
Baba was right. She should leave Tehran.

"Of course we will go. We'll go together, Baba Jan," Roya said.
Her body had lost its form; she floated above the breakfast table
like a ghost.

Though it felt like going to the moon, this was a guarantee
that she could avoid Bahman, at least for a few more years. She'd
get her sense back. She'd be away from the spot where Mr. Fakhri
had fallen and from the charred remains of the shop, which someone had said would be rebuilt as the branch of a bank. She'd study
and then return as one of the few women in the country with a
university degree, from America, no less. She would truly join the
rank of the newly educated modernized class. She would be the pi-
oneer. Why not her? What else did she have to do here? As for
Zari, Roya would make sure to take care of her little sister. They
would do this. Others before them had done what had at first
seemed absurd. The country was changing. Why not be on the
front lines of education? They would come back when they had
finished their studies, and to hell then with everyone who had
given her those looks of pity and judgment.

Baba nodded and said he would ask his boss for the paperwork for the applications. He said it in a small voice, as though he
was both amazed and slightly ashamed. Maman stared first at
Roya, then at Zari, and burst into tears.

~*~

"Look, you don't have to do this," Roya said to her sister that night
as they got ready for bed.

"Baba won't let you go alone."

"There is something with you and Yousof, yes? You've been awfully quiet about him lately. What's going on with you two? It's not like you to not divulge every detail. Why so quiet? Look, I know you're not saying anything because you're worried about how I might react. Well, don't worry! If you're happy, I'm happy for you. You don't have to protect me. If you're in love, then you should stay in Tehran."

Zari removed pins from her hair. Ever since Mrs. Aslan had called to tell Roya about Bahman's wedding plans, Zari had stopped wrapping her hair in newspaper strips to create waves. She pinned her hair to the sides during the day. It made her look older, more mature. It befitted a girl in her last year of high school studying English on the side. Roya marveled at how much older her little sister looked in these past six months. It was as if the breakup of Roya and Bahman and the death of Mr. Fakhri had forced Zari to grow up faster too.

"Never you mind, Sister." Zari's hands stayed at the nape of her neck. She looked like a sculpture described in an ancient poem.

"You're willing to leave everything behind?"

"If you go, I go. We'll start together. And anyway. It's only for a few years, right? Maybe I should try to make something of myself too. It's a new world. We are the pioneers of the new generation of liberated young Iranian women!" She imitated Baba perfectly.

Stunned and secretly relieved by her sister's willingness to accompany her on this journey, Roya went to bed feeling as though she were about to dive off a cliff into freezing, choppy waters.

∽

The letters arrived by post at the beginning of summer. Baba took them to his boss, who translated them for him. Yes, his boss reassured him, the letters said yes. Both Roya and Zari had been ac-

cepted to the small women's college in California that Baba's boss
had recommended because it had a special scholarship program
for international students. Yes, each had gotten a spot. They would
start in the same class because Roya had waited a year after her own
high school graduation, and yes, yes, yes, indeed, they had been accepted. No, they wouldn't be the only Iranian women there, a few
others had gotten accepted this year! Probably the Shah's relatives,
Maman said with worry. But she stayed up late sewing the girls new
clothes, making each of them a trunkful of blouses and skirts and
blazers. Her daughters would not go to Amrika without the finest
clothes that she could sew. She made each of them a dress (light
green for Roya and pastel blue for Zari) from the finest, softest cotton she could get at the bazaar, darting her needle around the col-
lars to add her unique embroidery of tiny flowers. She cut batiste
fabric and worked late into the evening stitching together blouses
in four different colors for each of them: cream, white, light pink,
and a baby yellow. She bought blazers and pleated skirts from the
shops in the north of town and ironed them painstakingly. At the
bottom of each trunk, she carefully placed underwear and stockings bought at the bazaar. Roya and Zari helped Maman pack their
trunks with disbelief. All the rest of the savings that Baba had went
into the purchase of plane tickets and the portion of the tuition
not covered by the scholarships. He sold the collection of gold
sekeh coins that his own father had given him when he married. He
worked late hours for extra income. He even asked Maman to take
the small inheritance she had from her parents' deaths and send it
to America with the girls.

On the day of their departure, Maman held a Quran above
their heads. Roya and Zari paced under it three times, then kissed
the book for good luck on their voyage. It was a small ritual to ensure safety for all trips. Roya and Zari had performed this supersti-

tious rite growing up whenever their family was going on vacation to the city of Yazd or Isfahan or Shiraz. They had held the book above the heads of relatives who were returning to villages up north after visiting them in Tehran. But Roya had never expected to go under the Quran for a voyage that would take her to America.

The pain over Bahman and the death of Mr. Fakhri had been so raw at first; Roya felt like her skin had been torn off. But over time, in place of the exposed skin, a veneer had formed. By the time she boarded the plane, Roya was aware of her skin and bones and eyes and limbs, but her heart was locked away. An enormous amount of what she used to believe had been erased. Her heart would be closed off, this she promised herself. Her hair was carefully set, the handle of a suitcase dug into her palm—and somehow, her feet were moving, one in front of the other. She could see that Zari looked concerned but also slightly thrilled. She heard Maman cry, watched Baba count money—a fistful of unfamiliar green bills that he had gotten from the bank—and hand it to them. She registered all this as though in a dream.

On the ride to the airport, the sky was the color of gunmetal and it looked like rain would come; the clouds were so full. But the gray puffs remained just low and heavy. They drove by familiar buildings and streets, the shops they'd walked past countless times. Café Ghanadi, their old school, and Maman's childhood home on Soraya Street. Baba took a long route and gave them one last look at this city that would be invisible soon for them—at least for a while. He deliberately avoided Sepah Square and the location of the Stationery Shop. Roya felt a surge of love for her home and for her parents and all she was leaving behind.

"We'll love the campus, won't we, Roya?" Zari squeezed her hand.

Roya nodded.

"It's not worth staying in this country anymore anyway." Baba tried to sound like he believed it. "They toppled our true democratic leader. Now the foreign powers and their lackeys can do whatever the hell they want with us. Not worth it for now. Go. Go and be free. Learn everything you can. Better than being here with your throat choked by a dictator and with a government that can shoot at will."

Roya waited for Maman to stop him and say, "Mehdi, stop the nonsense. Enough with your anti-Shah rhetoric." But she just fought back sobs in the car and said not a word.

The girls boarded the plane. And as they swerved above the city, they held each other's hands, not quite sure that they wouldn't just die. How did this thing stay in the air? When the plane picked up speed and magically rose in the sky, Roya felt like she could almost, but not quite, touch the clouds that carried in them torrents of rain. As they rose higher and higher, she wanted the bloated clouds hanging low over Tehran to finally release their deluge, to break down and give out and soak the entire city and everyone in it with a tsunami of tears. But maybe the gray puffs above Tehran just kept it all inside and didn't release one drop of rain. It stunned her to think as she soared farther and farther away that there would be so much about her hometown that she would now just never know . . .

Part Three

Chapter Seventeen

California Coffee Shop

California was new and shiny. Everything in it looked like a toy that had just been bought and opened. Sun-drenched buildings, sparkling streets, gleaming shops, tight shirts on men's bodies and glamorous clothes on the women could have come out of a film at Cinema Metropole. Despite the dazzling sunniness of her new home, Roya was beset by a chronic homesickness. Zari was all that tied her to her previous life.

The two sisters relied on each other to survive. They learned how to live in their new boardinghouse and how to navigate the campus of Mills College in the Bay Area. Together they learned how to practice their new language. At first Roya felt like a mime, hand motions and exaggerated shrugs making up for her lack of English words. All she lacked were painted tears.

Being in a new country felt like being plunged into a darkened room. In the beginning, nothing was distinguishable; it was all blurry blobs at best. But eventually, her eyes adjusted. Forms that were previously incoherent came into slow, painstaking focus.

Roya and Zari guided each other even though it was often the blind leading the blind. They smiled politely at their landlady, Mrs. Kishpaugh, in whose home they boarded along with several other female students.

Roya hadn't wanted to leave Tehran behind, even with all its pain and heartbreak and its political mess. Yet she had no choice but to create—stitch by stitch—a new life. She had to move forward. And Zari surprised her. In Tehran, Roya had often thought of her sister as vain and self-absorbed. But in this fresh chapter of their lives, and with a focus that bordered on obsession, Zari absorbed the new American culture as though she were inhaling the air that would keep her from drowning. By their second year at the women's college, both Roya and Zari were doing well in their studies and had a small group of friends with whom they went to the movies and ate dinner and sometimes shared strawberry milkshakes. Even through the homesickness.

Successfully mastering the language and her classes in chemistry and biology was more than enough. Roya had sworn off men. But Zari remained open and giggly and silly even as she thrust herself into America. Soon a young man, Jack Bishop, whom she'd met at a classmate's house, spent more and more time with Zari. Yousof, not to mention all the Hassans and Hosseins and Cyruses back home, didn't seem to hold a candle to this Jack. Jack looked like a lumberjack: he had broad shoulders, a stocky build, and dirty-blond hair that needed a cut. He was constantly smoking and grinning and shaking his hair out of his eyes. His father was a traveling salesman, but Jack wanted to break the yoke of capitalism and get to know the works of Walt Whitman better. Zari was swept off her dainty feet. Roya watched her sister transform from the busybody Iranian girl who wanted to go to fancy parties and marry a rich man to a girl who wanted nothing more than to understand why Jack Bishop loved poetry so. Roya realized, not for the first time, the fickleness and unpredictability of young love. Zari levitated in Jack's presence. Just like that, she fell hard in love.

⌘

At a round table in a café on Telegraph Avenue in Berkeley, behind her stack of books, Roya wrote in her lab notebook, trying to make sense of the chemistry problems that plagued her, avoiding eye contact with others, wanting more than anything to head back to her room in Mrs. Kishpaugh's house to sleep. It was late afternoon and the clamor and din in the café did little to calm her nerves even though she had specifically come here hoping the background noise would somehow help make studying less arduous. On Tuesday morning at 9 a.m.—in three short days—she would take her chemistry final. She felt completely behind and unprepared as she tried to make sense of the words and symbols and numbers in her textbook. She should have studied a lot earlier; she had left too much for these last few days. Now she was drowning in material and had to catch up. Baba often sent encouraging letters from Iran: he was so proud of his scientist daughters studying cutting-edge topics that would ensure their place in the world! And they both were mastering English so fast even though it was such a difficult language! Roya had never really *wanted* to be a scientist. But after the horror of the coup and Bahman's betrayal and her heartsickness in Tehran, it had become clear that what she wanted mattered little. She needed to survive. What good had the poetry books and foreign novels done her? She ferociously pursued science at Mills College not just to please Baba but because a degree in chemistry could maybe inoculate her against at least some of the uncertainties in life.

But the elements and molecules in her textbook made her

head spin. Her body was in knots at the thought of Tuesday morning, 9 a.m. How on earth would she be ready for that exam? She took a chug of her strong coffee, put the cup down, and stirred the liquid nervously with her teaspoon. She could not fail. She had to get good grades and attain that chemistry degree with honors. Baba and Maman had sacrificed so much for her to be here.

He walked in wearing a blue blazer and gray pants, his hair like a sand dune on top of his head: a blond version of Tintin from the French comic series. Gold buttons shone on his blazer, and he moved with ease in the line and placed an order.

She tried not to stare at him. She had loved those Tintin comics as a child, and Mr. Fakhri had even stocked the stationery shop with a few of them. But this young man was far more handsome than the comic book character. She was inexplicably transfixed by his good looks. So much so that her teaspoon fell out of her hand and onto the floor. Oh God. She bent over, picked it up, and walked to the counter to get a new one from the basket near the jugs of milk and cream and the sugar dispensers. When she reached for a spoon, her elbow knocked over a cup of coffee. The cup bounced on the floor, dark liquid spilling everywhere, soaking the tiles, landing in streaks all over. Roya's squeal was high-pitched, so Persian, a *"Vaaaaay"* that came out of embarrassment and shock. She grabbed a few napkins and squatted on the floor, mopping up the mess she'd made, but it only made things worse. The napkins disintegrated as she tried to soak up her mistake.

"Hey, it's okay. I'll take care of it."

She looked up and saw Tintin kneeling eye-level to her. His eyes were Sinatra blue. "Don't worry about it," he said gently.

His gray pants were wool, she saw now, as they knelt together in close proximity. Who wore wool in California? Roya hadn't seen wool since she left Tehran.

"I am so sorry," she mumbled. Oh, how she must look, squatting as if poised over an old-style Iranian toilet, mopping up her humiliating spill. Please let the café fully resume its clatter and noise. Please let the attention fall on anything but her.

"It's really no big deal. You know what? I wanted a different coffee anyway." The blue-eyed man smiled.

Roya was relieved when the din around them picked up again. Café staff who'd glanced their way went back to taking orders, leaving the mess to the two of them. They both wiped the spilled coffee with napkins. He smelled like shampoo, the kind they sold in American supermarkets that created gigantic foamy bubbles and frothed between your fingers.

"Tell you what. I'm going to get another cup of coffee. And you're going to just stop feeling bad about this. Sound like a plan?"

It didn't sound like a plan of any sort that Roya knew, but she was charmed by his simple way of putting things. She nodded and smiled and nodded again, aware that she was "nodding like a foreigner," as Zari would have put it. She went back to her table and slid onto the chair and pressed her pen into the notebook again, drawing hexagonal shapes for molecules. UC Berkeley students dominated the café, but there were a fair number from Mills College as well. The air was sharp with caffeine and stress. Everyone was cramming for finals. Christmas vacation loomed like a mirage beyond torturous obstacles—so much work to get through before that much-needed break.

Suddenly the shapes in her notebook were darkened by a shadow. She looked up, and the man in the blue blazer was standing next to her table.

"If I may?" That smile again.

She wasn't sure what to say.

"This coffee shop is more crowded than usual today, don't you think?"

Coffee shop. The phrase seemed intensely American, as wholesome as small towns in the Midwest she had never been to but had seen in movies. *Coffee shop.* Who spoke that way? *Café, café, café* was all she and Zari ever said. Here was this blond Tintin with his coffee-shop smile, in a blazer that was out of a Robert Mitchum film, wearing flannel trousers that belonged in London, not Berkeley, California.

"Please." Roya piled her books in a neat stack to make room on the table. She felt like she was parting the sea. She wasn't sure if she was being too forward. But wouldn't it have been rude to say no? She wished she knew the rules in this country. Sometimes there didn't seem to *be* any rules. It had been far easier in Iran where tradition and *tarof* and who your grandfather was often dictated how to behave.

"Walter. I'm from Boston." His hand was extended.

Should she shake it? They did that here. Americans liked to shake hands, as if they were business partners, making a deal, sealing some contract. She placed her hand in his, and his easy grip surprised her. She was sure her face went red. It had been a while since she'd felt a man's hand around hers. When he sat down across from her, she was a trifle alarmed by his audacity, but that was how it was here, wasn't it, everything easy-peasy—no strict social mores that would shame your entire family if you broke them, no crazy rules like back home.

She expected him to pull out his own books, to huddle behind them like most of the other students, to sigh and complain about all the upcoming finals. But instead he stirred his fresh cup of coffee and sipped it as if he were on a piazza in Italy overlooking the mountains, as if he had all the time in the world and nothing too pressing. Everything about him was clean and well tended. Clearly she could not study with him sitting there. Why had she said yes to him? When he asked her what year she was in, Roya imagined soap bubbles coming out of his mouth. This man was freshly showered; she could not see him ever sweating. But it wasn't his picture-perfect image that impressed her. It was his manner. Even the way he sipped his coffee was measured and relaxed and without haste. He seemed . . . safe.

She had known a boy of haste once, had been swept up in his passion and fervor and unpredictability. She would not make that mistake again. Excitement was overrated. In fact, after Bahman and his betrayal, Roya had vowed never to tether herself to a man. She would study very hard in America, return to Iran, get a good job, and be financially independent, living a spinster life of equations and experiments and pure science. She would stand her ground with reserve and a steeliness that made even the most determined give up and leave for easier, less thorny prey.

But this man, this blue-blazered coffee-shop boy, was simply sweet, and she had let him sit at her table. He smiled and made polite conversation that was stunning in its purity. There were no innuendos, hardly any flirting. There was respect. He simply asked her questions, questions she answered. She flinched at the idea of being drawn to anyone. She could never again be that malleable, putty-like girl in Bahman's arms.

"And do you find the chemistry satisfying?" Walter looked at her earnestly.

"I beg your pardon?"

"You're taking the advanced chemistry, correct?" He pointed at her textbook. "Is it what you expected? Because a classmate of mine, Omar Said, hails from Lebanon. And he tells me that what he was studying in Beirut was actually more in depth than what we offer here. So I was just wondering . . ."

"Well, I never went to university in Iran. I only went to high school there. So yes, this is quite . . . deep. I mean, satisfying. The chemistry. The class." Why was she flustered talking to this boy? For crying out loud.

He studied her for a moment, then leaned in and whispered, "This California culture is a bit new to me too."

Of course he would have assumed her newness from her accent, her dark hair and eyes. But did she give off foreignness in everything? She imagined a waft of rosewater and saffron hovering above her wherever she went. He continued to talk to her in an easy way, however, as though nothing about her was strange. He told her how he had moved to the West Coast for his undergrad education but felt like a foreigner in California. He spoke of New England, and winters spent sledding, and summers at the Cape, eating lobster rolls and cheering for a team called "the Red Socks." The Red Socks? What an absurd name for a team. Walter's description of his New England childhood reminded Roya of scenes from an American film she had seen at Cinema Metropole with Bahman.

She focused on what Walter said. He was comforting, it was surprising just how much. He was like a character from a family TV show. He hadn't left a country whose prime minister had been overthrown in a coup. He hadn't seen men shot at his feet. He went sledding and drank hot chocolate. Behind the blue blazer he wore, Roya was aware of an innocence that most people would give anything to own. She envied him this simplicity, this lack of complication.

As they sat together, she listened mostly and shared a little. In her still halting English, she continued to answer questions about her background, the boardinghouse where she lived, her sister, Zari. Yes, she wanted to be a scientist.

When he finished his coffee, Walter got up and came back with two more. As he handed her a cup, she remembered another man standing in a café handing her coffee, asking her if she liked it. She quickly took the cup from Walter and sipped, even though it was too hot. They continued to talk. Sitting across from him, listening to him, something in her opened. The tension she'd been holding on to for so long loosened just a bit. She felt more relaxed than she had in a very long time. An hour went by with very few hexagonal molecules being drawn. He asked if he could maybe take her to the Powerhouse Gallery after finals were over, before he went back to Boston for the break. Sound like a plan? he asked her.

His blue eyes met hers.

It sounded exactly like a plan should.

Chapter Eighteen

Alternate Plan

*Most days I walk home from work through Baharestan
Square. The lady dressed in red stands by the fountain, still.
Her eyes are smeared with kohl, her hair is matted and dry.
They say she hasn't changed her dress since she was stood
up by her lover all those years ago. And she goes there every
day—poor lost soul.*

*I shouldn't walk through that square; there are other
ways to get home. But I can't help it. I am filled again with
longing and regret. This endless desire to turn back time.*

*I remember the expression in your eyes in the Stationery
Shop the day we met. I remember your shoes. I remember
how being with you made me happier than I'd ever been.*

*Mother's mood swings have decreased. She's calmer, but
almost too calm. The wild rages and angry lashings-out are
mostly gone. But she has a low-level chronic sadness. She
nurses her inner wounds quietly now. Mr. Fakhri's death hit
her so hard.*

Roya Joon, how I wish you hadn't changed your mind. How I wish her mental state had been tolerable for you. But you made your choice, and I wasn't going to force myself into your life.

Gozasht, it's past.

So Mossadegh is gone. The Shah has more and more control. A younger version of myself would be outraged and want to fight. But I am done with fighting. It's been four years since the coup. People lament the loss of a leader, but all I feel is the loss of you.

I don't know if Jahangir told you that my father passed away about a year ago? I'm so glad that you and Jahangir still telephone occasionally, by the way—it's my only way to get news of you. We held a small funeral for my father. Mother wrote elaborate invitations and sent them to the family who had shunned us all these years. She learned to read and write from my father. Her family was poor, illiterate. His family was learned. Their marriage broke class boundaries; it was a disgrace for my father's family. He was outcast for the decision. But he loved her! I know that he loved her. He loved her when she was young and he loved her when they experienced indescribable loss and he loved her through her depression.

That is the unconditional love I have strived to give her too, hard as it's been at times. I thought you could grow to love her too. Despite it all.

Others saw my father as weak, but I no longer do. He was intelligent, devoted. He tried very hard to be fair. In many ways, he didn't belong in the patriarchal system of our society. He respected my mother. He tried to help her through her sorrows and moods. He did not judge her in the harsh way that our culture judges those who struggle with their mental state.

Because they both married outside of their class, I always thought, albeit foolishly, that my mother would respect love. Marrying for love. I know it's seen as romantic nonsense by some. The poets, our own, wrote so much of love, and the American films are obsessed with it. But of course there still stands the tradition of marriage as a contract to attain or maintain status.

After I met you, I was engulfed—drowned in you. All I could see was you. I dared to imagine a future together. My hopes soared as our plans solidified. I couldn't think of anyone but you. But my mother kept insisting on Shahla.

So I told her I was in love with you.

She was doing calligraphy when I told her—I'll never forget it. It calmed her to copy the letters and the doctor had recommended it for her nerves. For a brief moment a look of tenderness crossed her face. But then she stiffened and said, "Basseh."

Enough, she said. Stop the nonsense.

Our financial situation was wobbly, much as my mother liked to boast about our "villa" by the sea. I knew her boasting drove you crazy. It made me want to melt with shame when she said those things about our "wealth" in front of you. Even now, I want to disappear just thinking of some of the things she said to you. But the truth is that my father had been passed up for promotions. He stagnated at his engineering job. Even though he came from a wealthy family, his relatives' rejection of him after he married my mother meant he could never ask them for help of any kind, especially financial. Over the years, my mother's mental state was all the more reason to avoid his relatives, because the few times his sisters did see us, they made it clear her illness only confirmed that she had been wrong for him all along.

Shahla's family is rich because of the Shah and her own father's powerful position, and my mother saw marriage to her as helpful, almost essential. They buy their dresses and pearls from Paris, my mother said. As though I cared a rat's hair about all that. I was worried about our country. I supported Mossadegh because he promised progress and democracy and autonomy. I couldn't stand the Shah's cowering to foreigners, his lack of spine. I admired Mossadegh's independent strength. But I digress. Suffice it to say that Shahla did not fit into my view of my future at all.

You did.

When I got your last letter, when you said that you didn't want to spend your life with me after all, that my mother's condition was just too much for you to bear, that you could not marry into a family with this mental instability—what could I do? I wasn't going to force my family on you. I couldn't change her condition, much as I would have liked to. I was so hurt, Roya Joon, by your shunning of her, of me. What could I say to that? She's my mother, and there was no possible way she would not be in our lives. I didn't want to stop your dreams. I had to let you go. You didn't want to see me and I respected that.

I wish I'd fought harder for you. I wish I could have shown you that it is not her fault. I wish I had shared with you some of her past and what made her this way. But I was too ashamed. And so hurt.

The day Jahangir told me you'd left, I felt like someone had torn off my skin. I can't even imagine California. But how amazing is that, Roya Joon, to think that you are there in the land of Cary Grant and Lauren Bacall and Humphrey Bogart and Ernest Hemingway and President Eisenhower. I'm running out of Americans to mention. I won't mention the CIA. I'll be good. Though it still boils my blood to think they had a hand in our coup. I want to be happy for you there in America, and I am. But what the government of your new home did to us . . . One day it will be proven. One day the world will know that the government over there overthrew our government over here. For what? The lives lost, the suffering caused—was it worth it?

I will never understand the turn of events for us in 1953. For you and me, I mean—let alone the whole damn country. If I live to be one hundred, I won't truly absorb it.

We are, I think, a lost cause in this country.

What did our generation learn that summer? That even if we did all the right things to bring about political change, in one day, one afternoon, foreign powers and corrupt Iranians could destroy it all.

I have relived the order of events of the 28th of Mordad (or August 19 in your Western calendar) over and over. Even now, I want to see you in that square, to feel you next to me, to hold you. We would have gone to the Office of Marriage and Divorce. I had planned it all down to the minute when we would arrive at the office. The clerk I'd arranged it with said he'd be ready with the paperwork.

Jahangir must have told you I work at the petroleum company now. Just another cog in the wheels of capitalism. We don't always match up to our own expectations of who we wanted to be when we were younger, that's for sure. Mr. Fakhri, God bless his soul, used to call me "the boy who would change the world." I think of the idealistic young boy I used to be and I am not embarrassed so much as bereft.

I wish I could clean life of the sadness in all its crevices. I want to accept that you made the choices you made for a reason. You will be a lady scientist after all. I hope you are healthy and happy. I truly do.

And Roya Joon, believe it or not, I will become a father this winter. I thought Mother would be delighted at the news, but she has been surprisingly quiet and in retreat.

When the baby is, God willing, born, it will have been four and a half years since I waited for you at the square.

Chapter Nineteen

Cooking Lessons

Roya never did learn to eat like an American.

In Tehran she had been raised, in its city streets she spent her childhood, in its schools she was educated, and right there on one of its main squares her heart broke. She pushed away the time when she was in love with Bahman.

But American food was surprisingly harder to adjust to than she'd expected: chicken was rubbery, meat occasionally pink, potatoes mashed into a puree. In the boardinghouse, they were polite about the meals Mrs. Kishpaugh prepared; how could they protest? They couldn't be rude and ungrateful. But Roya missed Persian food every day.

A few months after their first encounter at the coffee shop, Roya and Walter went on a double date with Zari and Jack. Jack refused to eat in a "pretentious joint," as he put it, so they ate at a diner that served burgers, fries, and milkshakes. Roya carefully cut her hamburger with a knife and fork while Jack sat back and smoked, shaking his head at her and saying, "Oh boy."

Roya gasped at the pink liquid running out of the middle of her burger.

"And what did you eat back in Iran? Lamb burgers?" Jack sucked his cigarette.

"Silly Jack!" Zari giggled.

The jukebox played Rosemary Clooney. The diner was overlit and the puffy plastic booth made Roya feel like she was sitting on a sticky balloon.

"Actually, you are not wrong." Forming English sentences still made her head hurt at times, but she had improved. "We have the ground lamb kebabs. They are not in the bread like this, though." She held up the soggy hamburger bun. "Our kebabs are longer. Thinner. Like tube."

"Are they, now." Jack blew smoke out of the side of his mouth and smirked.

"I think the ancient culture of Persia is renowned for a fine and fragrant cuisine," Walter said.

"Yeah, buddy? Name one other thing from that fine and fragrant cuisine."

"Well. I do believe . . ."

"They got kebabs!" Jack leaned back into the booth. "That's what they got."

Zari and Roya exchanged a look. Oh dear no. No, no. Roya wished her English was better so she could quickly regale him with a list of what she wanted to eat right now: chicken marinated in lime with saffron nestled into basmati rice sprinkled with slivers of almonds and barberries (the dish that the guests in another life had loved at her engagement party). Pomegranate and walnut *khoresh*. Fried eggplants with tomatoes, small sour grapes, and meat served with rice. Thick *aush* soup with noodles and greens and beans. Her mother's *ghormeh sabzi* stew. Grape leaf *dolmehs* stuffed with ground beef and herbs, wrapped by hand and simmered with cardamom.

Roya squeezed the bread bun in her hand. It disintegrated into clumps. "You will come to our boardinghouse. We ask permission from Mrs. Kishpaugh, our landlady. We cook for you."

"No." Zari shook her head. "We shouldn't cook there."

"We cook for you," Roya repeated, with a glare at Zari.

"Well, isn't that swell? Why, I would enjoy that very much!" Walter beamed.

"Sure you would, chump." Jack slung his arm around Zari's shoulders. "But I'll skip the cooking demonstration, if that's all right with you. I got my fragrant Persian cuisine right here." He tightened his hold on Zari.

Zari's cheeks reddened and for a minute she stiffened. Then she melted into his embrace.

Walter concentrated on his plate and cleared his throat.

"*You* come then, Walter. I cook for you," Roya said.

⁓

Their first lesson was on a Saturday evening. Mrs. Kishpaugh made meals for boarders on weeknights and Sundays, but on Saturdays everyone was on their own. Most of the girls were taken out on dates then anyway. And Mrs. Kishpaugh enjoyed visiting her daughter on Saturdays, coming back with long and detailed anecdotes about the antics of her grandchildren. Roya had asked for permission to use the kitchen, and Mrs. Kishpaugh had said fine as long as you clean everything, not a spot, make it as though it didn't happen.

Zari's date with Jack that evening was to go see James Dean in *Rebel Without a Cause*. Roya snorted when Zari told her the movie title and said it was fitting for the both of them. She had prepared for this night carefully. Earlier in the week, she'd made a pilgrimage to a Turkish/Armenian food shop in San Francisco. Since arriving in California, Roya's link to Iranian spices was tenuous. At the beginning of the semester, in chemistry lab, she'd met a girl named Seda Kebabjian. (The fact that Seda had the word *kebab* in her last name made Roya immediately warm to her.) They became friends. One day as they stood at the lab sink washing beakers, Seda had told Roya that her uncle had opened a delicatessen in the Richmond District of San Francisco where he sold spices and teas and jams from the old country. Roya's beaker overflowed as she stood in a trance, listening.

"Take me there," she whispered.

When she and Seda arrived at the small delicatessen in the city, Roya stepped inside, closed her eyes, and inhaled the familiar combination of scents. Then she opened her eyes. All at once, she wanted to devour the entire store. She wanted to sweep everything on the shelves into her skirt and run off, carrying jars of every single spice that she had missed so much. A piece of her had come home.

She bought yellow split peas. Cardamom. Cumin. Cinnamon (the one here was far closer to what cinnamon *should* smell like than anything she'd found so far in America). Crushed rose petals. Rosewater. Orange blossom water. And (was she dreaming?) the shop had actual dried Persian limes and saffron threads! Roya greedily grabbed all the ingredients. Baba had been dutifully sending money to America whenever he could. Now she would eat up his well-earned *tomans* on her one excursion.

⁓

Walter smelled of aftershave and soap when he arrived for the cooking demonstration on Saturday night. He wore his wool trousers, his blue blazer, and a porkpie hat. When he took off the hat, it was clear his hair had been washed and carefully combed for the occasion.

Roya led him into the kitchen and didn't say a word about him not taking off his shoes. It was pointless in Mrs. Kishpaugh's boardinghouse anyway. No one took off shoes indoors in this country, which was baffling and slightly disgusting, but she'd adjusted.

She offered Walter a seat and asked him what he'd like to drink.

"Oh, I'll have a Coca-Cola if it's not too much trouble, thanks."

If he'd been Iranian, he would have said, *Oh, no thank you, I couldn't trouble you, I'm fine.* She would have asked again, and he would have refused and said he was just fine, thanks, no need for anything. She would have served the tea that she had already brewed first thing. She would have prepared a big bowl of nuts and seeds, a platter of fruit, a tray filled with small chickpea cookies and other sweets. If he had been Iranian, she would have heaped fruit on a plate and peeled a cucumber for him and poured his tea into an *estekan* and offered him sugar cubes to put between his teeth as he sipped the hot tea. In the beginning she had wanted to do all these things for anyone who visited her in Mrs. Kishpaugh's house, for classmates who came over to study, for Zari's Jack even. But she was limited by what she could do in a house that wasn't her own, in a kitchen where there was no samovar, in a place where people did not consider cucumbers to be fruit and did not think that fruit should be eaten in heaps before dinner. When Seda Kebabjian had come over to review their chem lab notes and Roya had apologized for not offering her more, Seda had held up her hand and said, "Stop! It's not like that here Roya, it's not like it is back in both our homes. You do not have to constantly offer and cajole, the guests will say yes when you ask them, and you do not have to worry so much about being the perfect hostess."

So Walter's "Oh, I'll have a Coca-Cola if it's not too much trouble, thanks," did not come as a shock. She had already lived here for more than a year. She knew these American ways well enough now. She knew it was not rude that he didn't politely refuse her offerings at first. She knew that Persian *tarof*—that ritual of constant back-and-forth offering and refusal, often buttressed with flowery language and exaggerated flattery—was not the custom here.

She came back with the Coca-Cola. The other boarders and Mrs. Kishpaugh were all out. She and Walter had the kitchen and the house to themselves. It was strange to be with him, alone in a large house. In Iran, such a thing would never be allowed. But this was Walter. He was so well behaved; he would never force himself on her. She told herself not to think silly thoughts. "Come, it's time to cook, no?"

He followed her into the kitchen. Roya had prepared all the ingredients before Walter's arrival. She showed them to him and explained a little about the dish she was making.

"It's called *khoresh-e-bademjan*. We usually make it with beef."

He just nodded.

Blood rushed to her face. "But I couldn't get beef. So we'll make it with chicken today."

"Sounds like a plan!" Walter smiled.

She sliced an onion thinly, chopped it, then sautéed it in a large pot until the onion was just transparent. With a mortar and pestle that Mrs. Kishpaugh kept on the top shelf, she crushed precious threads of saffron till they were ground into a fine powder.

Walter sat at the kitchen table and watched with a delighted expression. "You should see my mom on Sundays when she's making the roast," he said. "She likes to cook too."

"Yes? See now, this is the saffron. You see how it is . . . crushing?" She pressed the saffron threads against the mortar with the pestle. "See?"

"I sure do see it crushing. That's neat."

Her self-consciousness began to evaporate as she cooked. Just like in the café with him, and at their few dinners with Zari and Jack, she actually felt comfortable. It had never been her intention to spend time in America with someone so cheerful. She found too much good cheer undesirable, smacking of falseness. How did Americans keep up their good spirits day in, day out, year-round? It had to be the brand-shiny-newness of their country. It had to be all that freedom. No thousands of years' worth of stultifying rules to observe. Just easy-peasy rolling with the flow. But she'd get used to the good cheer. She liked Walter, and his positive mood made her feel good.

Suddenly she remembered Bahman, but with a pang she pushed him out. It would be ridiculous to feel anything that dangerous again.

She added a few teaspoons of boiled water to the saffron and mixed. Walter couldn't possibly care about her recipe as much as he let on, but he nodded as she did it, as though he were watching an important event. Then he got up. "Would you like me to cut the chicken?" he asked gently.

She hadn't expected his participation. Not once had Baba cooked. Iranian men loved to eat, but she knew very few who loved to cook. In fact, she'd known none who cooked until . . . Of course she'd been surprised at how Mr. Aslan and Bahman bustled in and out of the kitchen in their home. With Mrs. Aslan so unwell, her moods paralyzing her, they had no choice. She took a knife and rinsed it. Here was Walter, waiting to help. Here was Walter, waiting. She had better things to do than think of anyone else. She handed Walter the knife and proceeded to describe, as best she could, how the chicken needed to be cut.

He obeyed her instructions and made sure the sullied knife didn't touch anything else. He washed his hands with soap when he was done. She was impressed at how diligent he was and how he worked with such care. That he genuinely worried about the size of the chicken pieces because he knew it mattered to her. A part of her couldn't help but be moved by his thoughtfulness.

When he finished, Roya dropped the chicken pieces into the pot of sautéed onions. The chicken sizzled. They stood next to each other, but not touching. Other than shaking his hand at the café that first day, at the "coffee shop," she had not touched Walter. He was a perfect gentleman on all their dates.

"We add the salt and the pepper now. And the secret ingredient," she said. It was getting hot standing near the stove. She had to stay focused.

"And what would that be?"

"This . . . turmeric." She wasn't sure how to pronounce *turmeric*. Walter's eyes twinkled, but she couldn't tell if she'd pronounced it incorrectly or if Walter had no idea what turmeric was. She sprinkled the yellow spice liberally onto the sautéing chicken.

"Without a doubt," Walter said, "this dish will be unlike anything I have ever tasted."

"Now we add water to the chicken and onions to cover them."

"I have made a note of it."

"I don't see you writing down."

"It's all here." He tapped his head.

"You let the water come to boil, then you lower heat and chicken can, um . . . what do you say? Cook . . . gently."

"Simmer?"

"Yes. Simmer." It was a big word, not because it was long but because it was the kind of word that made her feel like a native speaker. What Iranian woman in this country for less than two years walked around saying "simmer"? Turmeric, simmer—she was becoming quite the professional.

"As the chicken simmers"—Roya took care to use the correct verb tense—"we peel and slice eggplants. Then we add salt to eggplant, rinse them, dry them, and fry them. Yes?"

"Oh yes."

Together they peeled the eggplants. He handed them to her when done and watched how she sliced each one. He then lifted the knife carefully as though to ask if he could take a stab at slicing. She let him cut, impressed. He worked carefully at following her eggplant instructions, but she knew it would take too long to salt the eggplants the way she had seen Maman and Kazeb do back in their kitchen in Tehran and then wait for the bitterness to leach out. So she just took each slice from Walter and dropped it into another pan she'd heated with oil. They worked quietly in unison. Walter peeled and sliced, Roya dropped and fried. Meanwhile, the chicken simmered.

"To the chicken we also add some cinnamons, cardamoms, and saffron waters," Roya said. "And chopped tomatoes."

She made her way to the left burner on the stove, careful not to brush against Walter.

When she lifted the pot lid, steam billowed out and drenched her face and neck. She felt self-conscious and warm, knowing he watched her.

"The saffron mixed with water is like liquid gold. No? We call it liquid gold."

He looked confused.

"Because saffron is so expensive, you know?"

"I see."

"It's all still here?" She laughed and tapped her head just as Walter had done.

"Yes." He was staring at her. Then he placed his hand on his chest. "And right here. It's all right here."

The steam from the pot condensed into droplets of water on Roya's face. She felt the droplets roll down her face, her neck. This had to stop. She could not fall for a man again, even though this Walter was so very different from the boy who had betrayed her. She grabbed a Persian lime, placed it firmly on the counter, and stabbed it hard. A large jagged gash pierced its skin.

"Whoa!" Walter stepped back from the stove and from her.

"Sometimes you have to cut hard," Roya said sharply, "to get flavor out." She turned away from him. "Now we make the rice."

∽

They sat in the dining room as night fell. "Go ahead," she said, as she served him a plate of the chicken and eggplant *khoresh* they'd made together. "Try. Please."

It was a dish she had learned to cook at her mother's side in Iran. Kazeb always selected fresh vegetables at the market; sometimes she slew the chicken right in their own backyard, the limes drying in the sun next to the watering can in the garden, her mother on her haunches mixing the *advieh* spices. They would sit together—her and Baba and Maman and Zari—with their legs under the *korsi* on winter nights and share stories about their day as they ate.

Walter lifted a spoonful of her *khoresh,* her past. It should, if done right, be a mixture of sweet and tart, a fragrant, delicate combination of flavors.

She waited for him to try it.

"Wow," he said. He took another bite. "My God."

With each bite he took in the dining room of Mrs. Kishpaugh's boardinghouse, another layer of Roya's sturdy shell slipped away.

Chapter Twenty

To-Do

Walter's presence at the dining room table tasting her dishes became a mainstay of Roya's Saturday nights. When Zari heard of their ritual, she slapped the side of her mouth. "*Akhaaaay!* So cute! You cook for him and he devours it."

"Something like that," Roya mumbled.

The Tintin look-alike who had sauntered into that California café, who said to her "Sound like a plan?" whose memories of lobster summers and sledding winters seemed like they'd come straight out of an American film at Cinema Metropole, soothed her. Their courtship wasn't even supposed to happen; it was based on a feeling of goodwill, centered on feeling safe—it was just supposed to be a cooking lesson in Mrs. Kishpaugh's kitchen. She wasn't supposed to cautiously crave his calm.

When he asked for her hand, over extra-crispy *tahdig* rice served with *ghormeh sabzi* on a Saturday night about a year after the first cooking lesson, Roya felt again that dissociation, as if she was floating above the scene at hand, watching a girl in a movie play her role. She found it hard to breathe. She let Walter's proposal hang in the air for a moment, the smell of melted butter, saffron, and rice on his breath.

All of it—their gentle courtship, their growing affection for one another, the promise of a new life in New England—was a script for someone else's life. Someone better equipped for a relationship, someone less broken and foreign. She had somehow discovered the blueprints for things that happened to American people.

"Will you, Roya Joon . . ." She had taught him the term of endearment in Farsi, and he said it perfectly at the dining room table that evening. ". . . marry me?"

Her cheeks and ears burned. She was on alert, even alarmed. These were words said in the movies. Similar to words said to her in another language a lifetime ago.

"Think about it: Roya. Archer." Walter said the two names slowly, methodically, as though he had practiced saying them one after the other. "We could move back east. I got accepted to BU!"

"Beeyoo?"

"Boston University. You could work at a lab while I go to law school. There are so many hospitals and universities there. You could get the job you want. Roya. I want to spend the rest of my life with you. If you need time . . . look, maybe I'm being—"

"Yes."

It was as quick as a second.

Later she would replay the scene in her head. He had asked to marry her, and she had said yes. And to think she had faulted Bahman for jumping so quickly into the life his mother had scripted for him. Maybe they were both just following the fate invisibly etched on their foreheads.

Walter's breath on her neck was warm, Walter-ish. How excited he was when she said yes! Jittery, flushed. He almost tripped at the doorway when he turned for one more hug. After he drove off that night, Roya sat motionless in Mrs. Kishpaugh's living room with all the lights off. The other boarders, including Zari, were still out on their Saturday night dates. Mrs. Kishpaugh hadn't yet returned from visiting her daughter and grandchildren.

"*Such* a beautiful moon out there!" Zari said when she finally came home. She entered the living room, her voice giddy from her date with Jack. Roya could always sense the after-Jack aura around Zari.

"You should have heard Jack tonight, Sister!" Zari's lipstick flashed ruby red in the small stream of moonlight coming from the window. "Why are you sitting here in the dark? Oooh, smells so *wonderful* in this house! You made your *ghormeh sabzi*?"

Roya nodded, but she wasn't even sure if her sister could see that.

"These pumps are killing me." She heard Zari kick off one shoe and then the other. "Did you know Jack wrote a poem where every line starts with *p*? Every line except the third-to-last line, which then starts with *z*. Isn't that clever?"

"Genius."

"How was your night with Walter? Did you teach him how to cook *ghormeh sabzi*?"

"I'm marrying him." To anchor herself and not evaporate from the light-headedness that came from the enormity of what she'd agreed to, Roya clasped her onion-smelling hands on her lap. She had stumbled upon the role of fiancée to Walter, as though she'd been roaming the studios of a Hollywood lot, been mistaken for the lead actress, and then been asked to say the lines that someone else had written.

"What?" Zari stood still.

"You heard. Correctly."

"*Vaaaaay!* When?"

Roya shrugged.

Zari pranced over to her in stockinged feet. When she came in for a hug, she smelled of Jack's cologne. Of course her sister wanted details. Zari would have liked nothing more than for the two of them to talk into the night and process every moment of the evening: how Walter had proposed, what he'd said, breaking everything down word by word. But what was there to tell her? He had asked, and Roya had said yes. It was as simple as that.

"Good night, Zari." Roya patted her sister's back awkwardly. She wasn't ready for Zari's gushing. She felt drained.

"Oh my goodness, Sister! Married! Can you believe it? We have to tell Maman and Baba. Have you spoken to them? Did you ask their permission? Will you go back to Iran to have a wedding? How will they come here? What will we do? When will it be? I can help you. Do you want to have it here, in California? Should we tell Mrs. Kishpaugh? Will you move with him to Boston after graduation? Sister, what will I do without you? We'll be apart for the first time in our lives. You know I'm staying here, right? Mrs. Kishpaugh said I can stay even after graduation. I mean, I don't know what will happen with Jack. He wants to write poetry; he says San Francisco is too expensive. Sister, you will need a dress! You will have to speak to Baba. Oh my goodness! Walter! American! You should make a list of all that you have to do. You need to make a list. I'll write it up for you."

"*Yavash, yavash*—slow, slow," Roya said. Her head was spinning. Zari talked too much. It was happening quite fast. Walter's breath had smelled like saffron and butter. The *tahdig* rice had turned out golden and crispy that night. It was the perfect complement to the *ghormeh sabzi* stew. She'd been surprised. She had worried it would burn in Mrs. Kishpaugh's old pot and get stuck, but it had slid out perfectly. She hadn't thought about a dress. Or a list of to-dos. She wanted to lay her head on the back of Mrs. Kishpaugh's armchair and weep. She was tired. Zari was saying something about an engagement party, whether she would have one, and if she did then maybe they could invite the friends from chemistry class, and on and on. Roya didn't need an engagement party. The moonlight fell from the window in one small band. The rest of the room was dark.

"Sister, it's late, go to sleep, we'll figure it out eventually," Roya said.

Zari said a few more things about flowers and phone calls and petticoats and Jack. Then she got up, walked to the doorway in the dark, and fumbled on the floor first for one shoe and then the other. They dangled from her fingers as she walked out. Before she left the room, she whisper-shouted, "You know what this means? We are done with that boy for good!"

Shadows quivered like lace on the living room floor after Zari left. Roya couldn't force the to-do list out of her mind. How many boxes would she need to pack for New England? A heavy coat would have to be bought, of course. She would have to telephone her parents and let them know that a wedding was in order. Baba would want to meet Walter—he was supposed to approve first, they had done it all the wrong way, she had said yes before her parents' agreement. But everything was topsy-turvy in this country, and with Baba and Maman so far away, what choice did she have? Maybe they'd be relieved to hear she was engaged. Of course they had worried she would never marry after the breakup with Bahman. She wasn't considered as damaged as if she had been a divorcée, God forbid. But still. They had written off marriage for

her—at least, she had. It had been a public mess of a broken engagement. In their social circles, it was talked about for a while.
But Walter was American; he lived here, in this country. It was different here. Maybe it was all in the script. The forehead-written
fate.

She would need a dress, of course, Zari was right. She added
that item to the to-do list.

Sweet, dear Walter. He was very kind, wasn't he? He would
never betray her. She liked his mother—when Roya had met her at
homecoming weekend, she'd been reserved but polite. She kept
saying how much Walter's father would have loved to have been
there. His sister, Patricia, was cold, but Walter had merely
shrugged and whispered, "New England," as an explanation for her
demeanor. Roya willed her mind to focus only on Walter and her
to-do list.

But the lump in her throat wouldn't go away.

We are done with that boy for good.

She'd take Walter's lobster-roll life. A hundred times over.

We are done with that boy for good.

Roya held on to Mrs. Kishpaugh's armchair with her oniony
hands and waited for the lump in her throat to disappear and allow
her to swallow. With time. With time, it would go away.

Cream-colored roses covered banisters and tables in the hotel on
Cape Cod. It was midsummer, and the sky in New England was
gloriously blue. Roya walked down the aisle almost faint. Zari had
helped her find the dress at a shop in San Francisco. It was long
with a big poufy skirt that made her feel like a doll. The bodice
was made of lace, the skirt of creamy satin. Maman and Baba had
flown to America. In their embrace she had taken a quiet refuge,

dissolving into their arms at the airport. All this time she had missed them—more than she could admit. Their letters from Iran on airmail paper, their shouting on the phone long-distance, their making her promise that she and Zari would look after each other, could not take the place of holding her parents in her arms and smelling Maman's lemony scent. Baba had lost almost all his hair and was much smaller now, hunched. Maman still stood straight, but her hair was much more gray than Roya remembered. Inside the large American hotel, her parents were tiny, inconsequential: nodding and smiling at Walter's mother, shaking hands with tall, gargantuan, blond relatives of Walter's, looking a bit lost and needing constant translation and explanation.

"Smile, Sister, smile!" Zari flounced around the ballroom in a pale-pink organdy dress that cinched in the middle and showed off her figure. She tightened sashes and straightened tablecloths. She waltzed through and inspected each dish. Throughout the night, she pulled Roya to the dance floor and made sure that Walter's tie never got crooked.

"You look beautiful, dear," Walter's mother, Alice, said. "My, you are beautiful. Oh, Walter. How I wish your father were still alive."

Roya kissed Walter during the ceremony as was expected and waved at the clapping audience on cue. When they asked her if she was the happiest she'd ever been, Roya nodded and posed for photographs, keeping very still.

⁓

After Roya and Walter graduated from university, she from Mills College, he from UC Berkeley, Roya was supposed to go back to Iran. Years earlier, over breakfasts of *barbari* bread with feta cheese and sour cherry jam, Baba had said she would be the next Madame Curie or Helen Keller. But maybe now she could be a "lady scientist"—one who held beakers up to the light and solved problems and made steady discoveries that shifted the plates of the earth's knowledge—in New England.

In a suburb outside Boston, she and Walter purchased a small white colonial house with dark-green shutters. He was still in law school, but his mother helped with the down payment for the house in a very matter-of-fact way. Walter commuted to Boston University, and on weekends he showed Roya around her new town. Their home was a mile from the green where the American Revolution had begun, where minutemen fell to their deaths on the morning of April 19, 1775, where British redcoats antagonized the brave colonials and forced them to revolt. Walter relayed all of this with great pride. He took her to the spot of the shot heard around the world and pointed to stone monuments memorializing the dead. Roya stood on that pristine green grass wondering if one day, ever, there would be a memorial for those shot in the square in Tehran on that hot August day in 1953. Probably not. On the very green where her new country had started, Roya spread a picnic blanket and ate lobster rolls and drank ginger beer with her new husband. The spice of the ginger beer burned the back of her throat. She would have preferred water, but Walter told her that his swell girl would learn to love the taste. She nodded yes, she would.

Of course, her parents had gone back to Iran after the wedding. Roya could not talk to Maman and ask her how much tomato she should add to the *loobia polo* she was making—she could not dash over and pick up her mother for a quick run to the market. She could not read for her father the newspaper headlines or sit with him and laugh at the antics of this silly Lucille Ball who stuffed her face with chocolates. She wanted her parents to see the television set that Walter had bought. She wanted to be able to walk down the street to Maman's house and touch Maman's cheek and say, "Put on your shoes, let's go for a walk."

When Zari and Jack got married, Maman and Baba didn't even come to the wedding. Zari planned it in such a very quick three weeks and did not give guests enough notice. Besides, the trip for Roya's wedding had been expensive for Maman and Baba; they couldn't afford to come again so soon. Under the redwood trees of the Berkeley campus, Jack insisted that they exchange poems he had written while high. Roya flew out and watched the spectacle and hugged her sister and hoped that she and Jack didn't starve.

"Is he really going to be just a poet? That's not a reliable position."

"How harsh you sound!" Zari said. Then she whisper-shouted, "Don't worry, Sister! I've decided to introduce Jack to advertising. I think he would like it very much. He is so creative. Those poems? They can be advertising-product poems."

"If you say so." Roya was still worried.

The sisters started their married lives on opposite coasts and wrote letters and occasionally made phone calls to keep in touch. Roya settled deep into her Northeast life. Zari floated through California with Jack, at first camping out with his friends here and there. And then news came in a letter: *Jack has agreed to cut his hair. He's agreed to apply for a job in an advertising firm. He has to start from the bottom. But a creative genius like him won't stay at the bottom long, will he?*

Everybody waited for Roya's stomach to swell, for a baby to arrive. Walter's mother, Alice, smiled hopefully at Roya's waistline as though willing it to expand with life. It was very difficult to disappoint them.

One night, Walter's sister came to visit from her apartment in downtown Boston. Roya served meat loaf and boiled carrots, not wanting to bother Patricia with Persian cuisine. The last time she had served her chicken and prune *khoresh*, Patricia had moved the food around on her plate and sighed. It had annoyed Roya to scrape all that food off the plate into the garbage afterward. What a waste. Patricia clearly did not like her food, which was fine. But what hurt Roya more was that Walter's older sister clearly also did not like her.

"And what is new in the world of our lovely couple: Walter and Roya?" Patricia asked tentatively now at dinner, after sniffing the meat loaf on her plate.

"Walter is studying very much these days. And nights," Roya said.

"Well. It's completely understandable that he'd have to do so in law school, isn't it? You can't take it personally, Roya. He has to study hard. That's how it works over here."

"No, what I mean is that—" Roya started to say.

"Walter, are you getting enough rest? Enough to eat?" Patricia cut her off. "I can bring you a roast, if you like. Might be a nice break from . . . from the rest of it?"

"Oh, Roya is giving me everything I need. I'm all set. Thanks though, Patricia."

"Well then." Patricia smiled tightly. "Pardon me."

They continued to sit and eat in silence. After a few minutes, Patricia raised her fork and then said, "So?"

"So, what?" Walter responded wearily.

"Oh, do I have to spell it out for you two! So. Shall I be stitching initials on a baby blanket anytime soon?"

Roya's body went slack.

"See now, Patricia. What you need to understand is that Roya here is a modern woman. It's 1959, for the love of God." Walter took a gulp of his gin and tonic. "Roya wants to work," he said. "As a scientist. And she's very well qualified. You know that. She's been sending out her applications and looking for a position ever since we moved back east."

Patricia's fork stayed suspended in midair. Then she put it down and said, "Don't patronize me, Walter. As if I don't work! But if you are married, it makes sense to have children. That is all."

Patricia had never married. Five years older than Walter, she was employed by a bank in the financial district. She was known to be quite a whiz with numbers, and increasingly resentful of the secretarial work that she was relegated to doing.

"May I get you another drink, Patricia?" he asked.

Patricia glared and said something incomprehensible under her breath. Walter took that as a yes and went to the kitchen.

"I just want to work for a year or two," Roya said meekly when left alone with her sister-in-law. The things Patricia had said unnerved her. A wedding, a husband, a house in the suburbs: these things were easier to accomplish and had already been neatly checked off the list. But children terrified her. She was not ready for the role of mother.

Patricia took a bite of meat loaf, chewed, and swallowed. She carefully dabbed the corners of her mouth with her napkin. "You can't have everything fall into place for you just because you're in America now. It doesn't work that way."

"Oh, I know," Roya said. "I *sure do.*" She couldn't resist saying it in an exaggerated American accent.

Patricia just stared at her for a few seconds. Then she muttered, "Poor Walter."

Patricia had always made it clear that it was bad enough that her little brother had chosen a Persian bride over the many established WASPs in their social circle. To now have this little Iranian girl insist on *working,* for no good reason, seemed to truly rattle her.

"Not something *you* can control, now, is it?" Patricia said. "And there's Walter to consider."

"Pat, here you go!" Walter came back and handed his sister a fresh martini. His forced good cheer stopped when he saw Roya's face. "Did I miss something?"

"Nothing, Walter dear." Patricia took the drink. "Some people just think they control their own destinies, that is all. Too naïve and foolish to know better."

～

A few weeks later, Walter came home from law school and gave Roya a kiss as she stood at the stove cooking. "You know, one of my classmates has a sister who works at the business school. She's leaving her job to have a baby."

"Good for her," Roya said. After the disastrous dinner conversation with Patricia, she had repeated in private to Walter that she just wasn't ready for kids. He knew, he said. No rush. Don't let my sister mess with you.

Why was Walter bringing up somebody's baby now?

"Well, this fellow says that his sister's position is going to be available."

Roya stopped stirring the sauce on the stove.

"Look, I know it's in the business school, and that's not what you want. But it's a job, Roya. And—well, you may want to apply before others do. Soon it'll be officially opened up and loads of applications will come in."

"I don't want to be a secretary." She thought of Patricia in her pencil skirts and tight sweaters typing for men at the bank, seething with thwarted ambition.

"I know it's not a laboratory job. But, Roya, it's a good position."

It had proven far more difficult to get hired at a laboratory than even Roya had expected. Positions for women were few. She was willing to start at the bottom, as a technician. But laboratories didn't want her. One lab offered her the position of bottle washer: beakers and test tubes had to be washed by hand carefully, the interviewer said. Roya showed her transcripts of her near-perfect grades and her bachelor of science degree in chemistry. It was practically 1960, but it seemed that everywhere she went, male applicants got preference. And she was still—forever—the foreigner. She was in the minority of women who even *wanted* to work. Most of her cohorts in the Boston suburbs were happy to stay home and keep house for their husbands.

"Well, congratulations," Patricia said when she found out that Roya had gotten the secretarial job at the business school. "Now who will cook for and take care of poor Walter?"

"I will continue to cook for him, as always, Patricia. Don't you worry."

She chopped parsley, cilantro, spinach, and mint. She made the thickest *aush* soup, and she and Walter raised their glasses in celebration.

Despite Patricia's disapproval and the sad looks from Alice, Walter stood his ground with his sister and mother and respected Roya's desire to wait before trying for children.

Over the next year, every now and then, Walter gently asked if Roya had changed her mind. Roya didn't want to tell him that she was scared of creating another life and growing attached to it. She could not remove from her mind the ugly question: *What if something happens to the baby?*

Mrs. Aslan's strange refrain from a lifetime ago sometimes came back to her at the oddest moments. *Babies die,* she had said.

What crazy wife thought like Roya? Patricia was right. Poor Walter, indeed!

For years she thought that her biggest loss in life would be her first love. Or the stationer who had died at her feet. Little did she know that her future held a bigger loss: a loss that would make the summer of 1953 look like child's play.

Part Four

Chapter Twenty-One

I did not expect a son and a daughter at the same time!
It's a specific kind of joy blended with exhaustion: an
attachment that overwhelms. We are consumed by them. We
are blessed and in awe. May God protect them.

The other night I came home from work and the cook had
made a special egg and garlic dish popular in her village up
north and both of the twins started to cry at the same time,
and I could tell that had it not been for the servants and the
nurse, Shahla would have been at her wits' end. Mother came
to visit and she sat quietly and retreated into her corner.

I don't for a second forget any one of the number of things
she said to you that were cruel. I felt shame at her lack of
an emotional filter, at her forceful and cutting words. I
remember when you were at my parents' house and my
mother said things to hurt you. Cut you. Scare you. I was so
convinced that she was being cruel. And I can understand,
on my best days, why that would scare you away.

But here is the history you do not know:

I was not my parents' first child. I was not their second, nor their third. I was not my mother's fourth. I was the fifth child my mother had, and the others who preceded me all died. Two were stillborn, one died in my mother's eighth month of pregnancy, and one died in the first year of life. That my parents kept trying was a testament to their desire and the times. I don't know if my parents had more children after me. Maybe they did and I was too young to remember another one dying. My mother only told me about these other lost babies in a moment of extreme duress, on a day I'd rather forget. It was the day that changed everything for us. For you and me, you could say.

Of course, my mother wasn't alone in losing babies in those days, but others seem to have borne it better. Maybe it was that she lost so many in a row.

I attributed her melancholy to the loss of those babies. I attributed her depression and mood swings and instability—all of it—to that.

How was I supposed to know there was a loss that preceded all the others, that hung over everything?

I hope that you are well over there in America. Be good. Be safe. I hope you are healthy, happy. My children keep me going. Do you know of what I speak?

Chapter Twenty-Two

1962–1963

Marigold

Sister, Jack and I are expecting our first child. Also, I have learned how to make eggplant khoresh without the eggplant!

Roya read Zari's letter and filed it neatly on her desk in the pile of to-dos. She wrote back in Farsi and added "Congratulations" in English in block letters at the bottom of the page. As she licked the envelope and sealed it shut, Roya reminded herself of her goals. She was working hard as a secretary at the business school. Her typing speed had soared. It was not the kind of job she had expected to be doing, but compromise was the name of the game in her new adult life. She simply had been unable to get a good (or any) job in science, and it was not for lack of trying. This was what it was to be a woman, she knew. She was already pushing boundaries by even insisting on working. And in science there was always the assumption that she would be taking the job from a well-qualified man. And as a foreigner—well, shouldn't she just be grateful to be in this country? That was the underlying message she often received from well-intentioned friends and neighbors. Roya scaled back her ambition.

At the back of her mind, a question nagged. Patricia was right: she should be starting a family. What was she so afraid of, for goodness' sake, why did she think something bad would happen? Roya walked to the post office and mailed the letter to Zari. She would call her later in the week, send a present, of course. Of course. She walked home quickly, remembering all she had to do. She was happy for Zari and Jack. She really was.

She was busy though, boy, wasn't she! So busy.

Sometimes in her dreams, Bahman would appear. His smile, the musky scent, the eyes filled with hope, his touch, how he leaned into her against the books at the Stationery Shop, the taste of that first espresso, the sweet pastry, the slope of his back next to hers . . . She willed herself to forget it all when she was awake. She could not allow it to interfere with the present script of her life. In the dreams he was always young, sometimes happy.

On the phone at Persian New Year, Jahangir told her that Bahman and Shahla were busy with their children now. Twins. Twins! The once-a-year phone call with Jahangir was the only way Roya ever heard news about Bahman. Maman and Baba certainly never talked of him. During her first two years in the US, she had exchanged letters with a few of the girls she'd gone to school with in Iran and with two of her cousins. But as months wore on, they stopped writing each other. Too much distance. Too much time. The only people she exchanged letters with anymore were her parents in Iran and Zari in California. But the annual phone call with Jahangir kept her connected to a past she couldn't bring herself to abandon, no matter how painful.

Walter studied hard, and Roya was happy—well, content—well, *settled* at her job at Harvard Business School. HBS, they called it. Everyone loved acronyms in America. Her coworkers were efficient and sometimes kind. It was satisfying to insert the paper in the typewriter every morning, to type letters to the dean and other professors, to take notes, file papers, put things in absolute order. She liked being on top of things. Everything was in its place: the files, the letters, sharpened pencils, manila folders. She controlled her world with precise care.

"So!" Patricia said when over for another dinner. "How is everything with you two? Anything exciting on the horizon?"

"May I get you a drink, Patricia?" Walter asked through gritted teeth.

"I'm holding one, but thanks." Patricia smiled. "Walter, remember Richard from the Cape cottage when we were growing up? His family and ours were very close." Patricia said the last bit to Roya in an explanatory tone as if bringing her up to date, even though Roya knew Richard. She and Walter had dinner with him and his wife regularly. "Well," Patricia went on, "he and his lovely wife—oh, I love Susan! she is so elegant!—are expecting their third child! Third!" Patricia sipped her drink.

Roya went to the kitchen and fried some onions for no reason at all. She sprinkled mint on them and ate them out of the pan as her body shook. She and Walter were in their midtwenties now. Most of their friends and acquaintances had at least one child. But it was not too late for them. Patricia was rude. Direct and interfering. It was none of her business. They had managed to wait, and wait they would.

~~~

She came on her own schedule. She was born in Mount Auburn Hospital on January 11, 1962, and when Roya held her, when she looked into eyes that were strangely alert, held the tiny milky, cheesy body pressed against her own, she was terrified. But Roya was also, in a strange way, real again. She was not an actress in an American movie. She was delirious and dizzy—yes—but amazingly grounded at the same time. For the first time in a long time, Roya was fully herself again.

When they came home from the hospital, Alice took care of the three of them. Alice, who smelled of potato salad and lotion, who was matter-of-fact with Roya and enchanted with her granddaughter. Roya missed Maman sorely but was grateful for Alice's presence, boiling everything in sight as a hedge against infection, providing good cheer, and making endless quantities of baked potatoes with sour cream.

Alice's face crumpled a year later when their baby stopped breathing. Alice cried in the car as they drove to the hospital in an icy panic.

The baby gasped for air. Marigold. Her name was Marigold. She'd landed in their lives, and for almost twelve months, Roya had lost layers of her reserve. She had never given Walter complete access to herself; she had a part of herself always locked away. He'd accepted it (he was Walter!), grateful just to have her there, to see her every morning. But Marigold—with her light brown hair, her gray eyes, her soft mewls as she breastfed, grabbing onto Roya with startling strength—Marigold broke through every single glacial wall Roya had built up and melted it with her toothless smile. For twelve months, Roya, exhausted and exhilarated, was purely herself. Even the romance of her youth fizzled in comparison; nothing had ever meant everything to her the way this baby did.

On the drive to the hospital, Walter clutched the steering wheel, silent. Snow steadily fell; snowbanks hardened and grayed. The sound of Alice's prayers filled the car: verses from the Bible and entreaties to God. Alice had driven from the Cape to visit them; they had been having Sunday dinner when Marigold's bad cough wouldn't stop, when the fever she'd had for days flared higher, when she wheezed and gasped for air. As Roya sat so still in the backseat with her burning baby in her arms, she felt like she might crack and splinter into pieces. *Just let my child be all right, please let the doctors bring down her fever, she will be better, of course, she has to be.* Marigold wheezed, and then out of desperation Roya sang her an old Persian folk song. Alice stopped praying and listened, and Walter just drove as fast as was possible on the ice.

The nurse who took Marigold from Roya's arms had a blond beehive under her white cap. Her breath smelled of cigarettes. Roya didn't want to give her daughter to this woman, she wanted to keep her close. The doctor who arrived had a pimple above his lip, ready to burst. Years later, as Roya walked the blocks around her house, she'd be furious for remembering the doctor's pimple and the nurse's cigarette smell—they had come between her and her baby, they had inserted themselves into the tragedy of her life, and they would forever haunt her memories on a loop.

Marigold was pronounced dead forty-three minutes after their arrival at the hospital.

On the linoleum floor, beneath the fluorescent lights, Roya's legs went numb. The doctor's voice was garbled. He was speaking through mud. Just like when she'd first arrived in America, English was incomprehensible. Beside her stood Walter; he hovered next to her, tall and silent, and in her peripheral vision she saw his huge hands shaking. Alice was diagonally across from her; everything about her mother-in-law was motionless except for her tears.

The three of them went home at dawn. There was no avoiding it, though Roya had considered simply staying in the hospital and not leaving and maybe starving to death on its linoleum floor. In that building, with its beeping and noise and a million other emergencies that could never have been as important as Marigold's life, in that place that smelled of death, they had sat for hours and Walter had signed paperwork and then they were told to leave. During the ride home, the snowbanks loomed. Limbs she did not have, she could not feel her arms or legs or her fingers; Roya knew it was someone other than herself in the car. She missed more than anything else Marigold's face against hers. Her grief would have no end, of this she was sure.

It was Walter, finally, who made her tea. It was Walter who got out of bed first every morning and made the hard-boiled eggs. He didn't whistle anymore. Something sour was always in the air now, rotting in the crater left in Marigold's wake.

⁂

"You didn't need to come," Roya said a few weeks later when Zari showed up, suitcase in hand, two tiny kids in tow. Roya stood at the doorway of her darkened house, dirty dishes in the sink in the kitchen behind her, laundry piled up, mustiness in the air.

"Oh, but I did, Sister."

Zari's son, Darius, was four now. His little sister, Leila, wriggled in Zari's arms. Leila was two. Twelve months Leila had lived that Marigold would never have. Everything—every detail, every word, every second, every person—reminded Roya of Marigold. Except that *reminded* wasn't the right word. *Reminded* meant that she had to forget to remember again. But she never forgot. Everything was linked to Marigold; nothing, really, could be separated from her ever. Not even words uttered by a crazy woman in Iran a lifetime ago. *Babies die.*

Here was Leila in Zari's arms. Here was her niece, chubby, happy, breathing, alive, a knitted pink bonnet on her head. A bonnet that Zari would have wrapped and placed in a package and mailed to Roya with a note saying, *Maman Joon knitted it and sent it. Leila's outgrown it. Marigold should wear it now.*

Marigold should.

If.

Darius squealed and ran to the kitchen. Zari took her shoes off and shouted at Darius to not run through the house with wet boots. Roya stared out at the snow as her sister and niece and nephew rushed past her. The world dared go on in cold, spiteful glee.

~

To reform Jack, Zari had moved mountains. Under Zari's expert stewardship, Jack the beat poet transformed into a corporate hack. He wrote jingles for ads, first for print and eventually for television, and if the former idealist poet was saddened by this transformation, one could not tell. Whenever Roya had seen him, Jack was beaming, his kids hanging off him like zoo monkeys, his formerly long hair in a buzz cut. In his suits and thin ties, he was the epitome of a 1960s advertising employee. How had Zari managed to mold her man into this, what wonder drug did she give her Jack, what kept that smile on his face? *Oh, Sister, we both know in the end it comes down to what happens in bed, don't we? That's how you get anything done, let's face it! I am no fool and I know what to do.*

At the thought of beds and sheets and lovemaking, Roya simply felt numb now.

Zari cleaned the house. The kind of thorough cleaning normally reserved for Persian New Year, the first day of spring. But it wasn't spring, it was still winter, the ice and snow were everywhere. Zari didn't care; she cleaned. And Roya thought of all the rituals with which they had been raised to celebrate the first day of spring—all useless now. As if she would ever again have the wherewithal to prepare a *Haft Seen* table for Persian New Year, to set it with items beginning with *s* that were symbolic of rebirth and renewal. No. To soak lentils in water so they could grow green sprouts, to paint eggs to celebrate fertility—never. Persian New Year, the first day of spring, Nowruz—meaningless now, all of it. Walter and Roya wouldn't celebrate it, or Christmas or Thanksgiving either. What was the point?

Zari washed her windows (in February! in New England! why bother? they'd be covered by snow and frost anyway). Zari washed all the clothes too. She went to the store and bought fresh ingredients and cooked and sautéed and fried and basted and filled Roya's freezer with *khoreshes* and rice dishes and stuffed grape leaf *dolmehs* and meat patty *kotelets* and potato quiche *kukus*. She opened the windows and let in fresh air (freezing air was more like it). Zari even insisted on melting sugar in a saucepan, then adding a few drops of lemon juice and warm water to create a wax with which she wanted to remove the hair on Roya's legs.

"Do you honestly think I care about that right now?"

"It's not for you."

"I can assure you that Walter does not care. I can assure you there is no reason he would even know there is some hair on my legs."

"Please. At some point you have to . . ."

Roya's body heaved with the familiar grief. She wanted to disappear. What difference did it make? No one could make it different.

During Zari's two-week visit, Roya sat once on the floor to play with her niece and nephew. She listened to their giggles and chortles. Then she got up. She climbed into bed and stayed there for the rest of the evening.

When Zari brought up a tray for dinner, she lingered at the edge of Roya's bed. "I had no choice, Roya Joon. I had to come with them. I couldn't leave them with anyone. Jack works into the night; he is no help."

This was how it would be now. People would apologize for the presence of their children, tuck away their happiness from her, become self-conscious of their joy. This was her new destiny.

During those two weeks, in addition to cleaning the house and stocking Roya's fridge, Zari entered the nursery. She did ask first, and Roya could barely muster up a shrug. Zari brazenly boxed up Marigold's clothes, put toys in bags, and visited the church with donations. She had the audacity to tell Roya that she'd saved a few outfits for her to look at later, when she was ready. She'd never be ready.

"Thank you, Zari, thank you," Walter said again and again. "Aren't you kind. So kind of you to do this. You have no idea how much we appreciate it."

Uber-polite, wimpy Walter. The hell with both of them. The hell with Walter's manners and Zari's zeal. What was the point of going through her child's clothes, of washing the blasted windows? Roya stayed in bed and stared at nothing. In the rocking chair where she had breastfed Marigold, Walter sat with his damn drink and rocked to and fro in silence.

When the day came for Zari's flight back to California, Roya did not cry. Or did she? She cried so much these days, it felt invisible, she couldn't tell sometimes. When she thought she'd wrung out the last possible tear, there was always a well of more.

"Bye," Roya said. So tidy, so American. Bye! Easy-peasy. See ya! Maybe there was something to these Americanisms. Breezy. Casual. They made everything seem like strawberry milkshakes and good times coming.

"I'll miss you, Sister," Zari whispered in Farsi as she wept into Roya's neck. "I'll miss you so much. You can always write to me. I'll telephone you. You know the next time I can come, I will. . . ."

"Bye!" Roya said it again. "Thanks!" She didn't know if she'd ever access gratitude or kindness in herself again. She wished she could stop the ice forming around her.

"I am so sorry." Zari smelled the same way she had when they were girls sharing a room in Iran. Like tea, like home. "You know you can always—"

"Go. You'll be late."

Little Leila made a fuss about leaving and Darius hid behind the couch in a game of hide-and-seek that no one was playing. After some cajoling and yelling, Zari scooped up her children and shepherded them into the taxicab waiting outside. Roya waved. Walter had said good-bye that morning with endless thanks and gestures of gratitude and apologies that he could not drive Zari to Logan Airport, he had a motion to prepare, the judge was relentless in this case.

Roya stood in the doorway and looked out at the snow as the cab took away her sister and nephew and niece. Behind her a spotless, organized house filled with food in the fridge. In front of her, nothing.

⁓

Nothing to do but go back to work. Eventually, you waxed your legs again. *Not one hair there to bother Walter, see, Sister?* In their grief, husband and wife slowly achieved a new equilibrium. They padded around each other carefully at first, and then with more spontaneity because, as it was said, life somehow went on.

Snow turned to spring. Roya couldn't bring herself to celebrate Persian New Year for the first day of spring though. No Nowruz. What was there to renew? What rebirth was there to celebrate? The seasons were indifferent to Marigold. Someone had mangled the script, taken the pages and burned them in a fire, destroyed all semblance of meaning and order. Someone had wrought this wrong. Happy spring!

She got home from work a little earlier than usual on the first day of spring and made some tea. Walter was working late, and Roya did her best to ignore Persian New Year. When the doorbell rang, she expected it to be Mrs. Michael from across the street (she sometimes came by with cookies or a pie—much more so in the past few months since Marigold had died). But when she opened the door, Roya was surprised to see not Mrs. Michael, but Patricia. Patricia wore a dark-blue coat with hexagonal buttons and carried a grocery bag. Her blue suede pumps were sensible and looked expensive.

"May I come in?" Patricia asked.

"Of course. Please." Roya stepped aside so Patricia could come into the foyer. Roya knew better than to ask her sister-in-law to remove her pumps. The first time Walter had mentioned that Roya preferred for people not to come inside with shoes on, Patricia had looked confused and said, "I didn't use up half my paycheck on footwear so I could walk around in my stockings."

Roya took Patricia's coat, hung it up in the foyer closet, led Patricia into the kitchen, and asked robotically if she'd like some tea.

"That would be lovely, thank you," Patricia said. She put down the grocery bag on the table and cleared her throat. Then she said, "I went to Mount Auburn after work."

Roya stiffened. Marigold was buried at Mount Auburn Cemetery.

"Mount Auburn Street. The shops there," Patricia went on. "I got you something. Some things."

Roya watched as Patricia removed items from her paper bag

and placed them carefully on the kitchen counter. There was a small pot of hyacinths in cellophane and a bag of apples. Chocolate coins wrapped in gold foil and a packet of sumac spice. A bottle of vinegar and a few cloves of garlic. There was even a bag of *senjed*, the dried fruit of the lotus tree.

These were all items that began with the letter *s* in Farsi, traditional items for the Persian New Year *Haft Seen* seven *s*'s table. Roya had carefully laid out these symbolic objects every single year growing up with Maman and Zari and Baba. It was a tradition she had hoped to share with Marigold one day. It was not a tradition she had ever expected Patricia to help her celebrate.

"Happy New Year, Roya," Patricia said gently.

A lump the size of all of New England rose in Roya's throat. A sheen of sweat coated her skin. She was filled with a huge wave of gratitude that made her want to fold over and cry. "Thank you, Patricia," Roya whispered.

Patricia turned to straighten the hyacinth and move the sumac spice over to the left a little. She was not one to express her feelings all too well—this much Roya knew. But when she turned around, Roya saw that her sister-in-law's eyes were filled with tears. "I am," Patricia said, "so very sorry."

Roya didn't know if she was giving condolences again for Marigold (so many people told her they were sorry whenever they saw her these days—it was the one thing she heard the most) or if Patricia was perhaps apologizing for anything she'd said in the past.

Roya just nodded.

Patricia reached into the paper bag and retrieved another item. It was a small see-through sachet filled with the thin crimson threads that Roya knew so well.

"Where did you find saffron?" Roya gasped.

"Oh, I did my research. I have my ways." Patricia came close and gently pressed the sachet of saffron into Roya's hands. For a minute she kept her hands around Roya's. Then she quickly straightened herself up and said in a loud and authoritative voice, "Now then! Where is that tea you promised me?"

They sat together that afternoon and drank the tea. Their conversation was halting at first, but slowly they opened up more. For the first time since she'd married Walter, Roya and Patricia even commiserated about Walter's obsession with the Red Sox.

"Thank you, Patricia," Roya said when Patricia got up to leave. "I do appreciate this. More than you know."

"No need to thank me." Patricia went to the foyer and got her coat. At the door, she hesitated. Then she said, "I may have been a bit hard on you over these past few years. Perhaps. You have to understand that Walter is my only sibling and I adore him. You could argue I love him to a fault. Mother says I mollycoddle him. No one is ever good enough for my little brother and all that. But . . ." Patricia fidgeted with the buttons on her coat and then looked up. "Well, Roya, we may have lost Marigold. But we are so very grateful to have you." She quickly walked out, went down the front steps, and slid into her car.

Roya stood at the doorway, and this time, she broke down into tears.

*

They became the couple that others turned their heads toward and gave a sad smile to, the couple prayed for at Alice's church, the ones who received cards in the mail filled with fountain-penned condolences. Roya continued to work at HBS, and she felt for Walter a strange kinship. They were united in pain. He spent every night drinking in the rocking chair before bed. She retreated into her shell. Ice frozen over a melted layer is even harder to break than before.

A routine of work and a few friends and, painstakingly, a semblance of return to the world. Eventually, Walter and Roya went out again to dinners at their neighbors'. Sure, she even got out the pots and pans again and cooked. For Walter. She forced herself to buy rice and soak it in lukewarm water and boil it, and one night when Walter came home from the office (he worked at a huge law firm now, in Boston, near the Prudential Center, he was successful, everyone told him so), he was able to smell again the fragrant saffron, thanks to Patricia. He held Roya close and inhaled her hair. She was glad that he didn't say something awful like "You're back."

For their anniversary a few months later, they went to a restaurant for the first time since. At the table, Walter took her hand.

"Roya Joon, we should try again."

The words landed like sharp needles against her scalp, her skin.

"Not if you're not ready. But, I don't know. We are so young, Roya Joon, aren't we? I'm not saying now. I'm saying when you're ready."

She would never be ready. She would never want in any way to replace Marigold. Why had she agreed to come out with Walter? She wasn't even ready to be out in public at a restaurant where everyone around them was having fun. All she wanted was her daughter. She wanted to feel her daughter's face against her cheek. She wanted to hold her and hear her laugh. She wanted Marigold.

Under the dim light of the restaurant, Walter's expression was pleading. Not for the first time, Roya saw how he'd aged. The Berkeley café coffee-cup-spilling incident was seven years ago. They'd been married now for five years. It was 1963. They were twenty-seven. But their loss had removed them from the normal scheme of things—they were part of an elite club who'd experienced a coup of the natural order of life. Marigold had come in their fourth year of marriage, unannounced and unexpected but oh so welcome when she arrived. Only to then disappear and prove Roya's every worst fear true.

"Honey."

She hated it when he called her *honey*. He only called her that when he was being patronizing. Roya Joon was what he called her when he was actually affectionate, but *honey* meant *I know better*. *Honey* meant *you're not thinking clearly, of course we'll have another child*. *Honey* meant that he had no idea that the only reason she hadn't quit *it all* was out of obligation to him.

"I can't. No," she said.

He got up, and she thought that he was going to the bathroom. Maybe he was even leaving the restaurant. He had every right to get away from her. She had been impossible since Marigold's death: selfish and quiet and withdrawn. Maybe he would go to the restroom and gather his wits in his very Walter-ish way and come back with a façade of good cheer—as much as he could muster in public—and they would go on eating their beef stroganoff amidst the clatter of the restaurant. They would pretend to be like any other couple there.

But he didn't leave. He came to her side of the table. He knelt down and gently took her face in both his hands. His blue eyes were filled with a sadness that was theirs alone.

"She will always be right here," Walter said. And he touched his chest just like he had during the first time Roya had cooked for him in Mrs. Kishpaugh's kitchen all those years ago. Then he rested his forehead against hers.

The waiters came and went. The other diners clanged their

utensils and chatted and guffawed every once in a while. Roya and Walter stayed that way—foreheads touching. Of his love she had never been more sure. For every ounce of grief that she had, Walter had the same. He had labored with her in this grief, felt his way through the darkness and the depth of it, and all the time as the world carried on, he was there by her side. Walter was always there. Reliable. Trustworthy. Steady. The love that she and Walter shared was a lifeline she did not want to do without.

At the end of the Christmas holidays, after Marigold had been gone for almost a year, she dragged the rocking chair down the stairs and to the curb. She knew Mrs. Michael was watching from her window across the street as she did it. In the town where America had begun, Roya deposited the rocking chair on the curb and left it there for someone new to pick up, take home, rock on.

Part Five

Chapter Twenty-Three

2013

Virtual Friends

If there was one thing Claire would ban, it was TV commercials. And if there was one thing she couldn't stop watching, it was these commercials. Her friends on Facebook told her to record her shows and just fast-forward through the advertisements or to download them from a streaming site, but Claire couldn't help but watch each program in real time with all the ads—almost in a masochistic way. Like dwelling on a wound, like itching a scab and feeling it sting.

Every night after she came home to her small apartment in Watertown, Claire made herself a dinner of pita bread with turkey and tomato or Top Ramen noodles or microwaved packaged rice and a fried egg. She turned on the TV and prepared to feel the sting. She didn't watch the shows her friends on Facebook watched—the dramas on cable that won all the awards: sexy, well-written, edgy shows that warranted social media status updates and spoiler alerts and virtual water-cooler conversations. She watched instead—almost with horror—reality shows featuring plastic-surgeried housewives fighting in expensive restaurants or families with twenty happy children going through scripted mayhem. During the commercials, Claire would lie under her beige blanket as buddies ate fast food together, parents and children found bliss with mobile phone apps, cute toddlers ran around in diapers, fathers tearfully watched their daughters grow up in a montage from baby-in-a-car-seat to teenager-behind-the-steering-wheel. Claire scoffed at the sentimentality and rejected it, but longed for it all the same. Years ago, she had been a long-legged undergrad at college majoring in English literature, convinced she'd end up as a successful and content university professor. But then her mother had called in tears saying, "It's positive." The tiny lump in her mother's breast ended up, even after removal, continuing its evil journey throughout her body, so that by the time Claire was twenty-four, her mother was in a graveyard in Bedford, Massachusetts, just a mile from the local Whole Foods, and Claire was tented in chronic grief. Her father had died in a car accident when she was just a toddler in those diapers constantly featured in the commercials she watched at nights alone now. Claire had felt, at a very young age, the stunning reality of being alone. Boyfriends came and went. None of them stuck, even though she had been convinced that she was in love once. Maybe twice.

Now, at age thirty, her friends from school were either married or in serious relationships. They were scattered all over the country and even the world. Her link to them was through social media, not through phone calls or that ancient ritual of actually seeing one another. She followed their colorful, happy, but oh-so-careful-to-be-self-deprecating lives online. She read status updates of "Yes, it's true, we have a bun in the oven!" and pressed "like" even though she sometimes felt empty and jealous. She saw the photos of her pregnant friends on beaches with their husbands' arms around them and pressed "like." She opened her laptop to see the babies born—small, scrunched-up newborns in hats—and read all the comments: "So happy for you, Jenna!" "OMG—he is GORGEOUS!" and pressed "like" and added her own "Congrats!" She scrolled through selfies of her former classmates vacationing in Costa Rica and Hawaii with their kids and was mired in a strange stew of envy and happiness for them. Then she turned on the TV and watched families drink hot chocolate and have fights and make up and fathers give car keys to their newly licensed daughters. And all she could think was just how much she missed her mom.

Her room was lined with books written by gurus and advice-givers who told her that she should look within and meditate and be grateful and count her blessings and write in a gratitude journal. Claire did. But once it became clear that her English literature degree from a small liberal arts college in Connecticut qualified her for administrative jobs and folding clothes at retail stores, once she realized that she was never going to have the courage to apply for a PhD program in English and become a professor, she took the money from her mom's life insurance, rented an apartment in Watertown, floated from retail job to administrative job, and found herself, one day, at age thirty, working as the assistant administrator at the Duxton Senior Center.

She liked her job. She liked being with people day in and day out who were close to exiting the stage, so to speak. She appreciated that they did not have, for the most part, the fake humility and the need to prove that they were happy happy happy. She loved that the old, grumpy men coughed and spat and snarled and made no pretense that life was good. She enjoyed helping the older ladies apply bright-pink lipstick with religious regularity, as if skipping that one act alone would mark complete surrender to their age. She helped Miss Emily roll her nylons up her blue-veined legs and she buttoned Mr. Rosenberg's cardigan with care. The ladies and gentlemen at the Duxton Senior Center were the only reason Claire hadn't given up. They were all she had left. Her friends from elementary school and high school and college were now simply "Friends on Facebook"—a new category, it seemed, in her mind: FOF—who existed only as digital images, whom she hadn't seen in years (she skipped the reunions), and who scrolled through life in happy, occasionally messy, but always exclamatory moments. Her father wasn't even a memory because she'd been too young to know him. Her most vivid image of him was from a photo her mother had attached to their fridge with an eggplant magnet: a tall, grinning man with blond hair standing by a picnic basket next to her mom. There had been no fancy wedding. Just a justice of the peace visit, her mom had said.

For years she'd had a mother, beautiful and kind—a mother who told her stories about her father and who lamented being an only child who'd given birth to an only child and how little family they had but they had each other, didn't they, and that's really all they needed, and her baby was her everything, her beautiful baby who gave her life meaning. She was her gorgeous little girl, wasn't she, I'm sorry if I'm embarrassing you, sweetheart, but it's true— you are my life—and you and me, girlie girl, we're going to take on the world, aren't we, Claire, and oh, how your father would've loved to see you now, sweetheart, and we can make it on this planet, girlie girl—we can—you are so smart and so talented and you just wait—you're going to be a big deal one day, you already are my pride and joy. And then cancer had wiped her mother from the world and Claire felt desperately, inexplicably, painfully, permanently alone. No mom to come home to, call on the phone, cook a favorite dish with. No mom to tell her that everything would be all right. And the strange, horrifying realization that things wouldn't be all right. Ever. Even if her FOF scaled mountains in Asia and raised perfect children and celebrated romantic anniversaries in faraway resorts. Everything wasn't all right for Claire. At thirty, she grasped this, owned this, knew this—she did not feel the need to pretend otherwise. The husbands and babies and romance and oh-my-gosh-look-at-my-messy-but-oh-so-full-and-beautiful-life! status updates were not in her future. Hers were nights of reality shows and days spent in the reality of people nearing death.

She loved her senior residents at the center, even the ones so close to going that every morning hearing them say "Well, hey there, Claire!" felt like a miracle. Mr. Rosenberg told her tales of his life in Queens, New York, "back in the day," and Mrs. Ventura was about to "step over to the other side" every single week, or so she said. Claire's favorite was a Mr. Bahman Aslan, who had been there for two years. She called him "Mr. Batman." He was always kind and she loved to hear his tales of his youth in Iran, his political adventures, the years he spent during the war. His great love. People like Mr. Batman—his jokes, complaints, sorrows, ailments, regrets, perspective, memories—were the reason Claire woke up every morning, ate a dry, stale-tasting protein bar, and drove in her seven-year-old Honda from Watertown to Duxton. The Duxton Senior Center was a combination of a senior center and a nursing home. Seniors could just visit to partake in activities or be boarders under a more traditional nursing-home model. Claire threw herself into the concerns of her seniors and residents. Thanksgiving was with them. Christmas was with them. Her life was with them. And outside of that, life was simply FOF and the damn shows and commercials on TV.

She would take the stories of her residents any day over all of that. Especially the memories and life anecdotes of Mr. Bahman Aslan.

Chapter Twenty-Four

1978–1981

Dispatches

August 1978

Cinema Rex was lit on fire the other day. More than four hundred people killed. People trapped and stuck, people running and striving to get out of that place only to find that they never could. I couldn't help but think of our dates at Cinema Metropole. It was twenty-five years to the day of the coup. And now, here we go again. Every day there are more and more demonstrations in the streets. My children believe the answer lies in Ayatollah Khomeini, the exiled religious cleric who has a huge following all of a sudden. I just don't know. The young here these days need something to latch on to, something to believe in, and for that something to not be the Shah.

History repeats itself. To watch these young students pour into the streets again, convinced that if they rid themselves

of the Shah all problems will be solved, is painful. Yes, he
was complicit in Prime Minister Mossadegh's ousting, and
the West then propped him up. But the youth today think
all their problems will be solved if the Shah just goes away.
I worry about what may follow. We want democracy but
never seem to get it. What if what follows is worse?

I wonder about you over there in America. I get some
news from Jahangir, and for that I'm very grateful. I'm
glad the two of you still talk. Amazing to think that in this
modern world we can communicate across oceans just by
picking up the telephone! Jahangir tells me that you are
working, that you have a job at Harvard? Bravo to you,
Roya Joon.

You were always destined to do great things.

March 1979

Now the Shah is gone. All I see in the faces of those of
us who remember 1953, who can feel under our skin that
awful disappointment of having the world plummet in
one day, is the return of trauma. The youth are so hopeful.
They think we got it right this time. They are glad the Shah
is gone. He's trying to get to America, but I hear your new
country won't let him. How, after everything he did for the
US, is your country not letting him in?

Maybe this time we'll get a true democratic government.
I'll believe it when I see it.

Do you remember the twilight on the evening when I
proposed, the purple of the sky? Do you think I have not
looked at the sky on a hundred other nights remembering
your kiss?

August 1981

Since Saddam Hussein attacked Iran last September, the war has only gotten worse and worse. We spend our nights in the basement bomb shelter. My children are frightened all the time. You would not recognize parts of this country now. We have been blown up. At night we cover our windows with aluminum foil so Saddam's planes cannot find our city and its lights. We live in perpetual fear. My children are in their early twenties, and I do not want my son to be drafted into the army, to be told to fight and kill Iraqis. For what? For this new Islamic government to feel powerful and rally us around the flag? And my daughter is forced to wear the hijab when she steps outside. What have we become? I can barely recognize my country anymore.

Roya Joon, Jahangir joined the army as a doctor. My dear Roya, he was killed at the front. His place is so empty here.

Chapter Twenty-Five

2013

Big Box

Zari's nose on the cell-phone screen was strangely magnified. One of the few reliefs left in life was phoning people without being *seen*, but Zari insisted on FaceTiming Roya every week. Call her old-fashioned, but Roya couldn't stand having her face shown on the phone. Just made no sense. But she had to admit it was a comfort to see Zari, even on a gadget. Her little sister was a grandmother now, had had hip replacement surgery, and engaged in almost daily arguments with her daughter-in-law.

"Walter needs paper clips and a shredder. I have to go, Zari."

"Okay, Sister. You know, it's amazing: you have the skin of a young lady. At seventy-seven! Thank God for our genes!"

"Say hello to Jack and Darius and Leila and all the grandkids."

"Will do. Hope to see you for Nowruz! Big hugs to Walter and Kyle from me."

〜

The years had had the audacity to pass by. It had been decades since Marigold had died of the croup, and decades since Mossadegh was overthrown in the coup. The world was something else entirely. Iran had had its Islamic Revolution in 1979—now her country was no longer ruled by the Shah but by religious clerics. The losses mounted, and Roya didn't have time to mourn them all. Walter followed the news carefully, but Roya would rather stick her head in the oven than watch the garbage that masqueraded as "news" on cable television these days.

But babies could not die. They could not disappear and just leave their belongings behind. Her baby wasn't dead. At the hospital, they'd wanted her to believe that a one-year-old child could die when minutes ago it had been breathing in her arms. Marigold wasn't just with her every day and night; Marigold was a part of her. She carried her daughter with her at all times. Babies do not leave you.

But, Sister, think of Kyle! Marigold died, but you have Kyle!

At the age of forty-two, after Roya had been working forever at her administrative job at Harvard Business School and had accepted never being a mother to another child—she was clearly not meant to be a mother—Kyle came along. What was considered impossible happened again. A surprise, an accident, a child. She and Walter felt that tiny soft face against theirs again. Again, they were overcome with joy and terror.

Kyle became her new world. On him she pinned her dreams. He brought out Roya's deep laugh again, woke her up. He was her purpose. For him, she made sure the world did not crumble.

After Kyle was all grown up (a doctor!), Roya's morning walks kept her sane, kept her moving. Cleared her head. She didn't walk with friends. Friends talked too much and Roya needed to be alone with her thoughts. Sure, there were neighborhood women who met up to walk at *the mall* when it was too cold outside. Roya received e-mails from the town Listserv inviting everyone to join in the fun: *Let's meet outside Cinnamon Station!* they read. In front of a stall that sold flavored, greasy fried dough. No thank you. Roya didn't want to go back and forth in a big box of a building, inhale stale air, pass bright stores that sold unnecessary merchandise. The vastness of the junk in the mall overwhelmed her. She'd stick to nature as long as she possibly could. As long as she was still able to move.

And she had to move. Some things stay with you, haunt you. Some embers nestle into your skin. Shots cannot be forgotten. And neither can that force of love.

Sometimes she could sense his breath on her ear at night. He could not have been the man she thought she saw almost always here and there in New England or even in California in the early years, when a rush, a person going past made her body buzz and from her peripheral vision, for a flash, she'd be sure it was him. Once at Filene's in Boston, while she was browsing through shirts for Walter, a man on the other side of the rack looked like Bahman. She felt sure it was Bahman, but of course it wasn't. Couldn't be. Another time, at an airport stopover, a young man had looked and walked exactly like Bahman. She had to lean on a pillar to catch her balance. That man was about twenty. As she caught her breath in the airport, she remembered she was in her forties. So Bahman was in his forties as well. Of course that young man couldn't be him. It was impossible not to always imagine him as young, impossible to muster him up as old. Would he have lost his hair? Gained weight? Walter hadn't lost his hair. He was "a stunner," Patricia liked to say, a verifiable Jimmy Stewart. What was Bahman? Which movie star did he look like? What had life served up for him? It was not her business to know.

When Kyle arrived, a small pocket of air had been let into their tightly wrapped bubble of privacy and pain. Soon that pocket of air expanded and let in the world again. Because of Kyle, Roya had tea with the other mothers. Because of him, she attended PTA meetings and sprang up when he hit the ball at baseball games. She accessed joy again, moved with ease again, made the scrambled eggs in the mornings and discussed soccer scores and pored over textbooks and report cards. Because of him, she learned about the world again.

"What happens when the blood in our veins runs out?"

Kyle's questions never stopped. He was endlessly curious. She took him to the library and sat him on her lap and read him book after book. In the early years, Kyle had her Iranian accent because her voice was most of what he heard. It disappeared once he started school. Other mothers complained that their children didn't pay attention, but Kyle listened. His appetite for understanding how the world worked was immense. When he was little, they were the two musketeers. The third musketeer—his older sister—was in Roya's heart always. Her Marigold.

Roya was thankful that they could afford for her to quit her job and be with Kyle. She wanted to spend as much time with him as possible. If only she could carry Kyle's heart in a padded tea cozy and protect it so it would not break. If only she could somehow shield him from danger, from loss, from grief. But she knew that the fate on his forehead was written with an ink she could not see and no amount of mothering or hovering or worrying could keep the dangers at bay.

She showed him tadpoles in the pond on Merriam Hill, learned the distance of the stars and moon just so she could teach him, traced the outlines of his favorite TV characters on sketch paper for him. With Walter's steady presence, she carved a life in

New England for the three of them and stuffed all that mattered into a colonial home with shutters on its windows.

Each year when Kyle blew out the candles on his birthday cake, Roya's mingled relief and anxiety wafted in the wisps of smoke that rose. They nestled into the baseboard molding of their dining room. They landed in every strand of their hair. Another year. Another year, and he was here.

⁓⁂⁓

The stationery store was 2.7 miles from their house; she knew because she liked to set the odometer to zero sometimes just for kicks. The big-box store was huge and overlit, a warehouse really. Part of a national chain. Stepping in with Walter, Roya steadied herself inside. The aisles smelled of chemicals and cheap carpeting, of corporate gluttony and weariness. Row after row of notebooks, Post-it notes, antiseptic wipes, plastic boxes, folders, envelopes, markers, crayons, popcorn. (Popcorn? Why?) It was what she used to love: stationery and sharpeners, pens and pencils. But nothing she wanted anymore, not like this, not spread out in this cavernous space without even an owner present. Pimply teenage boys wearing uniforms ignored her "excuse mes" until Walter had to blurt "Excuse us!" as though he were scolding them. Only then were they directed to the correct aisle for paper shredders. (Walter was determined to go through their old files and shred what wasn't needed so "when the time came" Kyle didn't have to do it: "Best we organize and get rid of all that paperwork we've saved over the years. We should do it now. While we still have our wits. Make it easier for when we're gone. Kyle doesn't need to be burdened with going through all our things.")

He picked out the shredder after much comparing and contrasting, and then led Roya through the chemically carpeted aisles until they found the correct place for paper clips. So much to choose from in various packaging. Just for paper clips. They finally selected a clear jar filled with clips of cheerful blue, grass green, bright yellow, and deep red.

In line for the cash register (one of eight—so many!), Roya picked up a small vessel of hand sanitizer from a bin. It had a rubber loop that allowed it to attach to a purse, a key chain, anything. She could ward off colds and flu and pneumonia and the latest diseases with this. Could Marigold have warded off the croup? she thought. With this little plastic vessel of antibacterial gel?

When they finally reached the front of the line, Roya grumbled, "This shop is so big and not one of those teenagers knows what he's doing."

The cashier's head bobbed up. She was probably in her late sixties, not that much younger than Roya. She had dark-blue eyes and soft gray curls. Roya worried she'd offended this woman by denigrating her fellow employees. But the cashier smiled.

"Don't I know it. They're good kids though. We constantly get new inventory. Can you blame them?"

"Of course. It's just so . . . huge," Roya murmured.

"Oh, this place is great for some. Got everything! Moms love it for back-to-school shopping. But it still dizzies me sometimes when I walk into work. Let me tell you"—she leaned in and whispered—"at the end of the day, I'm a small-neighborhood-shop gal myself. Don't tell my boss!"

Walter fumbled for his wallet and slipped out a credit card, swiped, and waited for his receipt.

"Those days are gone," Roya said. "The small neighborhood shops."

"Oh, there's one or two mom-and-pop stationery shops left here and there," the cashier said, bagging the paper clips and hand sanitizer while Walter loaded the paper shredder back into the shopping cart. "I'm not talking drugstores, now, with their stationery supplies in one aisle—cheap spiral notebooks and such. But you know. Old-school. Real shops. Like the one in Newton on Walnut Street. Best fountain pens there. Inkwells! Don't know how much longer they can stay open with all the competition from stores like ours. And online. But that one is a throwback, let me tell you."

"Well, thanks. Now, you have yourself a good day," Walter said, and signed the receipt and quickly steered his cart away from the cashier. He had no interest in her recommendation.

Roya felt a sudden pull toward this kind lady. "Thank you so much."

"Now, *you* have yourselves a good rest of the day," the cashier mimicked Walter, and winked at Roya.

Roya winked back and then followed Walter into the cold parking lot.

"She was an odd one," Walter groaned as he hauled the paper shredder into the car trunk.

"I thought she was very helpful."

"Poor lonely old bat," Walter said, and then added quickly, "I'm kidding!"

They drove home through the icy streets with the paper clip jar and the hand sanitizer in a plastic bag on Roya's lap.

The message on their answering machine was from Walter's podiatrist's office.

"Did you hear that, Walter?" Roya said. "You need new molds made for your orthopedic shoe inserts."

"New molds for the inserts. The fun never ends!" Walter said.

"That it doesn't," Roya said as she got out some fish sticks to bake. She was too tired to make Persian food so much these days. Some things just had to go in your seventies.

⁓

The following week, Roya waited with Walter in the orthopedic clinic. They always went to the clinic in Belmont, but it was under renovation and the podiatrist's secretary had directed them to a new clinic near the Newton-Wellesley Hospital instead. Roya shifted in her seat. It seemed like every high school athlete and obnoxious child from the suburbs had an appointment that day.

"You don't have to wait here. Go get some fresh air, Roya. We finally have some nice weather," Walter said.

"I can wait with you. I'm fine."

"You don't have to. Poke around the shops. Grab a coffee if you like. I've got my reading to keep me company." Walter patted a law journal. "This could take a while."

Roya was relieved to get out of the stuffy waiting room with its noisy children and teenagers glued to their phones. Outside, the air was almost pleasant. Walter was right: it was the warmest it had been in months. What a rare day in the middle of January! She hadn't been able to walk outside for weeks. *And why you don't just leave that freezing place and move to California is beyond me, Sister!*

Roya walked the blocks outside of the orthopedic clinic carefully. Last thing they needed was for her to lose her balance. Thank goodness she had her good shoes on: the thick-soled gray ones with the small bows on top. After a few blocks she reached the heart of the neighborhood center. Behind the glass of a bagel shop, a cat lounged and gazed lazily at her. Outside an old-fashioned cobbler's, shoes stood in rows next to tins of polish. She liked this part of Newton. It was less fancy than the other shopping centers and felt more authentic. No big-box stores here.

As she walked past a tiny pizza place, the smell of sweet tomato sauce tempted her to stop and get a slice. She was pondering whether she should go inside and indulge when a sign down the block caught her eye. From a second-floor trellis hung a sign with gold lettering on a black background. Spelled out in curlicue letters were the words THE STATIONERY SHOP.

Best fountain pens there. Inkwells! The words of the cashier from the big-box store rang in her head. Was she on Walnut Street? She must be. Propelled by a force she couldn't explain, she headed toward the sign.

When she opened the door of the shop, a familiar chime rang out. It had been a long time since she'd been in a store with one of those bells. My goodness, all those old-fashioned bells sounded the same.

It took a few beats for her eyes to adjust to the slightly dark, musty interior. But when they did, she saw shelves filled with colored journals and notebooks in all shapes and sizes. On her left was a table stacked with gifts and gadgets: alarm clocks, puzzles, tea mugs, fancy soap. In the middle of the shop, pens and pencils of all kinds sat in small boxes on the shelves. She walked through the aisle of writing utensils. People had tried out the pens with multiple squiggles: *hellos* and doodles were scribbled on the sides of the small cardboard boxes holding the pens. Old-fashioned sharpeners and fancy new pencil cases lay in neat rows.

She walked along one aisle and then another, as if in a dream. In front of the main counter, she stopped short. There within a big glass case lay shiny fountain pens and inkwells, just as the cashier had said. They were arranged like jewelry: the ink bottles shone in sapphire blue and emerald green, even purple. One bottle held ink the color of pomegranates. She wanted to unscrew a fountain pen and pump its cartridge carefully with ink, glide it across a fresh, clean page. She'd had a special blotter for those letters she'd written so long ago so the ink wouldn't run, so not one word could be smudged before she placed it in an envelope to be hidden in a Rumi book of poetry.

"Find everything okay?"

She turned as if she'd been caught stealing. A man with salt-and-pepper hair, olive skin, and dark eyes stood by a door in the back.

"Oh yes—" Her voice caught. She was suddenly dizzy. Her chest tightened and the room began to swim.

"Are you all right?" the man asked. His voice. His voice was like something she should know.

"Of course." But she was sinking. "Please, may I sit?"

He came to her and gently took her arm. He helped her behind the counter to a chair with a pink cushion. She slid onto the chair with relief and leaned back. Her forehead throbbed.

"Ma'am? Can I get you some water?"

"No, no. I just need to catch my breath."

"Let me get you some water."

His insistence, his politeness, something about his body language was just so familiar. Then she realized what she wanted to ask. The dark eyes, olive skin. A slight accent. "Are you Iranian?"

"*Khanom, salam.*" He bowed his head. "*Man fekr kardam shoma ham Irani hasteed.* Miss, hello. I thought you were Iranian as well."

"*Hastam.* I am."

"I'll be right back," he said in Farsi. "Let me get you something to drink."

He went through a door behind the counter. She rested her head against the back of the chair. He came back after several minutes holding a tray with a *chai estekan* and a saucer of sugar cubes.

"You didn't have to," she said. "I am fine."

"It's no trouble. We have a small samovar in the back. You know how it is. Persians have to have their tea." His Farsi was impeccable. He must have lived in Iran as a child or his parents had had the discipline to teach him the language.

He set the tray down. "*Befarmayeed*, this will make you feel better."

She sipped the tea. The flavors of bergamot and cardamom mixed with the slightest hint of rose petals took her home. "You certainly know how to make real tea. Thank you."

"My parents taught me." He shrugged.

Her head began to clear with the steam and fragrance of the tea. This man was probably in his late forties, maybe early fifties. He could have come here as an older child with his family as part of the wave of Iranians who immigrated after the 1979 revolution.

"Hope I didn't startle you," she said. "I just lost my balance for a minute. And my wits a little bit." She rested the tea glass on the tray and studied him. "Also, if I may, you just look so familiar to me."

"All us Iranians look alike, right?" He smiled.

And when he did, she was gripped by a tightness in her chest that felt like it could fold her over. She stared at the tea and then looked around the shop again. The shelves were aligned in diagonal rows, the glass case held the fountain pens in parallel lines. In one corner was a rack on its own, filled with paperback books. She hadn't noticed that rack before. She could make out the covers from where she sat: they all had artwork similar to Persian miniature paintings. The image of a turbaned man holding an old-fashioned *setar* instrument flashed from most of the covers.

"You sell books too?" she asked weakly.

"Oh, some," the man said. "Coloring books for kids. Craft books. Sticker books. Things like that."

"But those?" She pointed to the rack that should have held greeting cards, that should have been filled with calendars printed with photos of dogs and kittens and oceans. Instead it held slim volumes of a book series she recognized. She had bought those very books for Kyle so he could read in English the poetry she had loved since she was young, so he could see for himself the wisdom and passion in the words of her favorite poet of all time. "You sell Rumi?"

The man shrugged again. "It was kind of my dad's thing. He always had a very particular vision of what he wanted this place to be. Down to a T."

"He did?"

"Oh yes. It was tough setting it all up. And staying afloat over the years. But my sister and I have pushed through."

"Your sister?"

"Yeah, my twin. Anyway, Dad had his vision and we worked so hard at making it happen. And now . . . well, we like to keep it just how he wanted it." He smiled again. "We've managed to stick around."

Roya's heart suddenly beat so fast she thought she might have a heart attack. The shop fashioned like this. The slim Rumi volumes arranged on a circular rack. The blueprint. The vision. But it couldn't be. It could not be.

"Your father," she asked breathlessly. "May I ask his name?"

"Sure. We're originally from Tehran. My dad's name is Bahman Aslan."

Chapter Twenty-Six

2013

Appointment

By the time Roya walked back to Walter to hear about how the molding of the inserts had gone, she was flushed and ready to collapse. You might think that the world is complicated and full of lost souls, that people who've touched your life and disappeared will never be found, but in the end all of that can change. One shop, one glass of tea, and all of that can simply flip.

Bahman's son, Omid—he'd told her his name—had been easygoing. A benefit of living in America, a benefit of his generation. He was open and willing to share. Not guarded and suspicious the way he would have been if he'd been her age. When she told him that she had known his father once upon a time, his eyes widened. "Seriously? Wow. Are you kidding?" She couldn't bring herself to form the words to ask if he was alive or dead. Ever since Jahangir had passed away, she had lost news of Bahman. She had pushed him to the bottom of the bucket anyway.

But the son said, "Shall I tell him I saw you? He'd be tickled to know I met an old friend of his."

"That won't be necessary, absolutely not," she said. "Don't bother him. We were barely acquaintances. I'm just happy to know he is . . . well. And to meet his son. It was a pleasure to talk to you. Thank you for the tea. I have to go now. My husband waits."

"Oh, sure. He's at the Duxton Senior Center now, just so you know. He gets pretty lonely. My sister and I visit as much as we can. But you know how it is with these crazy busy lives."

She couldn't imagine the boy who would change the world in a nursing home. What had happened to Shahla? But she didn't dare ask this nice man about his mother. She said she had to go, and they both repeated over and over what a small world it was and how she should come again.

The new inserts were made of foam, Walter told her when she returned to the clinic. He said that even so they were surprisingly firm, how do you like that? They got in the car, and Walter groaned at the top-of-the-hour news. "Can't they ever get it right in Washington? We should vote them all out." And then: "What's the matter, Roya? You look pale. Roya? Roya, what's wrong?"

"Nothing. I just felt a little faint earlier, that's all."

"Should I stop?"

"No, Walter, carry on. Let's just carry on."

⌘

Once home, she was still winded, shaking.

"I'll heat up the coffee," Walter said. "It'll perk you up. No pun intended." He slipped on his moccasin slippers and headed to the coffeemaker. Drip. Not the fancy espresso machine with the pods, which Zari kept encouraging them to buy. Walter preferred coffee brewed in an old Mr. Coffee machine, left to stand in the pitcher all day long.

"Thanks. Just going to the bathroom!"

Walter's camel moccasins, beige fur peeking out around the ankles, were just a flash as she rushed past him.

Driven by an energy that was new and frightening, she climbed the stairs faster than she had in years. She hurried to the desk Walter had built in their bedroom, sat, and turned on their laptop. Her hands were sweaty (must be from the thermal gloves) and her heart pounded. Maybe these were symptoms of an impending heart attack after all. Like Mrs. Michael, their neighbor, she'd have a stroke, her head would fall on the keyboard, and Walter would find her, never knowing what she'd intended to type. Maybe she should stop. But tears ran down her cheeks as she heard again the bell from the Stationery Shop. She clicked on the browser just like Kyle had taught her. When the cursor hovered in the search bar, she typed: *Duxton Senior Center.*

How you haven't googled him in all these years is beyond me, Sister! Lord knows I've searched for every man I ever loved. Yousof from Tehran is a retired neurosurgeon in Maryland now—I saw his photograph on a website. Did you know? But you insist you want to leave the past in the past. As if that's possible!

Her fingers shook. Well, if she was going to have a stroke, then at least let her find out what had happened. By those jasmine-soaked bushes on that summer night, she had kissed him hard. From him, she had learned the tango. It was his letters that she'd run to get day after day that blasted summer, because of him that she had written page after page with a fountain pen in blue ink. For him, she had waited in the square.

Walter would be pouring a cup of oily coffee. Roya reached for her reading glasses.

Images and words came into focus on the screen. The Duxton Senior Center was a community center with its own assisted-living facility, in the heart of beautiful Duxton, Massachusetts. Photos of trees near a lake, seniors ballroom dancing, a close-up of a plate with beef stew and carrots and corn and the caption *Delicious homemade meals!* filled the website. She felt like she was witnessing something forbidden but also absolutely normal and mundane. The boy who had built their stationery shop in America was at this center—which, according to the directions she now googled, was 53.5 miles south of this house. The house where Walter waited. How do you like that?

The center had a phone number, a fax number, step-by-step directions on how to arrive at its front doors from north, south, east, and west. Roya pressed the corners of her eyes. Ridiculous old lady revisiting something she thought she had reconciled a thousand years ago.

She got up to go downstairs to Walter.

But then, with a pull that outdid any kind of gravity, she landed back on the chair again. Just to ask him *why*. Why did he lie? Why did he leave her there? Why did he break it all off so abruptly? Why did he change his mind? She deserved that, at least, after all these years. Who knew when the heart could attack? Let her just know once and for all.

She clicked on the "Contact Us" link and there was the phone number.

But she didn't call. Instead, she went downstairs. Walter asked again what was wrong.

In the early days of their courtship in California, she had mentioned to Walter that she'd had a beau back in Tehran. Just a high school crush. No biggie, nothing doing. Didn't we all?

It felt strange to mention the Newton stationery shop to Walter now, as though she were revealing someone else's secret, not her own, as though she were pulling back the curtain on something sacred and sweet but filled with danger.

In the days that followed, she would cry for no reason. Out of nowhere, out of the blue, every time she thought of that shop sitting on Walnut Street for all these years, in the state in which she lived, a few towns down from where she spent her days, not that far from her colonial home with its shutters on the windows— she fell apart. She was losing it in her old age. And now when she thought of Bahman's son, Omid, arranging the inventory in the shop, she was filled with a sense of the surreal, with a mix of nostalgia and disbelief. She remembered more than ever the kind stationer who had guided her in that shop in Tehran in the first place. Trauma and loss never went away—of course those memories had always been with her. But now she cried like she hadn't cried in years, not since the early years after Marigold died. She was grieving all over again for something she thought she had finished with years ago.

Get a grip, Sister! Zari would have said.

But with each passing day, she would also remember the son's kind comment: "Shall I tell him I saw you? He'd be tickled to know I met an old friend of his."

She wanted to see him. Just to ask *why*. Just so she could know once and for all. And so, a week after her visit to the stationery shop on Walnut Street, and six decades after she had last seen the boy from the Stationery Shop in Tehran, she picked up the phone.

A receptionist. *How can I help you* and *hold on, let me see, I will speak to him and get back to you,* and then another phone call, and *yes, please do come, Mr. Aslan will be expecting you.*

Just like that.

After the phone call, she waited for the floors to crack open, for the walls to close in.

But Walter dried the dishes with a kitchen towel printed with a yellow chick holding an umbrella as she told him she had made an appointment to see that boy from long ago. And the world did not crack open.

And they would drive in the snow, she and Walter together. He had that in him—he was that kind. He said he didn't believe in his wife sitting around moping and crying. If she needed to talk to him, then she should. We're too old to suffer for no reason, he said. Lord knows that life is fragile enough.

And he would get out of the car to make sure her knitted scarf protected her nose and mouth against the wind, and they would climb the steps of the gray building labeled DUXTON SENIOR CENTER. Inside, a blond administrator would lead Roya to a hall where an old man in a wheelchair sat by the window, and she would see once again the boy whom she'd once believed would always be hers.

Chapter Twenty-Seven

2013

Reunion

When the administrator turned and clicked her way out, Roya and Bahman were alone in the overheated dining hall. He wheeled his chair around and smiled—his eyes still, somehow, filled with hope. "I've been waiting."

It was an effort not to fall. Her heart jumped, as if it mattered, as if it wasn't all just too late for the two of them. The gust of wind that blew through Mr. Fakhri's stationery shop when Bahman strode in that first Tuesday in January so many years earlier—the same force that held her then—seized her now. He was hers, he'd been hers, his voice was the same. It was as if she hadn't stopped hearing it for sixty years. Here was the boy who'd danced with her at Thursday night soirees, who'd kissed her by the jasmine bushes when they decided to marry, who'd written love letters that summer of the coup.

She looked down, and the sight of her gray little-old-lady shoes with thick soles and tiny bows jolted her back to the present. She was seventy-seven. No longer seventeen and in love for the first time, anticipating a life with this boy who was going to change the world. An old sadness rose up like bile. "I see. But all I've wanted to ask you is why on earth didn't you wait last time?"

She was dizzy again; she had to sit. She walked over to the plastic chair by the window and plopped into it. She couldn't fall flat onto the floor in front of him. He said nothing, but there was the whir of his electric wheelchair, and then he was next to her. They sat like that, side by side, facing the window. She didn't dare look at him. It would have been like staring directly at the sun or into the beam of a strong flashlight. It hurt too much.

The glass pane was thick and wavy. Or was that just her vision blurring? The clangs from the radiator and Bahman's heavy, labored breathing filled the room. Flake by flake she watched snow accumulate on the windowsill, on the hoods of the cars in the lot, on the roof of the other wing of the building, on crevices in the sidewalks, on the tops of the trees in Duxton. Her thoughts were like the snow: they needed to land and gather for this new scene. She and Bahman were together again. They were alone. After sixty years, they sat together alone.

She had, of course, imagined seeing him over the years. People bumped into each other all the time. She was married to Walter because her elbow had spun his coffee cup off a counter, wasn't she? *Look at you, Sister, sitting like a fool in that beef-stinky place looking out the window! Talk to him at least! Look at him!*

"I worried about seeing you. I was so nervous. But it's you. *Khodeti*. It's you." He spoke again in Farsi, in that voice she'd never stopped hearing.

A lifetime ago, Bahman had not shown up; he'd married another and not looked back. She would say what she'd come to say.

"I forgive you."

It came out clear and lucid, as if she'd practiced in front of a mirror. But it was not what she'd planned on saying at all. *Why?* she had wanted to ask him. But now that she was here, right next to him, the answer to that question no longer seemed important. They were in the evening of their lives; they were beyond all that and then some.

"I beg your pardon?"

Was it a question, or a plea for forgiveness? She turned to take him in; she'd bear the glare, squint if needed. He looked vulnerable, shaken. "I forgive you, Bahman." It felt odd to say his name to his face again, to say his name at all. "We were kids. What did we know?"

His eyes were confused. Had he not heard her? Maybe he had a hearing aid he never used, like so many friends she and Walter knew.

"I'm not here to find fault, Bahman," she said louder. "I don't even want an explanation. Maybe I did before. But not anymore."

"You forgive me?"

"Yes."

"I don't understand."

"Look, my regret lies in myself."

"For what?"

"For thinking it could be different. All I'm saying is that life happens and I forgive you and I wanted to see you again. Just to see you. To think we didn't talk all those years. Why? Of course, I heard your news from Jahangir—may God rest his soul—I knew for a while how you were. Until I later learned from Zari that Jahangir, poor Jahangir, died in the war. But we're too old to hold grudges. I just wanted to let you know." She had the urge to reach over and pat his hand. But she didn't dare. It was *him*, and he still had power over her, she could barely believe it, but in his presence—it was quite astonishing—she was filled with love. To see him so old! Her Bahman. The boy who would change the world in this wheelchair, in this place.

Yes, she loved him. The truth of that was like a wave that washed over and submerged her in salty torrents, knotting her hair and stinging her nose, pulling the life out from under her. Of course she loved him. The earth was round, day turned into night, he was in front of her and she loved him. She could see, in his face, the kindness she remembered. How he had taken care of her and trusted her, shared with her everything. How he'd rested his head on her shoulder when he was filled with sadness at his mother's rage and lack of reason. Ultimately, his mother had more power over him than Roya ever did. But what could either of them have done at seventeen? Fate had its own plans.

"You forgive me?" His voice sounded far away.

Another unexpected wave hit. This time it was icy, cruel. Of course. He kept repeating things. Why had she expected anything different? Memory loss. Possibly dementia. It was quite likely Bahman didn't even remember her. Maybe she'd come too late after all.

"Bahman?" she said slowly, as if she were talking to a child. She should just reach out and hold him. He had held her so many times.

"You don't know how happy you've made me by coming here," he said. "I've dreamed of seeing you. It was my dream." Without hesitation, he took her hand.

She remembered, of course, his touch. It was so familiar, she ached. She could smell his woodsy cologne. Had he worn it for her visit? Were they like young teenagers eager to please each other again? She had certainly refused to wear snow boots, just to look good.

"I waited for you all afternoon."

"It's morning," she reminded him gently.

"No, I mean at the square."

"Excuse me?"

"I was so worried you got caught up with the mobs, that you'd been hurt. When you didn't come, I just prayed that nothing had happened to you. When I learned you were safe, it was a huge relief. That's what mattered, that you were okay. That's all that still matters.

"I want to know how you are now," he went on. "Tell me how you are. Tell me everything."

The cruelty of old age, degeneration of the mind! Poor man did not know their history.

"Shahla died," he suddenly said.

The tall, wavy-haired girl who'd sized her up at Café Ghanadi, who'd sidled up to her at Jahangir's house, who'd fumed at the chandelier and tangoed past them, was suddenly present in the room. The taste of the crushed melon at the party that night, the ice inside Roya's cheek. Death was nothing new, several of her friends had died in recent years; they'd both lost Mr. Fakhri—she'd lost her own child! But of course the words struck her with sadness. "I am so sorry," she said.

"We raised two wonderful children. Twins."

"My goodness. *Mashallah,*" she said. And then she forced herself to add, "I met your son, Omid." She didn't mention the shop. It would open up too many worlds to even ask him about the shop. She couldn't just yet.

"Omid told me. I'm glad you saw what we built. I wanted to"— he squeezed her hand—"just have our shop."

She felt like she might drown all over again. Remembering the shop in Newton also made her see the one in flames in Tehran. "What happened to Shahla?" she dared to ask.

"Thank God, she suffered not too long. They told us the Tuesday before Thanksgiving of 2004. By Nowruz, it was over."

"Cancer?"

"Pancreatic."

Nowruz would have been the first day of spring. Roya calculated four short months from diagnosis to death. "May God protect her soul."

"She was a good wife," he said, and then he paused. "But she wasn't you."

Roya looked at the floor.

"Tell me. How's your son?" he asked.

"How do you know I have a son?"

"I've searched for you on the Internet. He's a doctor, I saw. Congratulations. Forgive me, I hope you don't think I am snoopy. I couldn't help it. I know too that you are married to a Walter Archer, a retired lawyer with Lippinscott and Mackevy. The Internet . . . it knows everything!" He looked slightly uncomfortable as he said Walter's name. He pronounced it "Valter." He pronounced Lippinscott "Lee-peen-es-scot."

"Like Jahangir. He was our World Wide Web of info," she said.

Bahman's face lit up at the mention of his old friend. "Yes, he was always news central! Remember his parties?"

"How could I forget? Those songs on his gramophone!"

"Roya."

When he said her name, it did not matter: the decades, the children, the cancer, the betrayal, the loss, the coup, the rewritten history. He said her name the same way he had always said her name. They were Bahman and Roya again, the couple dancing, talking breathlessly as they leaned against the books in the shop. She held on to the seat of the plastic chair. It was not an option to fall.

His breathing grew louder as though his chest held a broken motor. She turned to the window. The snow had picked up even more. No one came into the hall—there was no bingo, no lunch was served even though the smell of beef stew hung in the air. They were utterly alone. Would the window be cold to touch? Even with all this heat cranked up inside, if she leaned over to touch the glass, would she feel ice? She was with a stranger here. She was with her love. She held these two truths in her mind at the same time and found it hard to speak.

"I missed you very much," he said.

Maybe old love just ran through the decades unfettered, unimpeded, even when denied.

"Me too."

"Are you comfortable here?"

"Of course." She shifted in her chair, not letting go of his hand.

"In America, your life."

"You bet," she said in the American way.

"Don't feel sorry for me for being in this place. I know it's looked down on in our culture. But my daughter and her family visit regularly. They live right here in Duxton. Omid and his wife and kids visit too. It was just too much to take care of me. They tried. But I didn't want to be a burden to them. Especially after my Parkinson's. This is a good place. They call me 'Mr. Batman' here."

"Parkinson's?" She stiffened. "You don't—"

"I don't shake? Rattle and roll, as the Americans say? Some days are better than others. I thought I'd be trembling all morning, seeing you. But in fact, I feel better."

"I didn't know. . . ."

"I feel better than I have in ages. It's because of you."

"Please, stop. We're not seventeen."

"We'll always be seventeen."

"Okay, mister." Now that they had warmed up a bit, it was easy to slip into the old banter, the teasing. But she couldn't go down this slippery slope too far. "So, tell me. How many grandchildren?"

"Six!"

"Oh my! May they live long lives with their parents' shadow guarding them." Thank goodness for old customs. These Persian expressions were a reflex and a relief when you didn't know what else to say.

"I haven't stopped thinking about you. What I'm trying to say, Roya Joon, is that I have not stopped thinking about you since that day in the square."

She dropped his hand. Then she just patted his arm, the arm that had once made her feel so safe. His sleeve was wooly and worn. "It's okay, Bahman, it's okay." This was all she could do. Never with Walter had she had to worry about memory loss. Nor with Zari, oh God, that would be a nightmare. A few of her friends sometimes complained of forgetting. But this—well, these were uncharted waters for her. She wasn't sure if she was supposed to just go along with his version of things. She'd heard that dementia patients could get violent from the rage of not being understood.

"That day at the square? Roya, I stood there for hours waiting for you. I wanted to see you so badly. I had all the paperwork set so we could go to the Office of Marriage and Divorce and get everything stamped and official. I waited as the thugs came and took over, when they marched to the prime minister's house. Pro-Mossadegh people in the crowd asked for my help, but I didn't join the fight. I didn't move. All I could think was what if you came and I wasn't there. I didn't want to leave you there. I waited for you. I waited because all I wanted was to see you, to explain everything, to hold you again. But you never came."

Roya tried to remember what she knew about Parkinson's.

Was this one of its symptoms? "I forgive you," she whispered again.

"Forgive me, but why? I would have given you everything. If only you had let me." His mouth turned down like a small boy's.

"You married Shahla. It's fine. We just . . . we just were not meant to be."

"I married her because I lost you."

"You lost me because you married her!"

Bahman's hand shook. "It was one thing to have Mossadegh toppled and Mr. Fakhri and so many people die. That was a huge loss. But the biggest loss for me? It was losing you. Nothing in my life has been more painful. I've thought about you constantly for sixty years."

He went on, "But I wasn't about to stand in your way. When you wrote to me that you couldn't, in the end, marry into my family with all the burdens and sacrifices my mother's moods and rages would entail, I was heartbroken. I was so very hurt. What could I do about her mental state, about her? I couldn't change it. We had already been shunned by my father's relatives because of it. I was used to being shunned. How could I not let you go? I didn't want to burden you with what was, back then, our shame. You didn't want to see my family and all its dysfunction anymore, and I didn't want to get in your way. Shahla didn't have the same bias against my mother's condition. She just didn't, and I suppose a part of me felt gratitude toward her for that. . . ."

Madness. He had completely lost it. Roya spoke kindly but firmly. "Bahman. I don't know what you're talking about. I know you may not remember everything. I never said those things. Never would I have said or felt anything like that. Leave you because of your mother? Shun you because of her mental instability?

I wanted to be there for you, to be with you every step of the way. To help you and your father. Your mother too! You are the one who told me you wanted to move on. Remember?"

Bahman did not move. He studied her face quietly for a few seconds. Then he suddenly took in a sharp breath that sounded like a strangled gasp.

She had to get this conversation back on track from his absurd ramblings before he worked himself up more. She said in as calm a voice as she could muster, "I was in the square. Okay? I worried *for you*. You're the one who didn't come. Your mother wanted Shahla for you; it was different times. Honestly, it's all right. Think of your children. Your grand—"

"No." His head and neck and shoulders trembled. "Oh my God."

"Look, it doesn't matter. Let's just let all of this go. Please."

His face twisted in pain. "You don't understand. Roya Joon—" A wheezing cough took over his body. It was so forceful, she was afraid he could have a heart attack right there. When he finished coughing, he looked at her again. "Where were you?"

"I've been here, in the US. You know I came to study in California. Remember? My father applied for one of the first college spots available to Iranian women in America?"

"Jahangir told me, yes, I know all of that. Roya Joon, where were you that day?"

She sighed. This was really so difficult, the poor man. "In the square."

"Which square?" He wasn't shaking anymore; he was still as a rod, his breathing less labored after his coughing fit. He looked like he was actually holding his breath.

"Where you told me to meet you. Sepah Square."

"I said Baharestan Square."

Oh dear. So he remembered some things, but not the details. He had his own version of reality, of the truth. It was so sad to see. She wanted to go back to Walter, to the safety of lobster rolls and uncomplicated histories, to Walter's steady memory. "You don't remember, it's okay," she murmured.

"The letters—"

The sound of clicking heels interrupted him. It was Claire; she walked in with a plastic bean-shaped tray filled with prescription bottles. "Mr. Batman, it's time for your meds!" As she came closer, her face went red. Bahman was on the verge of tears. "I'm sorry, I'm interrupting. I can come back in a few—"

Roya got up. "I should go anyway. I really should go. My husband is waiting."

"Stay," Bahman said. "You don't have to go."

"I'll come right back," Claire said.

"No, Roya, you. Please. You stay. We have a lot to discuss."

"My husband is waiting."

"I'm beginning to see," he whispered.

"Would you like lunch?" Claire asked her gently.

Roya stood there in her gray heavy-soled shoes. Seeing Bahman like this, with his mind half-gone, his memories jumbled up, his Parkinson's and dementia, broke her heart. She wanted the boy she used to know, the boy who would save the world. To think that she still loved him! She was suddenly exhausted.

"The snow," she finally said. "It's coming down so fast. We have a long drive ahead of us. I can't afford to wait. We don't want the conditions to get dangerous."

They had switched to English in front of Claire. That's what you did in front of Americans. It was strange to hear him speak it. She wanted to hug him good-bye, hug him hello, hug him for forgetting, hug him for remembering a little, just hug him again.

"Who tricked us, Roya? Someone did. I said Baharestan Square. Who was it that changed our letters?"

Claire looked at Roya and then at Bahman, the plastic tray in her hand almost tipping over.

"What about your sister? She never liked me. Was it Jahangir? Did you know, Roya Joon, that he later told me he was in love?" He looked at his hands. "With me." Then he looked up again. "Who did this to us? Shahla would never have had a hand in this. She couldn't have. Could she? Was it Mr. Fakhri? Not my mother, surely."

Roya's heart raced as the past came flooding back, as the people who had figured so prominently in their lives that summer swam in front of her eyes, as she listened to the man she'd loved who had lost so much, including his mind.

"Good-bye, Bahman."

"Come back. When you can. There is so much history you do not know."

Chapter Twenty-Eight

Bahman's letter came in the mail, addressed to Roya's home. Was it so easy to find the address of Mr. and Mrs. Walter and Roya Archer, nothing more than a neat searchable item on the Web? Roya opened the envelope with a strange feeling of déjà vu: that old familiar thrill coursing through her even as she sat in her kitchen—at seventy-seven!—waiting for Walter to come home from the grocery store.

> *Dearest Roya Joon,*
>
> *After our engagement party, I wanted to make it all up to you. The fact that my mother tried to sabotage our joyful celebration saddened me to no end. All I wanted was a normal mother, someone kind, someone who didn't dominate my life with her strategies and calculations and endless plans to manufacture the life she wanted for me. She wanted me to climb up in that fake, bourgeois world that she coveted. Her rage episodes left my father and me bereft. They*

barreled through like a force of nature, like a hurricane out
of control, and once whatever semblance of peace we had
in the home had been destroyed, we were left exhausted and
brittle. My mother was sick. She needed help. But we did not
know how to help her.

For days after our engagement party, she was restless,
agitated. My father recommended that she sit and do her
calligraphy. He had taught her in the hopes of having it
calm her—so she had an outlet, a pastime, a way to focus
her nervous energies on something positive. And she was
surprisingly fond of it. But she could never be as good as
those who had studied the art from a very young age.

Calligraphy was the skill of the best students of that
generation. Those in the top-notch schools had been trained
by masters in how to control their hand, produce their
strokes, hold their pens.

And, of course, I would later find out the damage this
skill could cause. The chasm that it created in our lives.
When you came here to the Duxton Center a few days ago,
it forced me to acknowledge what I think I had feared all
along. My mother changed our letters. Rather, she had them
altered, ensuring that you would go to one square and I to
another. No one could have wanted that but my mother,
Roya Joon. She was the one who felt her world would
collapse if her son didn't go through with the wedding she'd
planned for him. And how did my mother get her hands on
our letters? Oh, Roya. The answer to that question involves
the history you do not know. So here, as I sit in this assisted-
living center in the twilight of life, let me tell you what
happened that summer.

On the Friday that fell two weeks after our engagement

party, Mother could not sit still. She got up, paced the room. She complained of burning, of the heat keeping her up all night, of voices in her head. She demanded cool cucumber peels for her eyes. I peeled the cucumbers, what could I do, I pressed them against her eyelids. I fanned her with the bamboo kebab fan the way she liked. I fussed over her even as I seethed, hoping she'd just calm down, just relax, rein in her demons.

Nothing worked. She scratched the cucumber peels off and hurled them on the floor. She told me I had no idea the pain I was putting her through, how all she'd wanted was for her one son to have a life that was successful and filled with the right people in the best circles and that meant marrying Shahla. She went on about how she'd picked out Shahla for me, spoken to her parents, planned it all. Did I know what I was throwing away, what I was actually doing? She herself had been the daughter of a melon seller, and it was marriage to an engineer who was decent and good and most importantly from the upper class that saved her. Did I have any idea, she went on, what it meant to stagnate in life, to have no standing, to push and strive for a better life but to be stuck because of who your grandparents were, because your father was not educated, because of the class in which you'd been born? I was furious. She had busted out of the class into which she'd been born, and now, instead of letting me marry for love, she insisted that I just keep going as if I were an athlete grabbing her baton. I would not be allowed to stop running, would not be able to turn around, as if my marriage to someone I loved would somehow negate the "progress" she had made in fighting her fate.

I picked up the wilted cucumber peels from the floor.
They were warm from contact with her skin, soft and limp.
Touching them disgusted me. I argued for us. I told her how
clever you were, your excellent grades, how hard you worked
at school. I even emphasized your father's steady job as a
government clerk. And as I sit here in twilight writing this
letter, it pains me to think I even uttered those words. As if I
had any duty to convince her. As if our love alone shouldn't
have been enough. I am stunned by my own weakness.

My father got a fresh bottle of ink, pushed the calligraphy
pen closer to her, begged her to write out a few lines of
a favorite poem. Anything to have her concentrate on
something other than her rage.

"If Bahman marries that girl, I'll lose him, I know. Roya
won't be like Shahla. She won't let me stay close to him. As if
losing the others wasn't enough."

My father shrank when she said this, put his head in his
hands and stayed still.

She stormed off. We heard her open and close drawers
in the kitchen. Then we heard her bedroom door slam. Like
always.

We sat in our usual uncomfortable silence, my father
and I, waiting for her anger to dissipate, for the ugly storm
to pass. I closed my eyes and recited Rumi in my head to
distract myself. Eventually I smelled something sweet and
cloying. I opened my eyes. The air smelled like rotted roses.
My mother had come back into the living room fully dressed
and made-up. She had put on too much perfume. Layers of
thick rouge covered her cheeks. She held her handbag tightly.
She stormed out the front door before my father could say a
word, before I could beg her not to go.

Sometimes when she left the house, it felt like a suffocating layer of soot had suddenly lifted. But this time the discomfort remained. I couldn't move. For I don't know how long, I waited to get the energy back in my legs, to get up and go out after her. My father said nothing. He looked undone. Of course we had to go after her. Who knew what trouble she'd get into when she was in these moods? I worried for her sanity, for her safety, even for the looks on the faces of people in the street as she strode by. For the spectacle she could make of herself.

"I'll go," I said. "I'll bring her home."

I went out the gate. I had no idea where to turn first. I cursed myself for sitting on the couch longer than I should have, for not running after her immediately. I didn't know where she'd gone, which street she'd taken. Because it was the Friday holy day, most people were at home resting or at the mosque praying, and there were few passersby. And what would I ask of them anyway: Have you seen a woman smeared with rouge walking by in a rage?

All I wanted was to be with you. I wanted to see you, hold you, feel you next to me. I was tempted to walk to your house. But I had to find my mother. Once at the greengrocer's, she had bitten the tops off several eggplants because she said the greengrocer had treated her like a lowly peasant dahati. "You treat me like an animal, I'll act like one for you, how's that?" And I had melted in shame. Another time, she cornered the beet seller and his young daughter as they pushed their wagon down the street. He should never take his eye off his daughter, she told him, because she could easily become a whore, a slut, a piece of trash, pregnant before her time. When she was overtaken by these manic forces, my mother's cruel streak whipped out of her like a snake, unexpected and unable to be contained.

I couldn't find her. The shops were closed for the holiday and few people were around. Once or twice, I saw a woman from behind, but of course, it wasn't her. I searched and searched, going in circles and feeling more lost.

Worn out, my nerves jangled, I went to the one place that could calm me down. I knew Mr. Fakhri sometimes used Fridays to catch up on his inventory and to organize things in the back storage room of his shop. In my high school days, I'd even helped him unpack boxes of books on Fridays, proud to be his assistant of sorts.

The clear sound of the bell when I opened the door to the Stationery Shop was a relief. The door was unlocked, so Mr. Fakhri must be there then, working. I remembered how my mother had spoken to him at our engagement party. She'd been rude and forward, blaming him for helping our romance. I suppose I wanted to apologize on her behalf just as much as I wanted Mr. Fakhri's calm, soothing presence.

When I walked into the shop, muffled voices rose as if in argument. I looked around but I couldn't see anyone in the store. The familiar scent of dusty books and pamphlets was laced with something else. Withered roses. My mother's perfume.

I moved to the door leading to the back storage room. The voices grew louder. The floor felt suddenly uneven. The clock in the shop hiccuped as if it were broken. I hated the smell of that perfume; I wanted so badly to be wrong. But by now I recognized my mother's voice from behind the door.

"Tell me you love me," I heard her say.

"Don't do this, Badri." I had never heard Mr. Fakhri

sound so vulnerable. In that moment, I knew what he'd sounded like when he was a boy. Why did he call my mother by her first name? What was she doing here?

"Remember the sword my father used to slash the melons?" she said. "I was expert at it. I can use this right now and end all the pain you've caused. You were and always will be a useless, spineless coward who murders his child."

"Badri, please," Mr. Fakhri said.

It was then that I opened the door. My mother was standing on a small stepladder. Her arms were by her sides. In her right hand she held a large butcher's knife. My body went cold. I wanted to believe that the knife was simply hanging there by her thigh. It could not be attached to her hand. Where would she have gotten this knife—was it from our kitchen? Was it the one my father used to cleave chunks of meat, was it the one he kept at the back of the kitchen drawer? In its large sickle-shaped reflection, I saw Mr. Fakhri's spectacles.

In a swift move, she lifted the knife. Then she pierced her own throat.

I'm not sure how I made it across that room. I bulldozed through what must have been piles of books and boxes of magazines and pamphlets. I got to my mother and jumped. I grabbed the knife she held. When I landed, I held it so tightly that I thought my hand would break.

"Bahman?" The color drained from my mother's face.

A metallic, tinny taste filled my mouth. I thought I might be sick. All I could do was to wrap my arms around my mother's knees as she stood on the stepladder. I still held the knife.

Gently, she stroked my head. When I looked up, drops of blood had bubbled up on her neck.

I let go of the knife and it landed on the floor with a sharp clang.

I pulled her down from the stepladder. She was in a daze. Her tearstained face was red and blotchy. She put a hand on the wound in her throat and extended her arm, looking at the blood on her fingers. "Look what you made me do," she said. "Ali, it's all because of you."

Mr. Fakhri rocked back and forth and murmured a prayer. Then, with his perfectly polished shoe, he kicked my mother's knife out of his way. He walked closer to her. From his pocket, he took out a square handkerchief. He leaned in and held it as if to press it against her throat.

She recoiled and hissed, "Don't."

The small beads of blood from her wound expanded in diameter, in what seemed a strangely symmetrical line.

"First you, then me, right?" She smiled sadly at me. She wouldn't look at Mr. Fakhri. "You get your neck gashed in a demonstration, and I have to deal with the lies and betrayal of this traitor. Good thing we both know a good doctor. Do you think Jahangir's father will give us a family discount?"

I felt sick. The books I had knocked over in my rush to get to her were scattered on the floor. The knife lay next to a pile of political magazines. Her attempt at levity was for my benefit; I could see how afraid she was of my own fear. Why on God's earth was she this way? Why did she torment us, scare us, threaten us?

Then she wept freely, lost in an emotion so deep that the sounds she made were almost soft. I had seen her cry loudly, violently many times. I had never seen her cry like this. "It is too late," she said. "It is absolutely too late. It's too late for my child."

I thought she meant me. I thought she meant my upcoming marriage, of which she disapproved. I thought she meant, in her own warped way, that it was too late for me to have the life she'd planned.

"You made me kill my baby. By myself." She turned to Mr. Fakhri. "Because you are a coward."

My breath caught in my throat. I was planted to the floor.

"Badri, I beg of you," Mr. Fakhri said. "Don't do this now."

"After I killed it, my body was wrecked." She looked at her stomach as if she were talking to some force she had pleaded with before. "My body was so broken it killed all the others. All of them." She looked up at me. "Do you know how many children I buried? I should have told you before."

"Badri, stop," Mr. Fakhri whispered.

"They come out of you and you think they're whole. You think you will be able to love them, raise them, cherish them. But then you see. Well, they come out of you not how they should. Too soon, or they just come out . . . silent, warm, and dead."

I was burning with disbelief. I had never known my mother had lost children before. Neither she nor my father had told me. I was seventeen and only now finding out.

"You thought you could do whatever you wanted to me, Ali. Behind the mosque. In that square. You got away with everything. You had the money, the privilege. I had nothing." She wept into her hands. "I was a child!"

"I am so sorry," he said softly. "I am so, so sorry."

Dust motes moved in the shaft of sunlight that came

through the one small window in that storage room. What filled the space wasn't the smell of books or my mother's perfume or my own sour odor as I stood soaked in sweat. It was something different: something I couldn't quite define, that would forever cloak that day and all the days that followed. It was, I think, the scent of grief.

Mr. Fakhri walked over to her. She folded into him. In his arms, my mother wept. She spoke of babies lost and babies dead, and I learned from her disjointed, somber narrative that I was not the first child my mother had borne. I was not her second nor her third nor her fourth. I was the fifth child my mother gave birth to, the only one who lived, the one, I now slowly came to realize, into whom she poured the hopes and dreams she'd had for all of the others. And it was with a chilling shiver in that storage room that I realized that my mother's first baby—the one she'd aborted before it was due to be born, perhaps with her own hands—had been fathered by our soothing, calm stationer, Mr. Fakhri.

I stood among the fallen books, among the words of artists who'd spent happy, circuitous hours writing, honing their words for years. Mr. Fakhri bent over my mother like an animal wounded and lacerated himself.

I wanted to leave and not come back to that shop, to escape from the whole city, to run away and hide somewhere.

I rushed out. On the pavement I heaved forward and vomited and hid my tears as best I could from passersby.

⁂

When he saw my mother's laceration, my father sped us to Jahangir's. We couldn't go to a hospital in Tehran. There was so much shame back then in all of it, Roya Joon. In her sickness. In her attempt to take her own life. In even the idea of suicide.

Jahangir was home when we took my mother in to see his father. He hugged me and assured us that our secret was safe with him. Jahangir's father promised not to say a word about what she'd tried to do.

Thank goodness, she hadn't had a chance to puncture her skin deep enough. I had grabbed the knife in time. In the end, a gauze bandage and ichthyol ointment was all that was needed. "But one more second here and there, one little slip . . ." Jahangir's father shook his head.

She could have worn a scarf around her neck and gone about town. She could have stayed home until the wound had healed. But we were all—my mother, father, and I— completely stunned. Not just from what she had almost done, not just from knowing it took only "one second here and there" for a very different outcome. But I was still trying to process what had transpired between my mother and Mr. Fakhri. And I wondered if my father, in his own quiet way, knew.

It was Jahangir's idea that we go and stay in the villa up north. Just for a few days. Just until we got our bearings, until my mother healed, until we all regained some semblance of normalcy. He promised me he'd keep you up-to-date. I guess he wavered on that promise. Of course I knew Jahangir was in love with me—please, Roya, there is no more time for pretense. I won't pretend I didn't know. Though at that time, we never would have acknowledged it. We would not have put it into words. Necessarily.

But I loved you. All I wanted was you. I would have given anything for you. And Jahangir promised he'd make sure that you and I communicated. It was he who helped with the delivery of our correspondence. He was my conduit, my confidant, my go-between. He was good at heart, Roya Joon. He was trying to protect us. He wanted above all for me to be happy—I really do believe that. And who was it who ultimately changed the letters so we ended up at different squares? I want to say it was my mother. Lord knows she didn't want us married. Except, Roya Joon, my mother was in the villa with me up north all along. And even though she was suffering, I do not think it was she who did it. It was someone whom we both trusted but who felt he had a debt to pay.

She convinced Mr. Fakhri to do it. Of course, I only realize this now, decades later, trying to put the pieces together. Because he owed her. He owed her for completely abandoning her and leaving her with her unborn baby. Which she, well . . . there was no legal abortion in Iran then. She took matters into her own hands.

I wanted to tell you the very next day where I was. I thought I could find a telephone up there, call you, let you know. I wanted to have Jahangir tell you.

That next morning, in the villa, I walked into my mother's room. I didn't even have to say a word. I didn't have to tell her that I wanted to contact you. She took one look at me and said, "You call that girl, you tell that girl where we are, you let on to any of this, and guess what, Bahman?" A smile spread across her pale face. "I'll do it again. And this time, I'll do it all the way. I promise you."

She sucked in her breath and held her hand to her neck. "Just let her go, Bahman. For me. You communicate with her and I will do it again."

*I remember the wooden boards of the villa's main room
had a gap, and through this crack the wind blew, and at
night it got very cold. Even in summer: you know how those
nights up north can be. My father stuffed a shamad cloth
in the crack to seal it. It didn't help much. I sat night after
night and let the wind sting my back. I made sure I sat there
right at the gap so the wind cut through my spine.*

*I cooked. My mother eventually joined us for meals.
Delusion took over. She spoke constantly of my marriage to
Shahla. My father, to change the subject, talked about the
problems Prime Minister Mossadegh was having. I missed
you; I wanted so badly to see you. But I was too ashamed to
tell you that we had escaped the city because my mother had
tried to kill herself.*

*Misery seeped into that place and was impossible to
keep out, just like the wind that came in through the crack
between the wood panels, no matter how hard my father
tried to fill the gap. Your letters kept me going. I didn't want
to tell you all that had happened. It made me ashamed and
it made me confused. I wanted my mother to be normal, to
be like other mothers. I wanted her to care for and support
me, and I wanted her to be at our wedding and to let us
live our lives. I wanted that more than anything else. But
she was not like other mothers. She was herself. She had the
rage, she had the depression, she was violent, she was cruel,
she refused to let me live in peace. She wanted to control my
life, she told me she loved me so much that she wanted the
best for me. That she had been too poor and had given up too
much to have me squander it away.*

Was my father nothing more than a way for her to attain status? Did she ever even really love him?

I poured out my heart in those letters to you. Do you still have them, Roya Joon? Did you keep the letters? I suppose you wouldn't.

My father and I shouldn't have tried to handle all of it alone. I know that now. But I was too young to know better. I kept worrying about you. I still refused Shahla. The more my mother pushed her on me, the more I resisted. And I did not do so, despite what my mother may have believed, out of spite. I did not reject Shahla to rebel. All I could see was you standing in the shop, your hair in braids, your schoolbag on your shoulder. I only heard your voice. In your presence, I found a calm.

I was determined to marry you, despite the threats, the illness, the hell. That's why I wrote that last letter. She could not stop us. She could not end our happiness with the threat of suicide! I had had enough, and I had decided to escape. She was holding us hostage with her threats, and I didn't want her to have that power over me.

She knew I waited for you at the square. She knew I was heartsick with worry over you. And when I read your last letter and told her in anger and confusion that you had said you wanted to see no more of me (how could I tell her that the letter said you couldn't take her?), she laughed. She told me, "Good, I told you so, I told you that girl is no good," and she promised to starve herself to death if I tried to reconcile with you, if I tried to get you back.

I was supposed to be the "boy who would change the world." But life has a way of squashing dreams, plans, ideals. In the end, I barely served my country. I was an activist working to spread political material of the

National Front, sure. In 1953 I was active. But how disillusioned I became with politics and all the rest of it after the coup in '53. And I could barely rejoice as others did in 1979 to see the Shah gone. I was too worried that worse would follow. In the end, Jahangir did more than I did. He went to the front! He followed in his father's footsteps and became a doctor. And he treated soldiers and the wounded in Ahvaz during the war. He died in a bombing. So no, during those weeks apart I was not in prison. I was not in hiding for political reasons. I was simply trying to keep my mother alive and figure out how to solve this problem of her threats, of her closeness to doing it all again, of our irreconcilable plans.

Remember how much you used to worry that we would be jinxed by the evil eye? I scoffed at it all being just superstition back then. But I look at the life I have lived without you, and who knows? Maybe there is something to our culture's obsession with the evil eye. Look at what ended up happening with my mother.

Even after I received your last letter requesting that I never see you again, never contact you—I never stopped loving you. And I hate to think about the possibility there—was that really what you wrote? Because now I just don't know.

And, my dearest Roya, when we met here at the center last week, I could see in your eyes a certain worry that maybe I had lost my mind or my memory. But please know this. I may not remember certain things—what I ate for lunch two days ago or which darn pill to take when. For that, I need Claire's guidance. But my mind is sharp as a knife when it comes to remembering everything that happened that summer. When it comes to knowing my heart.

*The truth is, Roya Joon, I was never as happy as when
I was with you. So many wonderful moments with my
children and, yes, with Shahla, but I was never as happy
as I was with you. There have been years when you were
the first thing I thought about when I woke up. Just about
everything reminded me of you. Of course I knew you
belonged to another, as did I. But, Roya, you have always
been a part of me. Some things can't be helped.*

And now I find I must stop.

*It is when I think of the purple sky on the evening
of our engagement, and the moments we shared, that
I remember beauty in this world. But after what has
happened to our country, and really, when I look around
at this modern world, I can't help but think there is an
ugliness, a streak of cruelty in all of it. I have tried to
remain positive, as the Americans so encourage, I have
attempted to not be one of those grumpy old men! Claire
here at the Duxton Center has been good to me. She calls
me "Mr. Batman." She doesn't tire of my stories. I have
confided in her. Even told her about our young love. The
moments of beauty and connection keep me going. I see
my children and my grandchildren and I am happy. The
rest of it—the politics, the mental illness that drowned
my mother, the cruel twists and turns—well, there is a
fetid underside to life sometimes. When I think that way
is when I get the most hopeless.*

*I loved you. I loved you then, I love you now, I will always
love you.*

You are my love.
Bahman

Chapter Twenty-Nine

2013

Toothpaste Sheets

Roya found her phone and searched for the number of the center. Mrs. Aslan and Mr. Fakhri. A first baby who was never born. And then Mrs. Aslan's body turned on her and killed all the others. Except for one.

She could see Mrs. Aslan, the rouge on her cheeks that night at the engagement party. She knew how the loss of one child could render everything broken. To have lost four? *Oh, it was different times then, Sister, don't you remember? People lost children all the time.*

She had waited long enough, for goodness' sake. No matter the snow, forget it. She had to go there again and see him face-to-face.

"You don't have a lot of time, I'm afraid," Claire said on the phone.

"I'm sorry?"

"He's taken a turn for the worse, Mrs. Archer. His son and daughter have been here for the past two days."

"But I saw him less than two weeks ago. I got his letter. . . ."

"He wrote that as if his life depended on it. He asked me to mail it. Look, sometimes these are just scares. Sometimes there are dips, the Parkinson's flares up, and then he's fine again. We're hoping."

"Oh."

"But if you'd like to see him . . . well, I would come as soon as you can."

When she got to the center, the ice had barely melted. Snow still covered every corner of the parking lot, only it was gray now and dull, its crevices filled with dirt.

Once inside, Roya expected Claire to take her to the dining hall. The same stink of beef stew filled the lobby. (Did they ever eat anything else for lunch over here?) She wanted Claire to lead her down the corridor to the dining hall to see Bahman in his wheelchair by the window. They had probably placed a plastic chair for her in the same spot. They could look out at the parking lot again, at the snow, even though it was gray and dingy now. She'd pull out the letter from her purse, and Bahman's eyes would fill with that same damn hope, and she would talk to him about all the history she had not known until now.

But Claire led her down another hall entirely. It was the color of every hospital corridor she'd ever seen, the color of the place where she'd held Marigold one last time. She used all her effort to put one foot in front of the other. By the time they got to the room where Claire entered, Roya was sweating. She should have taken off the down coat she wore.

It was dark inside the room, the drapes drawn. As her eyes adjusted, she made out a bed, a chair next to it, a nightstand with a vase, a table in the corner by a sink. And in the bed lay Bahman, his breath like a broken machine.

"Let me help you with your coat." Claire pulled off one sleeve and then the other, and together they removed Roya's puffy coat. Roya made her way to the chair by the bed and sat down. She was so close to Bahman that she could now see the lines around his mouth. His eyes were closed. There were no plastic tubes coming out of his nose. He wasn't hooked up to volumes of liquid; he was fully there, her Bahman. He had to be fine.

"I'll be right in the lobby if you need anything. Just press the buzzer by the bed and I'll be here instantly. But, Mrs. Archer?"

"Yes?"

"Take your time."

"Oh," was what she said. But what she really wanted to say was: *Why is he in this bed and not in his chair, and please don't leave.*

When the click of Claire's heels receded, Roya was once again alone with him. His chest rose and fell under a white sheet and a blanket the color of turnips. She wanted to open the drapes, let light into the room.

"I've been waiting," he said. He opened his eyes. "How was your drive? How are you?" His voice was small, hoarse.

"It was all good. What happened, Bahman? What happened to you?"

"I'm just fine. Hanging in there, as the Americans say. My daughter was here this morning. She's coming back tonight."

Roya should have come sooner. She thought of him writing his letter to her. All those confessions. Suddenly none of it mattered. Someone had changed their letters when they were young. Whether it was Mr. Fakhri because of Mrs. Aslan, as Bahman seemed to suspect, or even Shahla or Jahangir, she might never know. She wanted him only to know that she, too, had days where he was the very first person she thought of, days where she had wanted nothing more than to be with him. Something had happened when they were young, something inexplicable and irreversible. They were bound, attached to each other in a way that was impossible to fight. She had loved him and her love for him had never quite stopped. She had tried to push it down, hide it, make it disappear. But it was always there. It floated in the branches of the trees outside her California college boardinghouse, it was in the layers of the clouds in New England, it had been in the red puffed-up chest of a bird that sang in winter. It was everywhere. Still.

"Bahman?"

His breathing had slowed. She took in the stubble on his face, the lines on his forehead.

"I missed you. Every single day," he said.

"I missed you too." As she said it, tears ran down her cheeks. She pulled her chair as close as possible to the bed and took his hand. It was dry and felt smaller than when she'd held it two weeks ago. A scent of pungent soil, a puddle of rain, came from the vase of flowers on the nightstand, like something forgotten.

She stood up. She balanced herself on her left foot and then with everything she had, she hoisted herself up onto the bed. His eyes widened when she lay next to him. She put her arm across his body. They fit perfectly next to each other. How natural this felt, to lie beside him. She nuzzled her head into his shoulder.

"Roya Joon."

The sheets smelled like toothpaste. He smelled like the wind, like water and salt, like all their time together when they were young.

In a parallel universe, the boy who had first shown her what it meant to fall in love, who promised he would wait for her, would have always been hers. She was in the bed in the center and she was pressed against the bookshelves for stolen kisses. She was in both places all the time. He would always be right there.

She held him under the toothpaste sheets and, too, in the pastry shops of a city long changed as they went through the lobby of Cinema Metropole with its red circular sofas to kiss under the sky. Before she knew it they were in Jahangir's living room, familiar patterns of navy-blue and white geometric shapes on the Persian rug as they practiced their dance steps. "Look at me." Bahman raised her chin gently. He interlaced his fingers with hers. The gramophone had a huge brass funnel through which tango music filled the room. Bahman could not have known what to do, how did he know what to do, but he took charge. Their movements were clumsy at first; they couldn't get their feet in sync. Couples around them danced as perspiration trickled down her spine. He held the small of her back; they caught the rhythm and then were one. It felt as though he carried her as they moved together in that hot living room. The music settled into the folds of Roya's green dress, landed in her hair. She was drunk on his scent. Together they swayed, their bodies against each other. He guided her face to his and kissed her. She thought it would have felt like flying, but no, it was like landing. In a place soft and sweet.

In the bed, beneath the toothpaste sheets, Roya stroked his chest, searched for his arms, the muscles she had known so well. She kissed his eyes, his cheekbones, his lips. She pressed her cheek against his heart and lay there, grateful for the time she'd had with him, however short or long it had been, grateful she had known him, grateful that once, when she was young, she had experienced a love so strong that it did not go away, that decades and distance and miles and children and lies and letters could never make it disappear. She held him in her arms and said to him all she needed to say.

For that fraction of time, he was entirely hers.

Chapter Thirty

2013

Blue Round Box

"It's fine. Some of his friends from the center will also be there."

"Oh, I can't, it would be too strange."

"You'll be seen as just another resident. Another friend."

"Yes, well, even so. Walter, he has a town meeting. And I don't like driving in this ice."

"Mrs. Archer, I can pick you up and drive you home. I think he would have wanted you there. Deal?"

Americans with their deals and their good plans. But there was something genuinely kind about this young woman, Claire. She insisted that no one would notice anything untoward about Roya being at the memorial service.

So Roya did go.

For decades she'd had no closure, no good-bye, so much unresolved with Bahman. But that last day with him alone—well, she would always be grateful for that time with him. She wanted to go to his service. She wanted to be there for him.

It was held at a Universalist church in Duxton. He'd asked to

be cremated. Bahman had never been religious; he did not practice. The white, sun-drenched steeple of the Universalist church
somehow fit him perfectly.

With Claire's help, Roya went up the stairs and into the
church. It was strange but also oddly comforting to see Omid and
a woman who looked a lot like him. Omid introduced her to his
twin sister, Sanaz. So Omid's sister had Bahman's smile too. It took
everything Roya had to keep it together as she walked up to Bahman's children to offer her condolences. Omid introduced Roya to
his sister as "an old friend of Dad's" and squeezed her hand.

For the service, Roya sat next to Claire in the pews. A minister went to the podium, thanked everyone for coming, and said
she'd like to start with a short verse from Mr. Aslan's favorite
poem. Blood rushed to Roya's face and throbbed in her ears as she
heard the words of the Rumi poem she and Bahman had first
shared in the Stationery Shop. Between the pages of the book
containing that poem, they had exchanged their letters.

> *Look at love*
> *How it tangles*
> *With the one fallen in love*

> *Look at spirit*
> *How it fuses with earth*
> *Giving it new life*

His children got up and spoke. They mentioned how loved
their father was, by his community, by his customers at the shop.
Through their speeches, Roya caught glimpses of Bahman's life.

"Mom and Dad loved to celebrate Nowruz," Omid's sister,
Sanaz, said. "Our home was always filled with the scent of Persian

rice, and Dad would make sure we set the table with the traditional *Haft Seen* objects signifying spring."

"Dad made sure we always worked hard," Omid told the assembled crowd. He couldn't say enough about their devoted father. "He always wanted to change the world."

Roya listened to these two competent, articulate adults. She could see that Bahman had changed the world, after all. Here they were, speaking from the podium, from their hearts. His children.

She had thought at times that what she shared with Bahman could take up all the space in the universe. It had felt that strong. But really, it was just a sliver, a tiny shard of his life. His children and their birthdays and their studies and their boyfriends and girlfriends and spouses and children. That was his life. His wife. She was his life.

When the service was over, they all moved to a reception hall inside the church. Claire quietly sobbed. Roya wanted to comfort her but wasn't sure what to do. As guests mingled, she noticed a table of refreshments. "I'll get you something to eat," she said to Claire as she patted her shoulder.

At the refreshment table, Sanaz arranged pastries on a platter. "These were always Dad's favorites," she said. She held out the platter for Roya. "He liked to call them 'elephant ears.'"

Roya wanted to say, *I know.* The boy who had brought her pastries at Café Ghanadi was right next to her, and always would be; she could smell the cinnamon and sugar in that crowded café. "Thank you." She put two elephant ears on a small paper plate and made her way back to Claire.

"What do you have there, Mrs. Archer?"

"Try these. He liked them."

Claire bit into an elephant-ear pastry, and Roya sank into a chair, astonished by the sweep of time.

Once the younger children were high on sugar, they started to run around the reception hall. The mood grew lighter, people ate and talked and laughed. It felt good to be here with these strangers, who were all connected to Bahman. She knew none of them save Claire, and barely Omid, but it was clear they all shared a fondness for Bahman, for his energy, his kindness. Snatches of conversation floated by: "Remember how much he loved to . . ." "Boy, did he make us crazy with that song he always whistled. . . ." As long as Roya stayed in this room, she could hear more about him, be with people who shared a love for him. Once she left, she'd be back to a life where no one else knew him. She wanted to cry. To distract herself, she tried to figure out which of the kids were Bahman's grandchildren. One teenage girl leaned against the wall, chewing gum. She was the spitting image of Mrs. Aslan.

At the end of the reception, Omid and Sanaz and their partners stood near the exit and shook hands with everyone and thanked them for coming. Strangely, Roya wanted to be near them for as long as she could. They were her only link to the boy she had loved. And she would never see any of them again.

"Ready?" Claire's eyes were red. "Let's take you home."

Claire pulled into the driveway of the colonial house with its dark-green shutters, and Roya undid her seat belt but did not get out. "Would you like to come in?"

She said it because it was the polite thing to do, but also because Claire knew more about Roya and Bahman than anyone else. She had been Bahman's confidante at the center. He had shared their history with her. Roya felt an inexplicable need to be with Claire. His kids weren't the only link to him. Claire was too.

"Oh." Claire looked surprised. "If you're sure it won't be any trouble...."

"No trouble at all," Roya said.

"All right. Thank you. I have something I was going to give you when I dropped you off. I'll give it to you inside then?"

"What is it?"

"He wanted you to have it. That's all I know."

Roya put the kettle on the stove and motioned for her guest to sit at the kitchen table. Walter wasn't due back from his town meeting for a while. Those meetings always ran over and went on for hours as people argued.

Once she was seated, Claire fumbled in her tote bag and took out a round blue tin box printed with pictures of Danish butter cookies.

Roya and Walter had shared many of those cookies over the years. There was a box just like it in Roya's closet. She kept her sewing things in it: spools of thread and pins and needles and thimbles and extra buttons.

"He was very insistent that this be given to you. His kids took all the rest of his belongings. But he was adamant that no one but you see this box."

Roya was feeling slightly faint. Claire pushed the box gently to her, and she pried the lid open, hands shaking.

Paper. A stack of onionskin paper. She took out a sheet and unfolded it. The handwriting was amazingly familiar but she couldn't place it. Then her heart stopped.

It was her own. She dropped the sheet and thumbed through the rest of the box's contents. These were the letters she had written to Bahman in the summer of 1953. These were the contents of her heart. She quickly put the first letter back in, as though touching it too long could burn her fingers. Then she closed the lid tight and put the box in the drawer of her kitchen desk.

Claire didn't say a word.

"Now then," Roya said. "What kind of tea can I get you?"

They spoke only about Bahman at first. Claire shared stories about him from the center, and Roya dared to share a few memories from 1953. Then Roya asked about Claire's own family. She had lost her mother to cancer and her father had died in a car accident when she was two. Something about Claire's bereft expression struck Roya. This young woman was especially alone.

"I should really go," Claire said after she had finished her Persian tea and baklava.

"Please, would you like to stay for dinner?"

Roya barely knew this young woman. What did they have in common but a fondness for the man Claire called Batman? But Walter wasn't home yet, and it was getting dark, and part of her worried that if Claire left, she would be alone with her grief. This girl looked like she shouldn't be alone. "Have you ever had Persian food?" she blurted out.

"There's a kebab place in Watertown," Claire mumbled.

"Oh, forget kebabs. Have you ever had *khoresh,* any of our stews? Have you ever had Persian-style mixed rice?"

"I've certainly heard Mr. Batman talk about them all the time. His favorite was something called allyballoo—"

"*Albaloo!* Sour cherry rice?"

"Yes. And he always talked about something *sabzi*?"

"*Ghormeh sabzi!* Look, I was going to bake frozen fish sticks tonight. Walter loves the fish sticks with ketchup and with mayonnaise. He's at the town meeting. They're discussing the override. It's good, you know, for him to stay involved? You have to stay involved. But if you like? We can surprise him with a nice dinner. If you stay."

That first night of cooking lessons at Mrs. Kishpaugh's boardinghouse, Walter had come with his perfectly combed hair under his porkpie hat and she had made him *khoresh-e-bademjan* with chicken. It was not usual to use chicken; it was supposed to be made with beef. But she'd made do and it had turned out so well and now, well, this young lady looked like she could use a good home-cooked meal. Why not? After all Claire had done for Bahman, the least Roya could do was make her a good dinner. My goodness, it had been ages since she'd showed someone how to cook Persian food. Patricia and Alice had never cared for it. But this young lady who sat in her kitchen, whose parents had died, who had taken the time to talk to Bahman, who had listened to him and taken care of him and gone above and beyond the dictates of her job, she deserved a good dinner. "If you help me?" she said again. "We could try."

Claire shrugged. "Tell me where to start."

Together they navigated the kitchen. Roya showed Claire where everything was. They washed the basmati rice and soaked it, and then Roya had Claire start the Persian rice cooker that Walter had ordered from Amazon. No more fumbling with a cloth under the lid to catch the steam the way Maman did to create the perfect bottom-of-pot crunchy *tahdig*. This rice cooker did that for you!

She got out a bag of dried Persian limes, yellow split peas, and from the fridge some chicken. She had made *khoresh-e-bademjan* with chicken for Walter that first night in Mrs. Kishpaugh's board-ing house, but tonight she had no eggplants so she'd make *khoresh-e-gheymeh* and use the yellow split peas. They cut and chopped and sautéed and added saffron and turmeric and Persian allspice. Claire opened up more and rattled on with tale after tale of Mr. Batman. How he had campaigned for the center to hold lessons in tango and had participated in them even in the wheelchair. How he had read every article he could get his hands on about depres-sion and anxiety and the effects of loss.

"He was determined to learn more about his mother's condi-tion. Told me that if only she'd been born in a different place at a different time, maybe she could have been diagnosed, treated." She paused. "Out of all the residents at the center, he was the one I connected to most. He wanted to share his stories. And I loved them. I loved his kindness."

In the end, his heart had simply given out. Roya had left the bed with him asleep, breathing. He had died later that evening when his daughter came. She would always be grateful for that hour in the bed with him at the end, for the time the two of them had to just be alone. She would always be grateful to Claire for giv-ing her that. And to Walter. For not standing in her way.

"Hello?" Walter's voice sounded from the foyer.

"We're in here!" Roya sang out. For some reason, she was hap-pier than she had been ever since the news of Bahman's death. Ac-tually, happier than she had been in a long time. It was just nice to be with Claire. Maybe it was the scent of saffron from the *khoresh* giving her a natural high. Zari always said saffron was a natural antidepressant. *Oh, and an aphrodisiac, Sister! Dissolve half a tea-spoon of saffron in a mug of hot water and drink up, and make sure to put extra in Walter's food.*

Walter came into the kitchen. "Oh, well, what do we have

here?" He looked at Roya and then at Claire and then at Roya again. "Roya, this house smells wonderful! I was wondering whose car that was outside! Hello, Claire."

"Hello, Mr. Archer."

"I thought I'd be coming home to the fish sticks which, I assure you, are quite the treat, but do I smell delicious *khoresh*?"

"I had a great assistant. I wanted to surprise you."

"Funny, because I have a surprise for you myself! Look who I saw pulling into our driveway."

Kyle's face was flushed from the cold as he entered the house, and he was in his socks, of course, because she had taught him to never wear shoes inside. She hadn't had the nerve to tell Claire to take off her shoes—it would have been a bit strange to insist on it that first time. Kyle must have had a busy few days because there was stubble on his cheeks, but it always suited him. Oh, this boy of hers, how handsome was he. "Kyle!" Roya rushed over to hug her son.

"How are you, Mom?"

"Oh, Kyle, this is Claire. She is—" She was going to say *the administrator at the center*. But she stopped herself. "She is my friend."

"Nice to meet you." Kyle walked over and shook Claire's hand. Claire went the color of crimson.

Walter set the plates and cutlery and Kyle made drinks and the four of them sat at the kitchen table and shared some *khoresh*. The scent of the rice and stew permeated the house; she was entirely at home in every sense. They hadn't downsized, hadn't moved to an assisted-living place even though Zari nagged her about it every chance she got. Roya wanted her kitchen, her own pots, her cookbooks, her armchair, the comfort of her large bedroom, the beauty of her backyard. She wanted to be in her own home for as long as she could. Would she and Walter end up at a place like the center? She didn't want to think about it.

The *khoresh* was just the right balance of tart and sweet, the rice fragrant and comforting, the flavors all blended together perfectly. For tonight she was happy to share this meal with Walter and Kyle and this sweet young woman who was smiling now and crunching on *tahdig*.

Kyle devoured the food. "It doesn't get better than this, Mom. Thank you."

⁓

Kyle put on his shoes in the foyer as Walter helped Claire with her coat and said, "Watch those steps. They can be slippery!"

"Oh my God, neither one of you has gloves. Your hands will freeze!" Roya said.

Roya and Walter stood side by side at the front door and watched as Claire and Kyle got into their separate cars and drove off.

"How're you holding up?" Walter asked after he closed the door and it was just the two of them again.

"Surprisingly okay."

"And the service?"

"His children were quite something."

"Right, then. I'll finish in the kitchen. You go on up. Sound like a plan?"

⁓

In her bedroom, Roya sat in the armchair that had replaced the rocking chair where she had first nursed Marigold. She had not thought, at the beginning of this winter, that memories from the past would floor her, that she would find that boy from another world, that she would actually go to the center and speak to him. She had thought nothing could get into her tightly sealed life at her age. But of course, it always could. Of course it was never too late for it all.

Just months ago, if someone had told her that she would sit next to Bahman Aslan again, hear his voice (the same voice!) discuss things that were long ago put away, she would not have believed it. She would not have understood, then, that time is not linear but circular. There is no past, present, future. Roya was the woman she was today and the seventeen-year-old girl in the Stationery Shop, always. She and Bahman were one, and she and Walter were united. Kyle was her soul and Marigold would never die.

The past was always there, lurking in the corners, winking at you when you thought you'd moved on, hanging on to your organs from the inside.

⁓

Later, Roya would open the blue round box and take out the letters one by one and read them. She would see what she'd written to Bahman all those years ago, and see, too, the last letter, which was not written by her but was written in her voice, in handwriting that looked like hers, from her to Bahman. She would know that someone had added that extra letter telling him she didn't want to see him ever again. She also read letter after letter from Bahman, the ones he'd written to her through the years. Updating her on his life, telling her about his job, his children, his days. Letters he had never sent. But saved up inside this blue round box along with the letters of her youth.

She added to the box the last letter Bahman had written to her, after their reunion at the Duxton Center.

The ice would melt. For the first day of spring, for Persian New Year, they would have the curtains washed and the windows cleaned. They would have the house scrubbed from top to bottom.

And celebrate rebirth and renewal. She thought of her parents in Iran, who hadn't gotten to know this son of hers. She thought of Zari and Jack and the kids and all their grandkids in California. She thought of Jahangir doing the tango with Bahman and dying in the Iran–Iraq War. She remembered the day of the coup, how she had stood in that square as the country fell apart around her. She thought of all the times her country had swelled with pride and hope and collapsed in fear and repression. Maybe one day it would be free. She thought of the daughter who should have been in this kitchen with her tonight and of the man with whom she had lain in bed on the last day of his life. She was suddenly wrecked by her love for him and for Walter and for all those who had gone and for those who remained.

Epilogue

The Keeper of Secrets

Others, even of his class, go to the main bazaar downtown every now and then. It's good for gold and rugs and bangles to adorn the thin wrists of elegant women like Atieh. Saffron is sold in heaps of crimson. Lingerie of lace is hung with clothespins on string. Colorful mosaic boxes are piled in pyramids for the masses. But Ali avoids the bazaar the way one would avoid heartache. To smell the fruit sitting in the sun, to hear the hawkers shout about their wares, to detect even the slightest scent of melon could make him blind. No need for shopping there. Why? The house is stocked. Atieh runs their home with regularity and reliability. His sons don't give him much grief. The daughters have grown and married well. What more could he even ask for? For God's sake. For all that is decent, Ali.

He opens the shop to help the young. He makes it a priority to carry books as much as stationery. Titles from all over the world, spines with lettering that beckon, words of the old greats and the new, tomes of knowledge and risk. This shop—this haven—has saved him, especially since his father's phlegmy laugh denied a future with the one whose melon-scented skin he *still* wants. Decorum and tradition and "for God's sake, for all that is decent, Ali" lead him to a marriage of stability and happy parents on either side. He and Atieh seal their future, and that girl who balanced the tub of melon rinds on her hip and kissed him in the square behind the bazaar is disposed. To be almost forgotten.

The children, when they come, happen in quick succession. Four in all, and all in good health, as it so happens, thanks be to God. Raised under the care of their mother and with his own guidance. Two sons who make their mark in scholarship (Ali's father feels vindicated to see at least his grandsons follow in his academic footsteps, even if Ali has stooped to selling wares "like a merchant, like a *bazaari*").

Today, Wednesday, 28 Mordad, he works alone. The prime minister has asked people to stay off the streets. The shop is quiet save for the scrape of the stepladder he drags across the floor of the back storage room. He is seized by the memory of Badri on that stepladder just a few weeks ago. The knife entering her throat. The droplets of blood on her skin.

He is suddenly drenched in sweat. It will pass—this rush of panic, this mess of his insides that mean minutes of immobilizing pain. It has to pass.

Forget the girl, Ali.

He needs to finish organizing books. He has to go home soon. Atieh is waiting, and sometimes when he is late, he can tell she suspects that he is seeing someone else.

Ali picks up the broom and sweeps the floor, and again she is with him. Stunning how he can carry her with him all the time. When she reentered his life right here in this shop, charging in with her young son after all those years, he was behind the garbage bins in the bazaar again. Had he really ever left that place? Where they had for themselves everything while the rest of the world held up their hands in prayer.

He misses her now. He misses her still. Why does he do the things he does for her? Why can he not say no to her? She tells him over and over again that Roya and Bahman cannot end up together.

She tells him to change the letters. She makes him swear to do it, and he does. Because he owes her. Because he slurped her up in that square behind the bazaar. He impregnated her, stole her honor, ended her innocence. Because he was a man—a young man, yes, but still a man—who took advantage of a fourteen-year-old. And then when he should have married her, he left and listened instead to his father and his mother and married Atieh. Atieh, whose skin is papery-thin and white. Atieh, whose personality is like yogurt. Atieh, who deserves better than a man who wants Badri.

He wants nothing more than to help these kids who come in so hungry for knowledge. He wants to save them from predictability and stagnation. Free them from the trap of custom. He disseminates the political speeches and treatises because he believes in democracy. He knows Prime Minister Mossadegh is a fair and just leader. When boys like Bahman Aslan come in (oh, that first day when his mother brought him in—the pain and pleasure of seeing Badri again), he wants to help them grow. Maybe he can guide these idealistic boys and girls to use their smarts and skills to better the country and themselves. Maybe he can save them.

All those days when Roya Kayhani rushed in after school, when she asked for book recommendations, he was fulfilled.

Nothing makes him happier than when he nurtures romances with letters in books. The love letters he passes along give so many young couples a mode of communication they would otherwise not have. A small release from the pressures of their parents and the suffocating mores under which they are—all of them—trapped. He transports those love notes for couples he knows cannot be seen with one another. Couples separated by class or religion or cultural dictates but not by desire. For girls whose clothes are too shabby for rich boys. For boys whose income prospects are too hopeless for elite girls. For Muslims in love with Jews. For communists in love with monarchists.

And he is happy to do it. He wants them to have that which was denied him: the freedom to love.

Abbas and Leila Gholami, one of the most philanthropic couples in Tehran, would not have been able to have their courtship without his assistance. Jaleh Tabatabayi and Cyrus Ghodoosi, a communist activist and a monarchist, will probably marry. He's done well by them. It helps to remember the ones he's helped. To hang on to the good.

And he helped Bahman and Roya fall in love. Hadn't he rushed off to the bank knowing they'd be alone together? Hadn't he gone to the back storage room again and again so they could speak in peace? He helps them along, gives them a sacred space of privacy. The time to be with each other. With delight, he watches Badri's son fall in love with Roya right there under his roof. And later he exchanges their letters.

Until she tells him to put an end to it.

Why doesn't his heart let go? Why do some people stay lodged in our souls, stuck in our throats, imprinted in our minds?

Forget the girl, Ali.

Roya is in the square now. Waiting.

God forgive him. God give exoneration.

Badri told him that she had aborted their own child with her own devices, that her body was wrecked for all the rest. Save Bahman. And so Ali tries to save Bahman. To give him all he wants: books, politics, love. But Badri does not want one thing for him and that is for her plan to go awry. For Bahman, she has plans. And they do not include Roya.

When she pierced her neck like that and almost died, when she went away to the north afterward to be by the sea, to recover, she continued to manipulate him. She made him promise.

And yes, at her bidding, he rewrote Bahman's letter. He changed but one word. That was all. Just the name of the square. But it was the cruelest word to change. To give them that hope, to have them wait at different locations, to not just end it. Badri wanted to draw it out. To see Roya suffer. She kept calling him on the telephone from up north by the sea to make sure he had done it just as she had demanded. She had enjoyed the drama of it. The danger and the cruelty. And to his dismay, Badri dictated two more letters: one from Bahman to Roya and another from Roya to Bahman, and made him promise to write them and mail them a few days before the kids were to "meet" at the squares. So each would receive the other's shortly after their planned meeting, while both were stung by being stood up.

So Badri could end it her way.

He had agreed. He had not wanted to, but he had agreed. He did as she said, in order to make up for his past failure. Although he knew he was creating even more heartbreak.

His penmanship was perfect—always had been. He could copy anything. Hadn't he been trained from a very young age at the best schools to master calligraphy, to train as a scholar? He was a product of the age when excellent handwriting signified status. Few could match the control of his hand.

Can God forgive him?

Badri would blame him if Bahman and Roya got married. And

then what would he do? What would she do? Would she kill herself? He couldn't live with that.

He sits on the stepladder, still shaking. Is he really just doing Badri's bidding? Or is there a part of him that, despite the best of intentions, is jealous of what those two kids would have? A life of love. What he never had.

He remembers how Roya looked at that boy in his shop.

He is drenched in sweat. And as he rests there with his head in his hands, he knows.

No. It is wrong.

He knows in his heart what he must do.

He closes the shop.

And he runs.

He runs and runs and runs. He has not moved this fast since he himself was young, since he himself was in love. With each yard covered, with each stride, there is a sense of new lightness in his heart. Badri is wrong. They cannot do this to the young couple. He cannot forget the girl. The girl who stands in the square.

The alleys and the streets and the swelling crowds of people are a blur as he runs. He finally reaches his destination, entirely out of breath. He pushes and shoves through the mob of people. So much for no more demonstrations. Will the people ever learn? *Roya. Roya. Roya.* Of course he knows where she stands. He pushes his way through. And then, in the middle of the mob and the chaos, he sees her. He forces himself past angry bodies to her. He grabs her shoulder.

"Roya!" He could cry with relief. He has found her. And he will tell her.

She looks worn out and tired. She is pale and her lips are dry. He is filled with a desire to protect her, help her, carry her away from this mess. He needs to tell her.

"Oh, thank God! Mr. Fakhri! Have you seen—"

"Roya Khanom, please listen to me. . . ." He clutches her shoulders with both hands.

"I just need to find Bahman," she says.

"Roya Khanom, I need for you to please know something—"

She moves away from his grasp. And then the force of a blast. He is sent up into the sky and onto the ground at the same time. He is shocked by the impact. He struggles to breathe. He knows only that he is now on the ground and his chest is wet and it won't stop being wet. He wants to find Roya to tell her what he did wrong to tell her she is in the wrong place because of him and that she should go to Bahman who is at Baharestan Square that they should go to the Office of Marriage and Divorce that they should seize this moment that they should not forgo their love that they should have many years together growing old together they will grow up and get older and softer and fuller together they will raise children they will do wonderful things they will grow into old age together he wants to tell her that he is sorry he wants to tell Badri he is sorry and he remembers the square behind the bazaar with the flies and the melon rinds and he remembers how he built that shop inch by inch book by book and he thinks of his children and their squeals of joy when they were young he is wrong and he sees Atieh sitting in her chair at night quietly sewing and he wants to burn onto this world that he is sorry and the child that Badri removed from her womb would be thirty-six years old this summer and he never got to know that child, he never got to hold its hand. And he is sorry. He is sorry. Roya's face is in front of him. And several others now. A man is pressing on his wet chest and he cannot breathe he is floating. Badri from the bazaar stands there, balanced on her toes for what seems like a snatch of time separate from all the rest. Her lips are warm and sticky on his face. She feels like a burst of fire. And now a snatch of melon cloth on his heart. Is he dreaming it? He looks in the direction of his stationery shop the one he built to make up for his sins to spread knowledge to nurture love and he thinks he sees smoke but he's sure it's not that. It will live on. People will walk into his stationery shop even after he is gone. He doesn't know how but he knows they will someone will not let it go someone will keep it going he is disappearing he is shrinking the sky is becoming darker the curtains are drawing closed from either side he is leaving but the love will continue to live the young will continue their hope the fight for democracy won't die his books the words the notes the letters the hope cannot ever end. It is a love from which we never recover.

Acknowledgments

For a long time I sat with this story alone, writing at my desk and shaping these characters from scratch. I was convinced they would only be mine. But once the draft was done and I dared to show it, the generosity of others stunned me. For all those whose time and energies played a role in bringing this story into the world, I am forever grateful.

Wendy Sherman has been with me since the very beginning and is an indefatigable supporter and brilliant superagent. She sat back when I needed time for these characters to bubble up and develop and gently encouraged me when I needed a push. I am so very lucky to have her in my life and am awed by the journey we've shared.

Writers dream of editors like Jackie Cantor who "get" their characters and story on a visceral level and whose wisdom and guidance come from the heart. When Jackie responded to my manuscript, it made me believe in magic. Her belief in this book and her intense commitment to it have made all the difference and I am so very thankful for her.

I owe a huge thanks to the entire team at Gallery Books, where this book was lucky enough to land. Thank you to Wendy Sheanin for a super exciting prepublication tour, to Meagan Harris and Michelle Podberezniak for all their publicity talents, and to Sara Quaranta for being there during every step. A special shout-out goes to copy editor Joal Hetherington, whose thoroughness is much appreciated, and to art director Lisa Litwack and her brilliant team for the book jacket design.

The coup d'etat of 1953 is seared in the memories of those who lived through it and the ripple effects of that event have affected the world. For historical research, *All the Shah's Men* by Stephen Kinzer (which opens with the same Harry Truman epigraph) was extremely helpful. For poetry, author Melody Moezzi helped me select Rumi verses translated by Nader Khalili, Coleman Barks, and her own brilliant self. And thank you to the elders in my family who put up with my endless questions about that tumultuous time, including my mother-in-law, Maman Pari, who shared fascinating anecdotes of her school days.

In the cold of Boston's winter after I thought my revision would be a puzzle I'd never solve, editor Denise Roy swooped in and lent her expert eye and brilliant mind to my draft. Her spot-on advice and guidance is much appreciated and I am so grateful for the conversations we shared. My friend and fellow author Susan Carlton met with me on many a winter's day and summer afternoon in the library and later over burgers and bagels. Her advice and support made such a difference and I don't know what I would have done without her. Thank you also to Maria Mutch for reading the first draft and for being such a source of joy and light in my life, to Ilan Mochari for his friendship and wisdom over the years, and to my classmates from the NYU MFA days who will always be my cohorts: Courtney Brkic, Cara Davis Conomos, Jeff Jackson, and Sophie Powell. A very special thank-you to the luminous Lara Wilson, who sat across from me at a serendipitous lunch and calmly suggested a plot twist (without having read a word of the manuscript). Thank you, dear Lara, for your friendship. And for being the first to read the finished book and to share their reactions before the advance copies came out, a huge glorious thank-you to Elinor Lipman and Whitney Scharer. Your early support means the world to me.

If there ever was a Hogwarts for writers, it is GrubStreet in Boston and I am so lucky to have found this community of fantastic artists. Thank you to Eve Bridburg for creating what is no doubt the best writer's organization in the country and for her friendship, to Christopher Castellani for always supporting me and being generous and kind and inspiring, to Sonya Larson and the entire staff at Grub for all they do, and to Dariel Suarez for giving me the opportunity to teach incredible writers. I am so proud of all my students and love being part of their journeys.

So much of my own growth as a writer was shaped by generous teachers whose words and advice I still carry: Charles Muscatine, Leonard Michaels, Maxine Hong Kingston, and Bharati Mukherjee at UC Berkeley; Alexander Chee, who believed in me when I was trying to find my way; and E. L. Doctorow, Chuck Wachtel, and Paule Marshall at my MFA program. And I would be remiss if I didn't include Mr. Garcia, my sixth-grade teacher at P.S. 144 in Forest Hills, Queens, who treated a newly arrived immigrant girl from Iran with respect and dignity and encouraged me to write and tell stories.

I also owe thanks to friends who keep me grounded: the entire Lavangar crew of Stephanie, Julia, Rachel, Abby, Lily, and David Lawrence (David is the photographer extraordinaire and his author photo has followed me around the world!), Victoria Fraser, Marjorie Travis, Pam, Peter, Jane, and Claire Lawrence, Alexandria Snyders Dykeman, Margaret Dykeman, Linda K. Wertheimer, Pam Wolfson, Kwi Young Choi, and Laurie Buchta. I will never forget Jay Buchta's generosity and he is dearly missed.

Thank you to the readers of my first novel, *Together Tea*: your notes and emails, as well as the many face-to-face interactions we had at readings and in book clubs, kept me going. A special shout-out to all the talented writers I've had the privilege of working with through *Solstice Literary Magazine* and the Arlington Author Salon. And thank you to poet and professor Persis Karim, who has supported my work and the work of so many Iranian-American writers.

My sister, Maryam, encouraged me to read and write when we took shelter in the basement as bombs fell on Tehran during our childhood and that's only the first time writing saved me. I love to laugh with her and see her beautiful girls grow and I am so grateful for our unbreakable bond. My mother's courage and good humor in the face of hardship inspire me every day. Her love has sustained me and I only hope to have half the stamina and strength she has. Thank you, dear Maman, for everything. You are everything. To my children, Mona and Rod: you fill my life with joy and your wit and your kindness are the best gifts in the world. I have loved all our days. There is no one whose company I enjoy more . . . except maybe your dad's. Thank you, Kamran Joon, for wiping my tears after I wrote certain sections, for listening, for being there, for believing in me from the start. I love you.

Above all, I want to thank my father, who spent hours talking to me about the city of his adolescence and its cafes, cinemas, demonstrations, and dances. He drew maps of old Tehran, explained history and geography, told me stories of poets and politicians, and amazed me with his knowledge and memory. Finishing this book brought me even closer to him and everything was worth it just for that. It was all an excuse just to hear your voice, dear Parpie. It was all because of you.